The kid's face was the worst. One half looked normal, maybe even handsome. But the burnt side was a horrible visage. Lips peeled back, exposing blackened teeth and charred gums in another sneer, this one much more gruesome than the last. His eyelid had burned away, but his eyeball stared back at Hamlin, an undamaged white orb.

Hamlin could see faint wisps of smoke rising from the blackened side of the kid's body. Despite being impossible, he was still burning. The kid must have been in intense pain.

"Jesus kid, let me help you. Let's get you to a hospital."

"No," The kids voice had become deeper, edged with slyness and barely contained desire. "I just need a good meal."

The boy charged forward, a half-normal, half-burned sneering smile on his face.

ALSO BY ERIK LYND

NOVELS

Asylum

The Collection

THE HAND OF PERDITION SERIES:

Book and Blade

Eater of Souls

The Demon Collector

SILAS ROBB SERIES:

Silas Robb: Of Saints and Sinners

Silas Robb: Hell Hath No Fury

SHORTER WORKS

The Hanging Tree

Dark on the Water

His Devil

Dreams

Siege of the Bone Children

In the Pit

RISE OF THE SOULLESS

BOOK FOUR OF THE HAND OF PERDITION

ERIK LYND

BROKEN GODS PRESS

Rise of the Soulless: Book Four of the Hand of Perdition
by Erik Lynd

Published 2018 by Broken Gods Press
www.brokengodspress.com
Cover design by Damonza Designs
ISBN-978-1-943069-15-6

For my family, both old and new.

1

With a crack like thunder the giant carved rock came loose. Ten men stood around the large stone as it shifted loose with a deep, grinding sound. The laborer turned off the stone saw; its twelve-inch blade spun to a stop and skittered back in case the giant rock decided to roll forward and crush him.

The other men, though well out of the path of the stone, tensed, ready to spring back. It was large, easily capable of killing or maiming anyone in its path.

The men were dressed in work pants and worn shirts, covered in sand and dust. It was hot, even deep underground in the tunnel, and sweat cut rivulets through the dirt and grime caking their faces. They had been working hard for over a year to find this piece of rock. It was their goal, but none of them had been told why. They were the largest and strongest of the men assigned to this excavation and it would be their task to haul the boulder out. The tunnels leading to this room were too small for modern hauling equipment. The men had chains, crowbars, and other manual tools to carefully move this stone up to the surface from deep beneath the Egyptian desert rock and sands. But the surly look on their faces told Max they all knew their main tool would be their muscle and even more hard work in the heat.

The chamber they stood in was large, easily big enough for them all to gather in and still have room to maneuver. The walls were covered with a combination of carved images depicting ancient scenes and the beginnings of the hieroglyphic alphabet Egypt was so famous for. The vast, underground tunnel complex had several similar rooms; the excavation team had discovered them all along the way, but they had no idea what the rooms had been used for, what old purpose they served.

At least Max and his fellow workers had no clue. Perhaps their employers were aware; this seemed likely considering they were paying for this dig. And there was no doubt, it was a large and costly project, the biggest that Max had ever been on, and he had been on a lot. There was good money for a laborer with experience in excavation. There were always professors looking for help digging up this or that.

That was another thing though. His employers were not professors. They did not talk to the help, except when necessary, but Max could tell. They didn't care about the history or the culture. They tore through the tunnels like they were hunting for treasure.

When they first opened a new room or tunnel they'd come to a screeching halt and the two men, dressed in khaki outfits complete with pocketed vests and high boots like villains from an Indiana Jones movie, would pull the crew back and venture into the room by themselves. More than one worker had been abruptly fired for going into the chamber before being given the okay from their fearless leaders.

But they were the bosses and they paid well. Max and his fellow laborers hung back from each new discovery until given the okay.

When they first opened this new room, the tunnel beyond had partially collapsed and it had taken them a while to clear the way through; they had shut the dig down for almost a week, the longest they had ever paused.

Max and the others didn't mind though. A week off from working in the hot tunnels below the sands was welcome. Once it was known that this break would be more than a day, that the bosses had found something they needed to study, many of the workers went home for a few days to spend some time with their families. Max, however, had stayed behind with the skeleton crew that supported the bosses and the camp.

Max was not his real name, but one the bosses found easier than his given one. So, he became Max when on the job. He had family: a wife who fit perfectly in his arms and heart and a beautiful little girl who made him laugh with joy every day. They were the reason he lived, the reason he worked as hard as he did. But they were far from here, further than most of his coworkers' families. And staying meant more money, and more money meant something better for his family, a better life, a better chance. He would do anything for them, even if it meant staying away a little longer so they could all be a little happier when he did return.

If he had known he would never see them again, he would have gone home for one last visit.

Much to the chagrin of the workers who had left, the bosses fired most of the laborers. They were at the end of their search and didn't need the bulk of their staff any longer. They kept the skeleton crew, and most of that was Max's group.

The break was over now, the bosses had done... whatever it is they had done alone here in the dark. The room was bare except for the carvings and the massive rock they had just pulled out of the wall. If the bosses had taken anything else out of here, they left no evidence. It was just a large, empty room.

The stone, the one they had detached, was different though, out of place amongst the old gray rock. It was as though all the other carvings were a pale imitation of this one. A masterpiece versus an amateur. It just felt better, more... present. Like it was the only real thing in the room. It made Max uneasy.

The bosses had selected the biggest, strongest of the crew for this work. Max was large and still had the strength of youth. He was only twenty-five, his wife four years younger. A young family, a young life just begun. It would be back breaking work to bring this rock up, but he could take it even if the bosses drove them hard.

With a nod from the boss they attacked the stone around the detached rock. With sledge hammers and large chisels, they began chipping the rock from around the edges of the target stone. The bosses, worried about damaging their discovery, didn't allow power tools or any type of explosive. The area they were working at was too small for all of them to get in at once, so they took shifts to maximize time.

Max could see the sudden impatience of the bosses. They had worked the men hard, tearing into this ancient tunnel complex, but they were also methodical, always making sure they had explored every new tunnel or room thoroughly, carefully deciding which direction to move next. As the dig went on however, their frustration started to show. Rooms were checked quickly; some only received cursory review before they moved on to the next one. They were not finding whatever it was they were looking for and the strain was showing.

Now however, they had found it and the excitement translated into even more impatience. The bosses promised triple the money if the crew could get the stone up to the surface in half the time is should have taken.

So Max and his fellow workers tore into the task. Triple money meant an easier few years for his family; he could work a little less and be closer to home. He could be with his wife and play with his daughter. It would be a good life.

The bosses didn't care about the surrounding stonework, so they smashed the priceless walls, pulling them down and away from their prize. Max wasn't the only one a little hesitant to destroy such artifacts, it just seemed wrong, but then he thought about the money and his family. That was all it took for him to swing his hammer the hardest.

It took them two days to carve enough of the wall away from the large stone to allow them to wrap their chains around it. One of his fellow workers almost crushed a leg while they chipped away at the ground beneath it. The rock had shifted suddenly. Max darted forward and pulled his colleague back like the man was a rag doll.

Driven by the sense of urgency, the boss supervising the work had charged forward, raging at the man who had almost been permanently maimed.

"You idiot, you could have damaged the sacred stone! It's more valuable than all our lives put together," the ridiculously dressed man roared. He screamed for five minutes, spittle flying from his mouth. Max thought that the stress, or whatever was driving this need, was taking its toll on him. It was driving the bosses half mad. "If you had broken it he would have..." The boss suddenly stopped as though realizing he was saying too much.

Max wondered who "he" was and what "he" would have done. Fire them? Sue them? Whatever they planned to do, Max did not like feeling threatened. For the first time he began to wonder if the money was worth it.

They wrapped their heavy chains around the stone, low on the back side. The bosses were insistent the rock not roll. The carvings could not be damaged. Once the chains, wrapped in thick canvas were in place, Max and his fellow laborers took up their spots along the length and heaved.

It was grueling work. They had to strain for every inch. Once they got it away from the wall they would use a small muscle powered lift to ease it into a hand-pulled trailer bed. It would make the transport easier, but to get the stone and trailer through the tunnels they would have to widen some of the narrower areas and shave off some corners near the turns. They had thought about digging straight down from above, but the depth and significantly dense stone underneath the desert sand made that approach impossible.

They had pulled the stone several feet before the cry came from the boss.

"Halt!" he cried. Then he approached the other side of the rock. They stopped, welcoming the rest even if they didn't understand it.

Max understood it though. He was closest to the stone and could see what had interested the boss. A passageway, half the height of a man, a large hole really, was revealed behind the stone. The darkness inside seemed a thicker black than normal—like the light of their lamps could not fully penetrate it. Cold air, unnaturally cold in this hot tunnel system, brushed up against Max. He shuddered, but not from the sudden chill. It just felt wrong somehow. Nothing came out of the hole, but Max had the sudden, irrational thought that it was filled with monsters.

"Go tell Mr. Smith to come immediately," the boss said to one of the workers. The man nodded and started off down the tunnel at a fast walk. "Run goddammit," the boss yelled, his words cracking like a whip. The man sprang forward, running as fast as he could.

"The rest of you take a long break while we investigate."

Not needing to be told twice, Max and his crew headed up top while the bosses did whatever it was they do in those rooms. Max didn't care; the job would be done soon and he would be home, flush with money. A few hours later the bosses brought them back down.

"We focus on bringing the stone up," the boss told them. "Nobody, and I mean nobody is to go into that room beyond the stone. If you do, you will be fired on the spot and we won't pay you the wages owed. Is that clear?"

There was nodding and grunts of general agreement all around. Max was curious, but not enough to risk setting off the bosses. Over the next few weeks as they struggled to bring the massive stone up to the surface they speculated and told stories. Some thought it was an old burial chamber; that speculation led the more superstitious workers to start warning of ghosts and the consequences of disturbing the dead.

"No good will come of this," Jon, the closest thing Max had to a friend on this dig, said one day. "There is something in that tunnel. All the other rooms, no problem; that one though, that is where the dead reside."

Max said nothing, but noted that despite his misgivings, Jon stayed for the money, so he must not be that concerned.

Then the accidents started.

They had the stone about halfway to the surface, cutting corners and widening passageways, when there was a partial collapse of a tunnel. While they chipped away at a corner, rounding it so the trailer could turn the ninety degrees, Max heard a deep rumbling. It was hard to hear over the noise of their work, but he recognized it immediately.

"The tunnel! The tunnel!" he cried, but there was nothing they could do. The ceiling behind the sacred stone—fortunately, the bosses said since the accident didn't slow them down—sloughed to one side. The wall sagged and the stone in the wall fell in a rush. A man, bringing up the rear had just enough time to look surprised, eyes widening in horrible realization as the stones in the ceiling came crashing down on his head.

The rubble covered only half his body, but it was enough. His head had been caved in by a large stone. His body moved in thrashes and jerks as nerves still fired off, but by the time they had fully dug him out he had stilled.

This sobered the workers. Max and his team had been focused on getting the job done, getting home quickly. Now they knew the cost of haste. But even as they resolved to be more careful and to plan the removal of the stone more carefully, the bosses drove them harder.

A few days later, when Max and others refused to work at the boss's hectic pace, the carrots were joined by the stick. If they didn't work twice as fast they wouldn't get their pay. They'd be forced to go home without their last paycheck.

This motivated most of them. Max was reluctant but what choice did he have? He couldn't walk away at this point.

After Jon was killed though, the men with the guns showed up.

A slip of the power chiseler. It skidded from the rock surface of a corner they were removing and straight into Jon's head. He had been bent over carving away at the base to "save time" when it happened. It had hit a harder than normal portion of the rock and skittered to the side and the man operating the chisel lost his grip as it slid from his hands. He had clawed after it, only catching hold as it plowed into Jon's head. The man could only watch in horror as his own weight drove the machine forward into Jon's skull, chiseling through flesh and bone.

Later the man said that he had been tired, probably shouldn't have been using that tool at all. But it didn't matter, Jon was dead. This time Max and his fellow laborers told the bosses to go fuck themselves. It was unsafe. They would finish the job in a safe way and they wanted the money they were owed now.

Max had been the one to step up and make the demands, but the team was on his side. The bosses tried to argue back, explaining that they had a timeline, a budget and these things could not be helped. Accidents happen.

Max and his team held firm. They would do this at their own pace and they would get paid.

The bosses realized they would not win this argument with the threat of withholding pay. Eventually they just nodded and told everyone to take a day off. Take some time to remove Jon's body and rest. They would start fresh in the morning.

Despite the death of two of their numbers, the workers relaxed. Max felt a little better, the bosses had listen.

The next morning the men with the guns had shown up.

Max woke to a commotion outside his tent. The sounds of men yelling and confusion pulled him from dreams of being in his wife's arms. He woke slowly; based on the light in the tent it was early, but after dawn. More yells made him throw the cover of his sleeping bag back and start to put on his pants and shoes. This did not sound good.

More yells, louder. Then a deafening crack from just outside his tent. It sounded like a rifle. He had heard many rifle reports growing up, but it had been a long time. It sent chills down his spine. There was only one reason to have gunfire out here in the middle of nowhere.

He finished putting on his pants and shoes quickly. A part of him didn't want to leave the tent, but he knew he had to. The canvas would not protect him for long. He carefully poked his head out of the front flap.

The bosses were there, standing in the middle of the camp and surrounding them were a handful of armed soldiers. They wore combat fatigues and carried assault rifles. Hardened faces surveyed the workers as they staggered from the tents. Max doubted they were real soldiers, despite the organized look. Most likely some kind of private security team. Guns for hire. And knowing the bosses, probably not too concerned with getting blood on their hands.

They herded the laborers to the center of the camp as they emerged from their tents. Those who hesitated got a rifle butt to the gut. Anybody who put up an actual fight got a rifle butt to the jaw.

Max was jerked from the tent and shoved toward the center of the camp. He didn't fight, they were out gunned. Silently he cursed himself. He should have seen this coming. He had ignored the warning signs.

He was almost to the center of camp when he saw the body. It was just at the edge of camp, face down in the sand, arms spayed out as though it had tried to crawl away. It was obvious that whoever it was —Max couldn't recognize the crumpled form at this distance—had been trying to escape. Perhaps he had been the first pulled from his tent and had been the first understand the soldiers' intent.

Whatever the reason, he hadn't made it. Now he served as a warning to the others. Everyone saw it, nobody tried to run. Not even Max.

When everybody was rounded up and forced into the center of the camp, when everybody was calm enough to listen, the bosses spoke. But no one really needed to listen to know what they were going to say.

They would go back into the tunnels and they would work as hard and as fast as they could to get the stone to the surface. They would do everything the bosses said as fast as they said to do it. The safety of the rock was the most important, speed was the next. It was made clear their lives were very low on the priority scale. The bosses told them they would still get paid when it was all done, but none of the workers believed them.

It began to dawn on Max that he would die on this dig, a bullet in his brain. And there was nothing he could do about it, at least not now. Their only chance was to bide time until they saw an opening.

But there was no opening.

The bosses became slave drivers. They worked the laborers so hard and so long they were too exhausted to plan an escape, let alone pull one off. The worked sometimes fifteen, twenty hours straight with breaks only for food and water, the guns always at their backs waiting for one of them to break.

Some did. Some snapped and ran, usually right in the middle of a long pull, dragging the rock on the sled. They would just run, silently as though nobody would notice. But the guards always did.

Sometimes they were cut down only three steps from the crew, a grim lesson as bullet holes peppered their backs and blood splattered the walls. Sometimes, because there were only a handful of guards that could fit in the tunnels with them, a runner would make it all the way out of the underground complex. But always they would see the body on display as they surfaced. A reminder of who was now in total control.

The bosses made Max and the others drag the bodies back to the hole behind the rock they had moved. Despite the partial cave ins and damage to the tunnels, the room of the stone was still reachable. He knew this was a bad sign, hiding the bodies. Max and his friends would be the only witnesses.

They didn't go very far into the hole the stone had exposed. Just enough to drag the bodies past the entrance and to the side. Max could feel the coldness in the room. So different than the other tunnels. He could not see the walls; the darkness was too thick, and he didn't really try to look around. It tuned his stomach and made him want to vomit.

No, more than that, it made him feel something was growing inside his gut, waiting to force its way out.

Based on the echo of the noise the bodies made, it was a large room. But beyond noticing those few things he had no desire to learn more about this room at the end—and he was sure it was the end; he somehow knew there was no other way out of this place.

When he and his partner had moved the most recent body into the room, Max took his flashlight and stashed it near the corpse closest to the door. He wasn't exactly sure why he did it, gut feeling maybe? His fellow pallbearer nodded, they could share his flashlight back to the surface. He, too, suspected where their fate lay. Max just hoped they would be able to put the flashlight to good use—if they weren't piled up with the other bodies.

It took them three more days to get the stone to the surface. They were exhausted and beaten, the unending work had been the whip. When they were done, there were only five of them left. The rest had been killed trying to escape or crushed by rocks or other accidents.

But their work was not done. A helicopter was on the way, and they had to prep the rock in a harness. Weary and aching, they worked the heavy stone onto a steel platform and trussed it up with strong straps. That done, they had to stand there, guns pointed warily at them.

By now all the remaining workers knew they would probably not be getting out of this. They did what they were told because they were human, delaying the inevitable. Every moment was a potential for escape, for rescue. But none of them took the first step; so many had died in front of them. They were truly broken.

While they waited Max tried to listen in on the bosses. Once the guns had shown up, they had become a little looser in the lips, talking openly in front of them.

Max knew this stone was a piece of a significant project run by a very powerful individual. Someone by the name of Golyat. He didn't hear any details, but the man could obviously afford a highly trained army of killers.

The helicopter came over the barren sand. They saw it long before they had heard it. It sped across the sand toward them quickly, like the devil was chasing it. It was pitch black like a smear of oil across the sky.

It landed close to the stone, sending the tents and sheets into the air, scattering part of the camp. Tables and chairs were knocked over, the cups and plates on them littered throughout the camp. Max's tent tore from the stakes from the wind pressure.

It didn't matter, they wouldn't need the tents any longer.

The helicopter kicked up a lot of sand, causing a blinding mini-sandstorm. Even the guards were distracted, using their hands to block the sand blasting across their faces. The guards had goggles to protect their eyes, but habits die hard. For a moment visibility was almost zero. One of Max's friends saw his opportunity and ran.

They saw him make a break for it and the guns came up firing, but he had disappeared into the sand cloud. At a command from the leader, two guards charged off in the direction the worker had disappeared. The rest leveled their guns at Max and the remaining members of his team.

This had all happened in the blink of an eye. There was no time for thought. Before Max could even consider running in the opposite direction there was a barrel at his temple.

"Don't even think about it," the guard yelled over the noise of the helicopter.

Max had thought, but too slowly. He had missed his opportunity. He peered in the direction the worker had run. The sand and debris were settling down, but the man and the guards chasing him were gone, lost somewhere over the dunes. Max didn't hear any gunshots, he took that as a good sign.

As the blades slowed, the side door opened and a small crane came out, just big enough to lift the stone and sled it was on. With a wave of the guns Max and his team secured the rock to the crane and helped maneuver it into the back of the aircraft. As soon as it was secure, the helicopter was off, not even waiting for the bosses to step away from it.

Max felt only a small bit of satisfaction hearing them curse at the pilot.

As the aircraft disappeared in the distance the bosses turned to Max and his team. They all knew what would happen next. But the how took Max by surprise.

After a brief phone call, presumably with this Golyat, the bosses spoke briefly and then turned to the workers.

They told them there were a few more things to bring up from the room beyond the stone. The bodies would stay there, and as long as Max and the last of his team remained quiet they would be paid and released once those items were on the surface.

None of them believed the bosses. They were going to die.

The guards surrounded them, and forced the captives back into the tunnels. Max and his team—there were only four left—walked through the stone tunnels of what was to be their tomb. Max thought frantically, his mind desperate to create a plan. A direct attack against the guards would be suicide and perhaps more painful than just letting the bosses execute them. There had to be another way.

Soon they were at the hole behind the stone and Max had come up with nothing. He found himself crying now. Thoughts of escape had slowly turned to thoughts of his wife and child; he hoped that the last time he had been with them had been enough, enough for them to know how much he loved them.

The laborer closest to Max leaned towards him.

"Don't forget Asif," he whispered quietly. "He got away, there is always hope."

Max wasn't sure Asif had gotten away, and he also wasn't sure what help he could bring even if he had managed to escape the guards. It was a long, perhaps impossible, walk across the desert to the nearest town. And any nearby town would not be equipped to mount an armed rescue.

But Max nodded. Hope was never a bad thing and who was he to take it away?

Prodded by the guns, Max and his team entered the room. They were given no light other than what came through the stone entryway. The bodies lying on the ground gave them a quiet welcome. They hadn't covered the corpses, so dead eyes stared up at them, as though to say welcome, make yourself comfortable, you'll be here a while.

"The artifacts are at the back of the room," one of the guards said.

"Can we get a light?" Max asked. But he knew it was all a charade. It didn't matter, this game they played.

"We'll bring in some light shortly. But you should be able to make out the items as it is now. Just work your way back.

Max sighed as they all shuffled toward the back. Max waited for the crack of the rifle, wondered if he would feel any pressure on the back of his head just before it all went dark. He could feel the back of his head itching, waiting. He could almost feel the muzzle pointed at him.

He wanted to scream.

But there was something. Out of the darkness he saw it, an ancient stone platform like an altar. On it were jars, lightly covered in dust. Relief flooded through him and he almost collapsed onto the floor. It was true, there were more things to bring up. They weren't going to be left here with a bullet in their heads. The man next to him cried out as realization struck. Max wanted to laugh.

He did a quick count, twelve jars, arranged in three rows. Four by three that seemed important. They were plain, although with the only light coming from the hole in the far wall, it was impossible to see any detail.

Canopic jars he guessed. Used to house organs removed from mummified ancient Egyptians. But there was no sarcophagus in the room. And if they were Canopic jars, only four were needed per body —each to house a major organ: stomach, intestines, lungs, and liver. All believed to be needed in the afterlife. That meant they were from three different mummies.

Max was no expert, never a scholar, but he had been on many digs and this was unusual. Usually the jars of an individual were by themselves, rarely in a group like this and never without a mummy nearby.

Suddenly a faint hiss came from behind them.

"Hey!" cried out the man to Max's right. He was looking back at the hole they had come through.

Max spun, his blood turned cold. He could see through the hole a bundle of red sticks sat on the floor. Only they weren't sticks, at least not wooden ones. They were the unmistakable red color of dynamite. And the little spark winding its way through the room was a fuse. Old school. Max could almost imagine the guard who had lit it using a cigar like in the movies.

Old school or not, it would still work.

"Behind the altar," Max cried out and vaulted over the stone. The others did the same, knocking over the jars as they jumped. The clay vessels fell over, their lids spilling open. Some crashed to the ground, cracking and splitting open, but they didn't shatter; it was as though whatever was inside was thick and held them together. But Max had no time to investigate.

They just made it over when the blast shook the room. The concussion echoed throughout, sending knives into their ears and knocking them back even as they crouched against the stone table. Max could feel the power of the blast whip through his body, and his head cracked against the stone. Everything went black.

He woke in what seemed like just seconds later. Around him he could faintly hear muffled moans. The blast had taken his most of his hearing.

It was pitch black; the blast must have collapsed the other room, blocking the tunnel. They were trapped. Although obvious, the realization came to him slowly as his mind tried to make sense of what he had just experienced. As soon as it hit, fear and panic flooded in. They were trapped! In the dark! Under meters of rock that might collapse at any moment.

A flailing hand hit against his chest briefly. He caught it and gave it a squeeze and was rewarded when he received a return squeeze. That simple act took a little of the fear away. He was able to calm himself.

He didn't know what hope they had, but without light or hearing, they would get nowhere. He squeezed the hand he held with what he hoped was a reassuring squeeze.

"I need to find a light, lie still," Max said. He tried to let go of the hand, but it clung to him. The man it belonged to might have said something, it was impossible to tell with his numb ears. Max gently, but firmly pulled the man's hand away from him. As he crawled away the hand grasped at his clothes, tugging frantically. Max tried to ignore it, there was nothing he could do without light.

He took a moment to orient himself and then made his best guess on the direction of the collapsed tunnel. Other hands grasped at him as he crawled by. In the silence and darkness Max imagined all his friends, half-buried in rubble, hands flailing about as the life slowly left them. Once he touched a leg and there was no movement. At least one of them hadn't made it; Max was not sure that was a bad thing. Even with a light, he had no idea how they could get out of this. They were trapped here until they ran out of water or oxygen, whichever came first.

But there was always hope. Asif had gotten away, he could bring help. It was a straw and Max grasped.

Just as he was thinking his silent crawl through the injured and dead would last forever, that he had died and was now in his own personal hell, his hand fell on a leg. It was ice cold, long dead. He had found one of the bodies.

He breathed a sigh of relief; he had been worried the bodies might have been covered by large stones. Trying to ignore his disgust, Max searched the body. His hands ran along the dirty clothes and clammy flesh. Thankfully, the odor of rot was faint; the coldness of the room had preserved the bodies.

His fingers hit plastic and he knew he had found what he sought. The flashlight was in his hands. Max turned it on and winced as the brightness. He wasn't sure how long he had blacked out or even how long he crawled around once he came to. But it seemed long enough for his eyes to be sensitive to the light.

As his eyes adjusted he stared around at the chaos. There were only three of them left. Fresh blood ran from a limp body surrounded by shattered rock. A large stone lay near his head, next to a bloody gash. The two others sat on the floor, hands shading their eyes from the brightness of his flashlight.

Their lips moved soundlessly. His ears were still numb, but if he concentrated he could almost hear them. The cries and panic were dulled, but there was no doubt they had also realized how dire their circumstances were. They had come around the alter crawling.

Something looked odd behind that stone table, but he couldn't see anything besides slowly moving shadows.

Moving?

The two men were still seated, faces in hands. Max thought he could hear them wailing, but with his ears it was hard to tell. The only thing he could tell for sure—they were definitely not casting those moving shadows.

Max quickly learned that they weren't shadows at all. Glistening black puddles reared up behind the altar. Like thick, flat snakes they arched into the air and shot forward, moving pools of shiny tar, launching themselves at the men sitting on the floor.

The others didn't see them of course, their backs were to the altar. Max cried out a warning, but of course they couldn't hear. Couldn't they see the fear on Max's face?

But it was too late. The first blackness fell, landing on the leg of the closest man. He looked at the liquid black in a confusion that quickly turned into a howl of pain. The liquid creature flowed around his calf and tightened.

Coming in dark waves, three more shiny puddles rolled over the man, each one causing him to writhe in pain. Max thought he could hear some of the dulled screams, though he could only imagine the wet sounds as the horrors latched onto the man's exposed flesh.

The other man had noticed Max's horror and seen the commotion from his friend. He was staring in shock at the scene unfolding, so engrossed in the horrible tableau in front of him, he did not see the other black blobs slithering to his feet and then leaping at him.

His mouth opened in a silent scream as the first shapeless leech attached to his exposed arm. A second one struck his face, wrapping itself around his head.

Both men had been swarmed by four of those things. That's when it clicked. Max looked back at the canopic jars broken on the altar. His flashlight lit up the stone and broken shards. The thick substance that had been holding them together was gone.

Max knew where the dark, liquid leeches had come from. Three sets of jars.

Three!

Max whipped the light around trying to find the rest of the things. A chill, so cold it felt like ice shards puncturing his skin, wrapped itself around his wrist. The flashlight flew from his hand sending a crazy strobe of light throughout the room.

In flashes Max saw one of his friends trying desperately to peel away the things. But pulling them away meant ripping off your own flesh once they were attached. Nevertheless, he clawed at them, even as one crested his head and slid across his face. He collapsed.

The light flashed on his other friend, body completely covered in the black things and levitating above the ground. He was not moving, just floating in the black death shroud.

All of this came in silent flashes of horror as the light spun. Then all Max could think about was the pain in his wrist. Another searing pain blossomed on his thigh, whatever they were, it tore through his jeans like they weren't even there, burning cold on his exposed skin. Another of the black things hit his chest. The fourth and final one landed on the side of his neck.

He could barely see, the flashlight had come to a stop and in the faint light he could only see his two friends lifted off the ground by the black shapes, looking as though they were draped in a thick, inky curtain.

The black thing on his neck stretched and covered half his face. He dug at the thing, ignoring the pain of peeling at his own skin. But it didn't work, they were on too tight. He could feel, rather than see, the shapes stretching and twisting around his body, joining together as though they were one. Perhaps they had been before being placed in the jars.

His body was completely engulfed in seconds and with a wet sucking sound, the black thing—it was more sludge than leech—flowed over his face and everything went dark.

His whole body was burning cold. It felt like ice on fire burrowing through him. It poured in through his mouth and nose.

Through all the pain Max had one clear thought. He pictured his wife and child. He remembered them clearly, everything about them. The way they felt to his touch, the way his wife smiled when he did something to make her laugh. These were the memories Max held onto as the darkness took him forever.

2

Apophis opened his eyes in the eyes of the new body. The blackness that was him was still seeping into the mortal shell, but he had full control. He had separated the soul that had inhabited this body. It was adrift inside him looking for a way out of the home Apophis had commandeered. He would deal with that soon enough.

He was lying on the ground, the stones cold beneath him. The cold did not bother him, he liked it. He had nothing inside that needed warmth.

He rose up and looked around, his brothers were waking beside him. He stepped on the flashlight the mortal had been carrying. It shattered under his foot. He hated the light, it obstructed one's ability to see in pure darkness. The absence of light around him was familiar, it would allow him to work better. His mortal eyes shifted and he could see the room around him clearly.

The ears of the mortal guise he wore were damaged. With a thought he healed them. The others were just coming to their feet as he strode over to the broken shards of the jars that had held his essence.

He picked them up and cradled them in his palms. The seams found each other and lit up a fiery red. They fused together as

Apophis pressed them together. The sacred jars became whole again. He set the first jar down and picked up the next, repeating the process to fix the containers.

Next to him his brothers picked up their respective jars, doing the same. Despite having been trapped for thousands of years beneath the earth, they did not speak to each other. They worked in silence. It was all they knew now.

When the mending of the jars was complete Apophis removed the lids and gently placed them on the stone alter. When he gazed inside he stared into the depths of something so fragile, yet so powerful. He opened his mouth above the jar opening. His mouth stretched open, widening.

He stood there for a moment then a glowing liquid bubbled up from his gut. The essence of the mortal that had been, in liquid form. The thick liquid rolled down Apophis' distended lip and poured slowly into the jar. When that jar was full Apophis grabbed the next, repeating the process. When he was done, a little essence of the mortal named Max was in the four separate canopic containers.

His brothers were doing the same. Their mortal's essences did not even fill all the jars just three out of the four. It was a measure of the man this Max had been, that he could fill all four of them. But Max was gone, there was only Apophis.

When the jars were full and sealed Apophis and his brothers—the Soulless, the ancient walkers—turned their attention to the pile of stones that blocked their exit. Again, without speaking, they moved the rocks out of the way. With one hand, they were each able to pick up rocks the size of two human heads and toss them to the other side of the room, each time careful to avoid the jars on the alter.

They worked silently, quickly moving the stones. They did not tire, nor need to drink or eat. They just worked like machines. And that is really what they were.

They were agents of destruction and they knew their purpose. To bring chaos and disorder. But they were not without some rudimentary emotions. And one emotion guided them above all else.

Revenge. Revenge against the one who had put them here.

Revenge against the one who hunts souls, the one who works for Hell.

3

The girl looked small, fragile. She rested on a hospital bed, her slight frame barely causing a lump in the sheets. She was pale —she had never been one for sunbathing—but this was more. She was almost translucent. That she was alone added to the illusion of fragility.

Her hair lay on the pillow in thin threads. They too seemed almost faded, although she was not losing her hair. It had just become fainter.

It was like she was very slowly disappearing.

She was alone, surrounded by machines that supposedly kept her alive. But that was debatable. As fragile as she looked, she might have stayed alive without them. She was a warrior deep down. But for now, an IV dripped into her arm, an oxygen tube ran to her nostrils, monitors of all sorts ran cables to her body, like she was some sort of machine.

Dark circles framed her eyes and sometimes her lips pulled back almost like she was smiling. Altogether she looked like a cadaver.

And Christopher was afraid.

He stood on the ledge outside the hospital window. His standard uniform—a coat made of shadows, the cowl of the hood so dark nobody could see his face—swirled about him in shifting patterns of black and gray. It was the uniform of the Hunter of Lost Souls, the Lord of Damnation, and a bunch of other titles he didn't want to think about.

And he was trying his best to not think of it. Trying not to think about his job now, hunting down the dark souls that had escaped from hell and reaping their souls with his blade to send them back to that infernal prison.

He was not hunting tonight, however; he was here to visit, just as he had done every day since he had brought her here. He raised his hand subconsciously and touched the window pane, knowing this was as close as close as he could get to her, wishing she would turn to him and smile. Okay, he didn't even need a smile, just some small movement, something to give him hope.

He knew she was still in there, he could see it in her aura, the faint light that was her soul. It was muted now as she struggled. And even deeper down inside Eris' dull-lighted soul Christopher could see the darkness that was the demon who shared her body, Dark Eris. Neither one knew how they came to share that body; they had hoped Christopher, recently named champion of Hell, could help them.

Now here they were in a hospital room on the edge of death. Some help he'd provided.

He did not dare go visit her properly, he couldn't go sit by her side touching her hand, willing her back from close. No, he had brought her here in all his raging, hellish glory. In his grief and rage the power had run wild from him. When he had come to this hospital it was an entrance like no other.

He had been careless and was not even sure if they had seen his face. Had he dropped the uniform in his mad dash to get her help? He didn't remember. He did remember the look of fear on the nurses' faces. He had seen the reluctance and sheer terror in the doctors' eyes when he pulled them away from their immediate patients to focus on Eris. He had put the fear of the devil into the entire staff and made clear the consequences of what would happen if she should die.

She had no records, a Jane Doe to them. They were working

blind. Dark Eris, trapped deep inside of Eris, could not help heal her with her power. Christopher had decided this was good as he was pretty sure he would not have been able to control the doctors if they had seen such a miracle at work.

As it was there were enough questions. They knew who he was, his fame proceeding him to some extent. Nobody truly knew who or what he was, just YouTube videos and speculation. He told them only that she had been an innocent who had been caught in the crossfire and that he just wanted to get her help. He told them she was nobody to him, just an innocent bystander.

Once she was getting the treatment she needed, and the cops and reporters started showing up, Christopher took his leave, jumping from a hospital window and into the night.

He could not risk being recognized or face the barrage of questions that would come from the doctors and reporters if he went in there to visit.

So here he was outside the window looking in, hoping she was winning the battle she was fighting. All this power and nothing he could do for her.

Three months later and still nothing he could do for her. Well that wasn't entirely true. Through his lawyers he was quickly able to make arrangements to pay for any treatment she needed: the private rooms, no expense spared kind of treatment. He had doctors come consult from all over the world.

No doubt the doctors here wondered who was paying for it all, if they suspected it was the mysterious man who had brought her in they didn't say anything.

In the end none of it mattered. There she lay, broken and beautiful.

Enough of this, he thought and shut the door on that emotion. He turned from the window and leapt from the building, sailing over the busy street below to land on the building across the street.

He wanted to be hunting, but it was getting late. He should return to the Lair. But a part of him, a relatively new part, wanted to go on, wanted him to unleash his Weapon and collect souls for Hell. Before, he had wished away this power; now he was starting to savor it. He pushed the desire back down. He knew it was related to the piece of Hellpower he had tied to his soul to complete it and give himself enough strength to defeat the Demon Collector. The one who had done this to Eris.

The Demon Collector had wanted the demon inside her and had tried to carve his way in. Christopher had stopped him, but not before Eris had suffered serious damage. He had been too slow.

Now he trained every day, sometimes twice a day, with the world's greatest warriors from ancient to modern times in the Library, the place of all knowledge and his home away from home. He was determined to get better as fast as he could; he could not risk being slow and ignorant any longer. This was his life now and many people depended on him. If he didn't get better, the world would go to Hell —literally. If he didn't retrieve the dark souls when they escaped, nobody else would.

These were the dark thoughts that powered his flight through the city. He looked down at those below him. Sometimes he found he didn't even see their faces anymore, just their auras, their souls on display. More importantly he saw and smelled their sin. The evil inside of them. The world had become different shades of black and gray, the color of corruption.

Sometimes Christopher thought he was balancing a fine line between madness and sanity.

He arrived back at the lair through the secret entrance in the park just outside the Bronx Zoo. Hamlin, the detective who helped him track down dark souls, wasn't there. Christopher guessed he had regular police work to attend to. Hamlin was also somewhat limited to when he could come to the lair; he couldn't use the entrance in the park, that only opened to Christopher, but there was a mundane, if somewhat hard to find, entrance from the zoo. Of course, that meant coming and going only during zoo hours and or involved a lot of sneaking around.

Juan was there but didn't look up when Christopher entered. He rarely did. He sat at the computer station in the middle of the main room. Monitors spread out in a wall of imagery. News and social media streams filled many of the screens. Some, the ones directly in front of him, contained black backgrounds with green writing scrolling past like a scene from the Matrix movies. Others had what he called a code editor, and programming code sprawled across these in a language so foreign to Christopher that it could've been written in Egyptian hieroglyphics for all he could understand of it.

Christopher knew a thing or two about computers, but Juan was at a whole other level. In the few months he had worked with them he had upgraded, redesigned, and rebuilt their information system from the ground up, spending millions—Christopher had given him a virtually unlimited budget—in the process. There were some pieces of tech Christopher's predecessor had installed that even Juan didn't understand. "Some top-secret NSA shit," he had called it. He left it where it was until he had time to examine it.

He lived here—he'd had nowhere else to go after Christopher rescued him. That too had been Eris' doing. As he had carried her to the hospital she had kept repeating Juan's name, where he was located and that he could do "the computer stuff like in the movies".

Apparently, he also thought of Christopher as his personal limo. Christopher must have spent half his time taking Juan through the cube room to the other lairs throughout the world so he could check out each system and upgrade where necessary. Not all the lairs, that would take too much time, just the main ones.

Juan was young, teenager young and an anarchist. When Christopher had pulled him from that wrecked bunker he had been a big ball of fear. He had been living in the bunker hacking into infrastructure systems while being controlled by Golyat—apparently Christopher's archnemesis, although he hadn't even known he had an archnemesis until a few months ago.

"Hey Juan," Christopher said.

He didn't respond right away, and for a moment Christopher thought he hadn't heard him.

"Hi boss," Juan finally replied, not even looking up from the computer. His focus could be disconcerting at times. You never knew if he was listening to you. And half the time he wasn't. "I'm gonna need you to shuttle me on another trip to Europe. I need to finish setting up the redundant data centers there. No need to upgrade the actual network conduit; whoever set it up planned ahead. We got some of the biggest data pipes in the world coming into these lairs."

"Not today, Juan," Christopher said. "What have you discovered about your former Days of Chaos friends?"

The Days of Chaos was an idea cooked up by the dark soul Golyat, apparently to disrupt and cause...well, chaos and destruction throughout the world. To what end they didn't know. Hamlin thought it was so they—the mysterious alliance Golyat was part of—could step in and take over the world. "It's all about power with these evil fucks," Hamlin had said. Christopher didn't know if it was that simple.

"Well..." Juan began, spinning in his chair to look at Christopher. Then he paused. "Since when do you traipse around the lair in full damnation regalia?"

"I forgot I was wearing it," Christopher said. He dismissed his uniform of coat and hood back to the shadows from where it came, and he was once again dressed in jeans and a hoodie.

Hellcat, the former hellhound that he had freed from being forever bound in the same body with a dark soul, materialized out of the shadows. She jumped up on the couch and curled into a sleeping position, taking up most of the couch in the process. She looked like a panther, but much larger and more menacing. Except when she was curled up purring or taking up more than her share of the bed when he was sleeping.

"You should really give her a name," Juan said.

"She has a name. Hellcat," Christopher said.

"No, like a real name. If a dog is born in New York, you don't name it New York Dog, do you? Hellcat isn't a name, it's a description, and a pretty obvious one at that."

"You didn't answer my question," Christopher said dropping the subject of naming Hellcat. There were more important things to worry about than naming a cat.

Juan sighed and looked worried for a moment, then he shook it off and turned back to the computer. "Most of the contacts I knew through Days of Chaos have disappeared. Like, went invisible, not a trace."

"So, they're gone?"

"Hardly. These are the kind of guys who can do that, disappear as if they never existed; doesn't mean they're gone. They just went invisible."

"And you haven't been able to track them?"

"I have a little. I shut down a lot of their systems, removed them from some of the more intricate and sensitive government installations. With me hunting them and the feds of pretty much every first world nation looking for them, they're laying low. You definitely set them back when you interfered in Mexico."

"Don't sell yourself short, you did your part to help set things right."

"Yeah, after helping those assholes and killing hundreds of people."

"I thought you were past the beating yourself up stage," Christopher said, perhaps a little colder than he meant. "You're helping me now, it's a kind of redemption."

Juan gave him an odd look then said, "Anyway. I think you slowed down the Days of Chaos plan, but when it does come it will be swift and firm. No more testing the waters. They know you and all the governments in the world are on alert."

"Well I guess our job is to be ready for them."

"Whatever you say."

Juan got up and went to pet Hellcat. It had taken him weeks to even be close to her and even then, only if he was close to an exit. Now he treated her like a fucking housecat. She responded to Juan's petting by pushing her head into his hands so he would scratch harder.

"Isn't that right, Fluffy?" Juan said.

Hellcat's purring turned to a low rumbling growl.

"Maybe not," said Juan and pulled his hands away quickly.

When Christopher had first brought Juan here, he had been a wreck. Christopher couldn't blame him. He had been under some powerful sort of mind control, most likely from the one called Golyat, that had bent his talents to their will. They had used him, along with others, to form terrorist hacking cells whose main purpose was to disrupt government and civilian infrastructure as part of this grand plan called "Days of Chaos".

Juan had been traumatized once the cloud of mind control and confusion was lifted from him. His coding skills had undermined everything from emergency services to air traffic control and caused the death of hundreds. And it would have been in the thousands or worse if Christopher and Eris hadn't come along. On the verge of suicide when he was found by Eris, she had managed to pull him back from the edge.

She had convinced him there was still a chance and had set him to work minimizing the damage he, and others like him, had wrought. While Christopher had focused on defeating the supernatural force behind it all, Juan had dealt with his own kind of magic as he struggled to bring normalcy back to the cyberworld.

Afterward though, he was broken. During Christopher's mad dash to get her to the hospital, Eris, near death in his arms, had told him where to find Juan and that she thought he was worth saving.

That was good enough for Christopher. He had found Juan, buried deep beneath the earth in some sort of techno bunker. His mind had been royally fucked by the dark soul. He wasn't exactly suicidal anymore, but on the verge of falling back into the pit of depression. Juan was an anarchist and hated any form of government, but he had been used in a way that disgusted him. He thought he was part of a bigger, nobler purpose, but he had been used as a weapon for power and control, the very essence of what he was against.

Christopher had offered him a path toward redemption and he had jumped at it. Well, jumped is probably not the right word. By the time Christopher had explained what was really going on in that techno bunker and who—or what—was running the show, Juan was on the edge of insanity again. He pulled himself together when he realized that Christopher wasn't going to throw him down some pit to Hell. But just barely.

It wasn't until Christopher had flown him to the US and shown him the lair with its impressive computer array that he had truly gotten excited.

"This is nice," Juan said when he saw the computer set up in the middle of the main room. "Older, but impressive."

"That's not the half of it; just follow me," Christopher said. He gave Juan a quick tour of the lair, ending at the cube room. It was the most unsettling and therefore last room.

The room itself was straightforward. A rock formation with a square hole in the middle like an empty doorway, a map etched along the wall showing the location of all the lairs throughout the world, and the cube on the pedestal to control it. The cube room allowed Christopher to travel to any of his lairs on the planet instantly. Although startled at the supernatural element involved, Juan's real shock came when Christopher informed him that he would be responsible for maintaining all the tech systems across all the lairs, by himself for the most part.

"It's impossible," he said. "That kind of infrastructure, the man hours for maintaining the cabling alone in all these locations would be astronomical. You may not be Google, but you're going to need at least a small IT organization."

"I am confident you'll find a way," said Christopher. "My predecessor was able to do it, and I have a network of various employees on payroll that maintain the areas around the lairs. Restaurant managers, janitors, and facilities managers for hotels. Discreet individuals who think I am working on covert business arrangements, again all set up by my predecessor. You can work with them for everything outside; they turn a blind eye to what exactly we're working on. You would just be responsible for the inside portion of the lairs and the overall architecture."

Still Juan had hesitated, perhaps it was just too much? But Christopher needed him. Even his predecessor knew tech was an essential part of the future and their job.

"You'll help me save a lot of lives and you will be working outside the law. I would think that would appeal to you." Christopher said quietly, and making a quick decision added, "And I'll pay you quite well."

"And there it is," said Juan. "The deal with the devil." Before Christopher could protest Juan continued, "I'll do it. I'll do it to make up for my crimes. But also, since Eris believes in you, perhaps I can learn something too. But for the record, so far you seem like an asshole."

And they had left it at that.

Christopher's phone rang.

"That'll be Hamlin," Juan said. Christopher gave him a questioning look and Juan continued a little sheepishly. "I've been monitoring police communications as part of my general media surveillance."

Christopher glanced down, it was indeed Hamlin.

"Hello," Christopher said.

"Hi kid, you busy? Any hunting?" asked Hamlin.

"No, taking it easy tonight. Spent two days training today, so I'm little beat. What's up?"

"Well... it might be nothing. But..."

"Please don't tell me another hellhound is on the loose."

Hellcat lifter her head off the couch and made a low growl in her throat.

"No, nothing like that... well something like that, but not a hellhound. Look, I'm not sure what it is, but it's nothing I've seen before and I'd like you to take a look at it. Just to rule out you know..."

"The X-Files shit?" That was one of the ways Hamlin referred to Christopher's line of work. Christopher had never seen an episode, but he got the drift.

"Yeah, exactly."

"Is there another crime scene you want me to visit? What's the address?"

There was a pause on the other end, then Hamlin said, "No, not a crime scene. I'm at the city morgue."

4

Christopher met Hamlin just inside the entrance to the morgue. It was a sterile looking place—a cross between an aging doctor's waiting room and a small DMV office. The room itself was small, just big enough to hold a few chairs, which made sense; it wasn't like this was a hospital waiting room. The patients here had a very final disease and weren't going home.

It smelled old too, musty with the chemical scent of formaldehyde and other embalming fluids. The insistent buzz of the fluorescent light filled the room as much as its pale white light did. Christopher supposed that decor for the dead was low on the city budget list.

A young man—not much older than Christopher's twenty-one years—wearing a white lab coat sat behind a desk, busily chomping on gum and trying to look busy. He alternated between shuffling through papers and poking at his computer keyboard. The cause of his nervousness seemed obvious. A patrol officer stood next to his desk speaking with Hamlin. But Christopher had to imagine the morgue workers were used to having cops around all hours of the night. This was New York after all. People were always dying.

Besides the three of them, the only other person in the room was a security guard sitting on a chair in the far corner.

Hamlin noticed Christopher's arrival and moved to intercept him. The detective wore the usual ill-fitting suit that looked like it he had slept in it. His eyes had deep circles under them, and his face showed the normal rough five o'clock shadow. He was a walking cliché, both Christopher and Eris had told him that on more than one occasion. Unfortunately, that only seemed to inspire him to play the part more.

Christopher had remembered to let go of his uniform before coming into the building, dismissing his hooded coat and clothes of shifting dark back to the shadows from which they came. Hellcat had also retreated to the shadows.

"Hey kid, thanks for coming," Hamlin said as he approached. "Something weird is going on."

Christopher nodded toward the uniformed officer. "I see. Do you guys usually have an officer on duty at the morgue?"

"No, not usually. They have their own security," Hamlin said quietly and nodded to the security guard. The guard ignored them, engrossed in his magazine. "But this is no usual night."

Christopher glanced at the patrolman. "I assume we are going with the psychic shtick again?"

"Well, it seems to be working. 'Course now I got a reputation at the station for being a little bit superstitious."

"There are worse reps," said Christopher.

"A few days ago, I found an anatomically correct voodoo doll with a pin in its penis."

Christopher smiled. "So... how's it hanging?"

"Don't you fucking start. Hey Marone," Hamlin said to the patrolman as they approached. "This is the K.C. Edgar I was telling you about. He's gonna take a look for me."

The patrolman smirked. "Right, the psychic. Gonna check out the vibes. Whatever you say, detective."

Christopher could hear the amused disdain in the man's voice. Suddenly Christopher was pissed. Hamlin had made a lot of sacrifices for him and this was his reward? A lack of respect? Christopher paused as they passed the officer. The man met his eyes and what he saw there caused the disdain and amusement to drain away.

Christopher let a little of the hellfire become visible in his eyes. He offered a small, very small glimpse into hell for the man. He could smell the sin on him. It was all he needed.

"Tell me officer, is fifty percent off a blow job the normal fee to let a prostitute off the hook? "

The officer's eyes widened, but he couldn't look away, Christopher wouldn't let him.

"Tell me officer, what is your usual fee for looking the other way when a deal is going down? Certainly not as much as when they pay you to be the actual lookout."

The officer's mouth opened and closed beneath his wide eyes, like he was trying to protest. Naked fear showed in his eyes and Christopher could smell the piss running down his leg.

"Keep it up Officer Marone. I'll be hunting you soon enough."

Christopher looked away, releasing the man from his hold and walking past him to the rear door. He heard a sob from behind and formed a slight smile.

Once they were through the door and into the hallway, Hamlin stopped him.

"What the fuck was that?"

"The truth. Besides, it pissed me off the way he smiled at us. He's an asshole."

"Were those things, about him taking money really true?"

"Yeah, of course. But I wouldn't worry, his sins were minor in the grand scheme of things. I don't think there's any need to turn him in; what I did to him was far more damaging than any punishment the law could impose." Christopher looked down the corridor. "Now please, lead the way."

Hamlin stared hard at him for a moment as though unsure what to do with him. Then with a grunt of frustration, he turned down the hall. "Autopsy room 4. Come on."

They passed down a series of hallways. Tiled floors, plain white plaster walls. There were a few more people here in the morgue proper, most wearing various gowns or medical jackets, but a few wore street clothes. In one case, Christopher saw a distraught man, tears in his eyes and running down his face. Christopher could guess as to why he was here. He hurried past the man.

They came to room 4. Christopher knew this even before seeing the plaque with the number because there was another patrolman outside the door. This had to be unusual.

"Why so many resources to guard a dead body?" asked Christopher.

"It was at my request, and I can only pull these resources for a short time before my captain starts asking questions. I didn't want anybody to access the body, at least until you see it. Just in case."

"In case what?"

"In case this is more your jurisdiction than the NYPD."

This patrolman was more professional. He nodded silently to Hamlin and limited his interaction with Christopher to a suspicious look. Hamlin pushed the door open, and they went inside.

The first thing Christopher noticed was the cold. The floors and walls were stark white, and that same sterile fluorescent light filled the room. The only furniture in the room, besides some cushioned stools and chairs, were stainless steel. All of this did nothing to make the place feel warmer. One of the fluorescent lights flickered. It made Christopher think of a horror movie.

There were three tables in the room, each one held a naked gray body. One woman and two men.

"Is it always this cold in here?" Christopher asked.

"They keep the temp down for obvious reasons, but this one is colder than usual."

"Almost feels like we're the ones in the cadaver coolers," said Christopher. He could feel something in the cold. He could smell there was something wrong. Not just the stench of death, but almost like the lack of something else. He smelled emptiness. That was the best way he could describe it.

"Something's not right here."

"Good, that's why I brought you. Come on, let's look at the body."

"Yes let's, it sounds like fun."

They approached the female first. She was gray, and death had aged her; it took Christopher a moment to realize she was probably only a little older than him. "How old is she?"

"We don't have an ID on her yet, but the doc says mid-twenties. It looks like death is taking its toll on her pretty quickly."

"How did she die?" Christopher asked.

"That's just it. The doc has no idea. No obvious signs of trauma, no contusions or broken bones. No sign of asphyxiation or disease. No signs of any heart damage. We still need to examine the brain in detail, but doc thinks it will turn up clean also," Hamlin said.

"So, what does he think did it?"

"Natural causes, but he can't find any causes that make sense. The only thing out of the ordinary is the rapid deterioration of the body. I'm hoping you can rule out supernatural causes."

"What about these others?" asked Christopher. The other bodies had the same look of accelerated deterioration. These, however, were different ages. One of the men looked like he was in his seventies, but it was hard to tell with the skin rotting so quickly.

"These bodies are the same. No marks, no heart issues—other than it stopped working—no normal signs of death, either. Just this old, withered look."

Something was very off about these bodies. Christopher could feel it. But what? And how the hell was he supposed to tell anyway? He wasn't a doctor, not even a supernatural one. He stepped closer to the girl. Ignoring the faint smell of decay, he sniffed deeply, leveraging the bestial side of his supernatural nature. At the same time, he let his eyes shift slightly focusing on the Shadow Side, as he now thought of it, in order to read the aura of her soul. But of course she didn't have one. She was dead.

But her soul had not simply departed. Christopher could still smell that strange scent of emptiness, which gave some sense to what he saw on the shadow side. It was like there was a hole where her aura should have been.

Christopher had not seen anything like this before. Most dead bodies became lifeless lumps of organic material, no different than a pile of meat and bones, the aura and soul gone to whatever final destination it was marked for. But this wasn't the natural fade away of a soul in death, this was the rending of a soul, torn out of a perfectly good body.

Even as he watched, the 'hole' faded. It would be gone in moments.

"I think you were right, these aren't natural deaths."

When Christopher didn't continue, Hamlin asked, "Well, what the hell happened to them?"

"It looks... you know I'm still very new to all this so I could be way the fuck off."

"Got it kid, standard disclaimer. Give me your best guess."

"It looks like their souls were taken from them. Not natural death type soul-leaving, more like ripped from their mortal shell soul-taking."

"And this would kill them?"

"Yes, probably. Anyhow, in this case it looks like it did."

Hamlin just looked at him.

"Hey, I told you I'm no expert, not yet," said Christopher.

Hamlin nodded.

"Anything else unusual about them? Besides the cause of death?" asked Christopher.

"Now that you mention it, yes. They were all found in the Bronx, each at a different park. Including one too close for comfort."

"I take it you mean River Park, close to the lair?"

Hamlin nodded. "Whoever or whatever did this is working close to your office. Coincidence?"

"If it's one thing I've learned from everything that's happened to me, it's that things are rarely a coincidence."

"Funny, being a detective has taught me that same thing."

Christopher took a closer look at the old man cadaver. A part of him was surprised that he could move so close to a dead body. A year ago, he wouldn't have even been able to set foot in a morgue, let alone examine a rotting corpse from a few feet away.

"How long ago did they die?" Christopher asked.

"Not sure. The Doc was having a hard time placing time of death. The bodies were just too... ambiguous. He did think they were killed a week or two apart."

"But they were found at the same time? Buried?"

"Nope. Just dumped there on the grass on the other side of the river. But yeah, we found them all on the same day, so he must have stored them somehow until he was ready to dump them."

"He? How do you know?"

"I don't. I'm just old with old habits. Besides most serial killers are men. That's a real statistic."

"But this isn't a serial killer, at least not a traditional one. This is some sort of supernatural entity. It has to be."

Hamlin nodded and asked, "Any ideas?"

Christopher shook his head, "Based on what we have experienced, it could be anything from a regular old serial killer with some occult skill to a gigantically fat dark soul with a God complex..."

Then a theory clicked in his head. "Hell, it could have been that girl that was with him—what's his name? Golyat?—she could manipulate souls, mine anyway. Of the usual suspects, we know she would be top of the list."

They had learned little of this mysterious group referred to as The Alliance. The best he and Hamlin could tell, it was a group of dark souls that had banded together for some purpose. They believed the leader of this group, or at least a member, was a rather large dark soul by the name of Golyat. Christopher had finally set eyes on him deep underground, beneath the slums of Mexico City. He had briefly fought Golyat, and it was clear he was outmatched. But a lot had changed in the months since that encounter.

Golyat had a girl with him in the cavern under the slums. She hadn't been a fellow dark soul. She had been mortal, albeit one with an unusual gift.

"You mean the little girl that almost killed you?"

"Well, I don't know if I would put it that way."

"Yeah, I think you said she was ten or something..."

"More like fifteen," Christopher corrected Hamlin. The detective was enjoying this way too much.

"Sure, whatever. You said she had been messing with your soul, right?"

"She was manipulating the shard of my soul that had been taken by the were-hellhound. She was somehow able to use that to hurt me. Almost control me."

"But she wasn't able to control you?" Hamlin asked, but he knew the answer.

"No, not yet. I was able to fight it. I closed that part of myself off by drawing on my power to fill the gap."

"I've meant to ask about that, you don't talk about it..."

Christopher cut him off, "It's not really important now. We can talk after we solve this little problem."

Hamlin stared at Christopher for a second as though debating something. Then he sighed. "My point is, she seemed untrained maybe? She's young, right?"

"Yeah, that's probably right."

"Well, maybe she's practicing?"

"You mean on these victims? To go from manipulating a small portion of a soul to stealing them from living humans seems like quite a jump to me."

"I agree, but if she has a former inmate of Hell or a group of them helping her? With the insane resources these guys have access to, they might be able to hurry her training along."

Christopher sighed. "Yeah, we know these dark souls all have different talents and abilities. If they are backing her, they might have found some way to speed up her development. But it could just as easily be a new dark soul that we haven't encountered yet, some newly escaped menace."

Hamlin nodded thoughtfully, "True. This girl as a suspect is just one theory. We can't get tunnel vision. That's detective work 101, it's just so hard to remember the basics in this new supernatural world I now live in."

"Tell me about it," Christopher mumbled.

"If only there were some sort of resource with unlimited knowledge that could maybe give us some guidance..." Hamlin said.

"Google?" Christopher asked.

Hamlin just raised an eyebrow.

"Okay Spock, I get it. You want me to ask the Librarian." Christopher said.

The Librarian was the only resident of an infinitely large library housed in another dimension. A library that contained all the knowledge in the universe and was accessible via the Book that Christopher had inherited when he assumed the office of the Lord of Damnation. The Librarian was kind of a consultant to Christopher's office. There was some debate over whether the Librarian was even real. That didn't seem to stop him from being a dick, however.

"I can ask him about this and the girl. I have a training session soon. I can speak with him then," said Christopher.

"You still training regularly?"

Christopher nodded, "At least once a day, sometimes two or three sessions a day."

"Jesus kid," said Hamlin, genuinely showing concern this time. "I've seen how you are after training. Don't kill yourself by overworking."

"I have to get better, Hamlin. That's the only way I'll be able to do my job. My prey isn't slowing down and I can't afford to, either."

"Maybe, but there is more to fighting this evil than being fast with that Weapon. If you're in too much pain or too exhausted, you might miss what's really important."

"Oh yeah, Hamlin? And what's that?"

Hamlin looked like he was about to answer, when a man walked into the room. He came up short when he noticed them standing next to the corpses.

"Oh, hello detective. I didn't expect to see you back again so soon. Did you forget something?" asked the man. He was older and wearing a white lab coat, thick glasses rested on his nose and his forehead cracked in veiny wrinkles when his eyes raised in surprise.

"No doc. I was just getting KC up to speed here. He's a...um..."

"Consultant. Specialist really," Christopher said.

"What kind of specialist?"

"Death, or rather what happens right afterward," said Christopher.

Now the doctor's eyes came together in a frown.

"He's a psychic," Hamlin offered. Christopher noted he said it much quieter than usual.

The doctor's face switched back to surprise with not a small amount of amusement. "I see. Any of these guys tell you what happened to them?"

"Speaking with the dead is a medium, I'm a psychic," Christopher said. He had no idea why he was getting angry at the doctor. Christopher was neither a medium nor a psychic. He just didn't like this man's smug-as-fuck looks.

"What's the difference?" asked the doctor.

"Here let me show you."

Christopher stepped toward the man. Then Hamlin was at his side grabbing his elbow.

"I think we've seen all we can here. Let's get out of the doctor's hair."

Christopher allowed Hamlin to guide him around the doctor and into the hallway beyond. It was for the best; there was no telling what he would do to the good doctor. He felt the anger bubbling up from his Hellpower inside, but he held it back.

This was not the first time he had felt the irrational anger burning him up on the inside, but he thought he was over it that last time. Apparently, the curse was still on him.

When they came back to the lobby, Officer Marone had moved to the other side of the room. As soon as Christopher came through the door, his eyes bolted down as though the ugly floor was some great work of art and he was frantically trying to analyze it for an upcoming art history class quiz. His pants were wet like he had tried to clean them off in the bathroom.

He still smelled like urine.

Outside the building, Hamlin hissed in Christopher's ear. "You can't go around starting something with folks just because they piss you off. It's called life. Sometimes you just need to ignore it. What's gotten into you?"

Christopher yanked his arm away from Hamlin's grip and gave him a cold look.

"I'll go to the Library and see what I can get out of my creepy friend there. What are you going to do?"

For a moment it looked like Hamlin was going to fight, give Christopher a piece of his mind. But then he just sighed, sounding like the oldest man in the world. "I'm gonna check all the locations where the bodies were found, see if there is any connection to our night job that the other officers missed."

Christopher nodded once and then turned down the street. He could feel Hamlin's lingering stare on his back. Christopher ignored it.

5

Christopher materialized in the Library standing in the middle of the study area. The Librarian was only a few feet away with his back to Christopher. This was a first, catching the Librarian by surprise. Although traveling to the Library was as simple as opening the Book and letting it transport him here, the actual journey, lasting a fraction of a second, was disorienting and strenuous, to say the least. It was getting easier, however; his first time he thought he was being torn apart mentally and physically. The pain was still there but dulled somewhat with experience.

The Library itself was the same extra-dimensional space it always was. Shelves stacked high, filled with obscure artifacts, scrolls, stone and wood tablets, but mostly books, reached up toward a ceiling obscured by mist and darkness. These shelves stretched off into an almost infinite number of rows.

The walls of the vast room were of old stone. Castle walls, Christopher thought. There were several doors and hallways from this room, but Christopher knew they just led to other rooms just as big or bigger. All the knowledge of the universe was stored in this place and couldn't be contained in earthly dimensions.

It smelled of ancient ideas and modern concepts—a scent of old, yet fresh at the same time. A fire burned in the hearth set in one wall, giving a slight wood smoke scent. Comfy wingback chairs stood next to it, and just behind them were a couch, table and large wooden desk with a well-cushioned chair behind it.

As daunting as this place was, Christopher had found it feeling more and more like home for him. He could never live here, but while visiting, he felt safe. He had been told this was all a metaphor for the true power of the Book. That this library had been created just for him to process and understand the knowledge represented by this powerful artifact. Therefore, it was a part of him.

The Librarian turned moments after Christopher had arrived.

"Interesting. Normally I know when you are on the way," the Librarian said. The Librarian was tall, draped in dark shadowy robes like the coat and clothes Christopher formed out of shadow for his uniform when hunting. The robe and hood covered his body entirely; Christopher had never seen a piece of the Librarian's skin, not even a hand from the sleeve and nothing could penetrate the darkness of his hood.

He didn't walk so much as float through the stacks; Christopher wasn't even sure he had feet. His voice was heavy, dark, and full of mystery.

If Christopher hadn't been used to the Librarian, he would have been scared shitless. As it was he only said, "I seem to have the drop on you for once. How's it hanging?" He was as much surprised as the Librarian.

"It is *hanging* just fine. I'm not surprised your comfort level with the Library has increased. You have become far more accustomed to your power and ability over the last few months."

"Thank you for the compliment," Christopher said. Any praise from the Librarian was very rare and usually ended in a backhanded compliment.

"I don't think it was a compliment," said the Librarian. Ignoring Christopher's puzzled stare, he went on, "What brings you to visit my little abode? I assume it wasn't just to sneak up on me and yell boo?"

Christopher walked over to the couch and dropped onto it. He slid into a slump with a sigh.

"Please make yourself comfortable," the Librarian said.

"Hamlin and I have come across a puzzle we were hoping you could help us with. Well, this is more Hamlin's show, but it does seem to tie into my work."

"Ah, the downtrodden detective and the work of the Hunter? You have my attention."

"He found a body, three bodies actually, that appeared to have their souls removed."

"That is typically what happens when mortals die. Have you been paying attention at all?"

Now it was time for Christopher to ignore the sarcasm. "These souls were removed before they died, presumably causing the death. There was no other medical reason."

"So, these souls were not removed through the typical means, such as a magic sword through the gut? Interesting."

"We, Hamlin and I, have a theory..."

"How is Eris?" the Librarian asked.

The question caught Christopher by surprise and for a moment he was nonplussed. The Librarian rarely showed interest in his companions in the real world. "No change. Still in a coma. Juan has hacked into her medical files, so I get a little information that way, but not a lot. I can't do much more than stare at her through a window at night. I send money for all the expenses of course, anonymously. She has the best care." He said that last part more defensively than he would have liked.

"Why do you ask? I mean you never really seemed to care about my friends before."

"Nonsense, I care about all those working with the Hunter of Lost Souls. I like to keep on top of your associates." The Librarian had glided closer to the fire and now loomed over Christopher. "And Eris is different, she is special."

"Because of the half-demon thing?"

"No, because I like her better than you."

"You haven't even met her. She can be a real pain in the ass."

"I know. From everything you have told me she seems very good for you. Both do."

"Look, can we get back to the topic at hand? Hamlin and I need help," said Christopher.

"Yes, unauthorized soul removal. Do you have any other details?"

"Just some guesses and instincts."

"From your lifetime of soul hunting experiences, I presume. Lay it on me, as the kids say these days."

While Christopher was pretty sure the kids did not say that line these days, correcting the Librarian wouldn't make a difference.

"Hamlin and I thought it might somehow be tied to the girl who had been working with Golyat. The one that was with him in Mexico."

"The one who had somehow ended up in possession of the piece of your soul that werehellhound had absconded with."

"Yeah, that's the one. I mean it's tenuous at best, but she was able to do some stuff to me by manipulating that piece. It's really the only lead we have."

"While I can't guarantee it is her, the connection is valid."

Christopher perked up. "Really?"

"Yes. I did some research when you first told me about her and based on what I have found, I think I might know what she is."

After a long pause, while Christopher sat literally on the edge of his seat, he finally asked: "And?"

"I hesitate because I am not one hundred percent certain, and I am not sure you are going to like it."

"Since when have you been considerate of my feelings?"

"Well, you've been through some shit as they say, and I am not sure how it is affecting your mental state. I suddenly feel the need to watch what I say."

"You're worried I'm on the verge of a nervous breakdown?"

"Nothing quite so mundane. Crack like an egg is more like it. Go mad. Batshit crazy. And that is the last thing this world needs. A dingbat with a magic sword."

Suddenly Christopher was angry. "Why the hell is everybody suddenly so concerned about my feelings and mental state? I'm fine. If anything, I'm better than fine. I am slowly but surely mastering my powers; I've become a much more efficient Hunter. I'm way better than I was before!"

"Before?" asked the Librarian.

"Before, you know *before*. Look, just don't hold anything back. I'm going to be just fine, and I need all the information you can give me. You're the Librarian, act like it!"

There was a long silence. Then the Librarian spoke.

"So be it. I believe this mortal girl child you encountered was a witch. And a very special one at that."

"You mean a cauldron and broomstick kind of witch?"

"Minus the cauldron and broomstick, yes. Witch is just one of the words used to describe any mortal, usually female, that has certain unexplainable abilities, usually termed magic. There are many kinds of these beings, but I think the one we are dealing with is a soul shaper."

"Sounds like the right name. What exactly do these types of witches do?"

"Didn't get it from the name? Alright. She can shape souls. Manipulate them and turn them to her desire. She can cause pain and suffering directly, as she did to you in Mexico. She can also twist and corrupt little parts of a soul. She can shift emotions and to some extent, control a victim's actions."

Christopher shuddered, remembering what she had done to him; the pain had been intense. It had almost killed him.

"Usually their power is limited unless they can actually gain access to a soul. There are all sorts of rituals for drawing souls to them when they pass and even to take a soul from a living being. Or as in your case, use a portion of one fetched by a werehellhound."

"You make it sound so trivial."

"Not my problem if you can't keep your soul together. It is not, however, trivial. These are rare and coveted beings. You, more than anyone, know the value of the soul. Imagine a being that can manipulate who you are fundamentally. Not mind control, soul control. It is the essence of who you are, not just a parlor trick."

"So, it's possible that she is the one taking these souls?"

"I'd say more than possible. Soul shapers are very rare. I know of none that have appeared in the modern era. It is doubtful there is another one or another being that has a similar power. Only..."

"Only?" asked Christopher.

"Only you said she was very young; and stealing souls—even manipulating you with the shard she had of your soul—is very advanced. From what I was able to ascertain only a highly gifted soul shaper would be able to do that at so young an age."

"She is working with the Alliance, at least with their leader Golyat, so she would have some powerful supernatural backing."

"She would be a strong weapon for them. No witches, soul shaper or otherwise, are necessarily born evil. But if she was corrupted by them, they could easily twist her to their will. My guess is Golyat is helping her obtain these souls to practice on."

"You mean she has the poor souls and is torturing them? For practice?"

"That is one theory. Although she is not necessarily torturing them. I doubt sadistic pleasure is her or Golyat's goal."

"If that's one theory, what's the other?"

"My dear boy, I don't think you understand the extent of the problem here. As much as it distracted you from saving Eris, causing you pain was the least of her potential. The real damage she did to you was the damage she did to your soul, the one you have now. You are changed. Yes, some of it you did yourself when you took in the Hellpower to replace what she had taken, but most of your personality change was from her manipulations."

"I haven't changed really, I've just gotten better at my job." Christopher paused and then added sheepishly, "Okay, perhaps I've changed a little, but you can't have a job like this and not change. It twists you all up inside."

"Yes, but you are changing fundamentally; it is far beyond just becoming jaded. Now imagine if you could somehow change someone in power, someone important. Make them... different. Take a family man, average, but a decent person, and then turn him into a homicidal maniac? Not just screw up his mental state, but make him crave evil deep down. No suggestion or mind control to wear off, it's just who they now are."

"A world leader. She could corrupt anybody, she could mess with someone who holds real power. The president even."

"Exactly. Not just corruption with power or money as you humans seem so fond of, but with real evil. Who needs an army, when you have the leaders of the world in your hand?" the Librarian asked.

"Jesus," Christopher whispered.

"You keep invoking that name. I am pretty sure he's not going to jump in to help the Lord of Damnation."

"So, what do I do?" Christopher asked. He liked it better when it was just a monster he had to look out for, not a teenage girl on a power trip.

"Seems pretty straightforward. Stick her with your sword," said the Librarian.

"It's gonna be that easy huh?" asked Christopher. Of course, he already knew the answer.

"It never is. She has her own power, the depths of which I don't know. She will have defenses that are not just tied to soul manipulation."

"Not to mention the full force of this Alliance of dark souls behind her," Christopher added.

It was quiet for a moment, neither spoke. It seemed like the weight of the office pressed down on Christopher's shoulders.

"Were you going to visit the journal room, perhaps pick up a hunt?"

"Fuck no. This is enough on my plate."

"Ah, training it is then?"

Christopher let out a groan. But he knew it was the right thing to do; he needed all the help he could get. And training via the library had some cool advantages.

"What will it be?" The Librarian asked. "I know this Mongol who could really help you get over your fear of pain..."

"Get over my fear of pain? You're a real salesman," said Christopher. "Besides, I can still feel the bruises from last time. Got anything more mellow?"

The Librarian seemed to think it over. "Come, follow me."

The Librarian glided back to the stacks with Christopher following close behind. They passed dusty volume after dusty volume and the occasional skull or other curiosity. Christopher had no idea how a skull, or really most of this other junk qualified as knowledge, but it must have been here for a reason.

They stopped at a row of books covered in what looked like Chinese. Even as he watched, the characters changed to English. He could understand any spoken language, and apparently that applied to the written word as well. He could make out the words Kung Fu, Tai Chi, and other Chinese words written in English, but he didn't recognize them.

"This is the book of one of the greatest Kung Fu masters to have ever lived," said the Librarian.

"Kung Fu doesn't sound mellow," said Christopher.

"You're learning to fight, kind of hard to find 'mellow.' Besides, he also has experience with the softer styles like Tai Chi. After all the months of training, many hours per day training with a dozen of the best warriors, I think you can handle this. It will probably be a walk in the park compared to what you've been through."

"You're right, just another day of training."

Christopher took the book and opened it. Then he was standing in an alley. He didn't recognize it—he spent a lot of time stalking alleys in his new role as Hunter—and he didn't think it was New York. Trash cans, overflowing, were propped up against one side next to a door that, based on the smell and noise, led to a Chinese restaurant.

There were a few other non-descript doors, paint peeling, one with a broken lock. There was only one other door with a small light just above it. A faded sign above it said 'gym.'

While he could hear the people talking inside the restaurant and the occasional car passed the alley mouth, Christopher knew he wasn't in the real world right now. This was just another pocket dimension where time did not pass for the Library or the real world. This was all just figments of some Kung Fu dude's memories. Here he could spend as long as he wanted training with the greatest warriors the world had ever seen.

There were times he had spent days in one of these dimensions, training as hard as he could, making himself better, learning how to wield the Weapon, how to fight the unknowable monsters that would populate his life.

The teachers he found here were not ghosts. They were not souls of long dead masters, nor were they truly real, but they might as well be. These books he stepped into represented the collective thoughts, ideas, skills, and life experiences of real people, in this case, warriors. They created this sort of virtual reality he could experience and that his mind could understand and interact with.

He could train with any fighter who had ever lived. It was an elegant solution for someone who had to learn to fight foes that would be different every time, with different weapons and skills. It was also hard as fuck. He was basically getting his ass kicked daily by a variety of people whose primary job was to perfect ass kicking.

The light above the door and faded sign flickered. That must have been where he was supposed to go. A gym sounded like as good a place as any to prepare for getting his ass handed to him.

The door opened easily under his hand into a large open space covered with the thinnest of mats. Martial art weapons hung from the walls. Nunchucks seemed to be the preferred weapon on display, many of them hung from hooks. The air smelled of stale sweat and maybe faintly of blood. It also smelled of wood—paneling covered the walls—and age.

There was a man across the room from him, he faced away from Christopher. He was short, but obviously wiry. He was shirtless and his pants were loose in a traditional martial style uniform. His back was packed with small, but defined muscles. The man's body fat percentage had to have been as close to zero as you can get. There was a tension in him even as he stood, like a tiger about to pounce.

He knew who it was even before the man turned around to confirm it. Christopher's mouth dropped open.

"You're Bruce Lee!" Christopher said. And all at once he knew this was not going to be the mellow session he had asked the Librarian for. "You're Bruce Lee," he said again, only this time it came out more like a moan.

6

Hamlin arrived at the scene of the first murder, at least the first one they had found. Without a cause of death or normal body deterioration, time of death estimates were not very precise.

It was hot out, even at midnight in Concrete Plant Park. He was hoping it would be cooler here by the river, but he was out of luck. The patrolman who had drawn the short straw to guard the place was long gone. Not that he abandoned his post; Hamlin was sure he had been told to head home.

There had been no obvious signs of foul play, just a girl dead and used up. Nobody cared. The assumption was that it she had died of natural causes, although exactly which natural causes were to be determined. Many on the force had concluded she was a runaway; the death was inevitable. A normal, rational cause would show up. It would be drugs or perhaps some sort of suicide. Either way, they only had so much time to dedicate to a case like this.

It made Hamlin angry. Of course, he couldn't go to the detective in charge of the case and explain to him why he knew this was no simple suicide or heart attack. He couldn't go to his superiors and tell them that the monsters that go bump in the night and the boogie man were real. That would be just as crazy as letting them know he was buddies with the guy that ran around town—and now the world—wielding a flaming magic sword and killing those monsters.

Despite the YouTube videos of the kid doing his thing, most people still chose to think it was an elaborate hoax. Although that disbelief was changing rapidly, the last thing Hamlin needed was to be playing Commissioner Gordon to Christopher's Batman.

Most of the police tape had been removed, but it had been a sloppy job. He could see strands of the tape still clinging to a tree. The evidence, what little there was, had been collected. The forensic team had done their usual thorough job and left. The girl was probably already forgotten.

Hamlin wasn't sure why he was here. It was unlikely he would find something the forensic guys had missed. He just felt frustrated. Hamlin knew there was a supernatural element at play, that this wasn't a simple cut and dry case. There was a bigger picture and he couldn't tell anyone.

Obviously, he could talk with the kid about all this, but even with him something was very different. Part of it might have been the realities of this new life forcing him to grow up quickly, becoming cynical, jaded. But there was something more wrong with the kid; he was changing, and not in a good way. Hamlin had no idea what to do about it.

Perhaps if he did some poking around at the scene, with his insider knowledge of what might really be behind all this, he could find some clue overlooked by the forensic teams. But after twenty minutes of kicking around through grass and peering at every dirty cup and cigarette butt with his flashlight, he knew it was useless. The place had been searched thoroughly.

He paused and leaned against a lamppost, thinking. Not for the first time tonight he wished he had a cigarette. That was the one bad habit he had been able to quit; all his others were going quite strong, thank you.

The theory that these deaths were supernatural was just that, a theory. He needed some sort of evidence. He needed a lead and was coming up empty.

Across a stretch of wild growing grass and a tall fence stood the abandoned shell of the old concrete plant that the park was named after. It was a dilapidated structure made of brick and wood but held together more by moss and dirt. Graffiti covered the walls. Despite the effort to rehabilitate the park, the artists managed to make it through the fence and paint those walls with tags and sometimes impressive murals.

A movement in one of the upper windows caught his attention. For a moment a cigarette cherry flared up and cast a red glow on a dirty, bearded face. Then the man, realizing he had been seen, ducked away from the open window frame. The glass had been gone for many years.

It had to have been some homeless man, a transient or drug user taking up residence in the abandoned structure. It happened all the time and in any other situation, Hamlin would have ignored it. This was New York, a huge city; cops didn't waste effort on rousting the homeless from old buildings. But he wondered how long the guy had been there. Had he been here the night of the murder?

Hamlin was walking down the path toward the building before he even finished the thought. There might be a witness. It didn't take him long to find a way in. A portion of the chain-link was only laying against a fence pole. He tapped it with his foot and it moved easily from the pole. He grabbed the chain and pulled it back, revealing an entryway big enough for a person to fit through. He didn't even have to crawl.

In moments he was at the door to the building. There was a padlock on the rusted steel door, but after a short inspection, he saw that the bolts holding the latch had been sheared off. It only appeared locked.

Hamlin wasn't going to call for back up, but he wasn't stupid either. Whoever was in this place had seen him. He drew his gun, then kicked the door open.

It flew open with a rusty screech of protest and banged against the wall. A hinge cracked and the whole door sagged with a moan. It would never close again.

The room beyond contained only the detritus of past visitors. Trash littered the floor: food containers, syringes, old newspapers, and some clothing items long since deteriorated and moldy. His flashlight traced the walls. There was more graffiti in here, but darker.

The outside work was filled with colors and, while crude in some cases, seemed as though the artist was trying to improve his canvas. In here the graffiti was filled with dark colors: blacks, grays, and browns. It seemed the artist who had made it inside had a darker side. Suicide, weapons, human figures with x's where their eyes should be—these were the images here. Sloppy, paint dripping images as though painted by someone not fully in control.

Besides his flashlight, the only light coming in the room was from the row of small windows at the back. Most were coated over with mold and grime to the point of being almost opaque. Several were cracked or completely broken out. The broken ones let in light from the city outside, mostly from the few lamps that lined the walking path in the park. It was through these windows that he had seen the figure.

But there was no one in the room now. Then he heard a something. A quick shambling sound, like someone shuffling through trash. Hamlin's flashlight, playing over the wall at the back of the room, found a doorway and hall beyond. Somebody had used a black spray can to paint a monster's head around the door, the doorway its mouth. It was the same dark-minded artist, and the eyes floating over the door looked almost real in their dark intensity and fury.

There was another noise from beyond the monster's mouth. This one like a short squeak and sputter; it reminded Hamlin of a kid playing hid and seek, trying to keep from laughing in a hiding spot as a friend searched nearby.

"Is someone there? I'm a detective with the NYPD," Hamlin said, voice raised. The acoustics in the room were odd. Dead sounding, like his words never reached the walls to bounce off. They were dull in his ears.

There was no response. Whoever was hiding in there wasn't coming out.

"Look, I just want to talk. I'm not going to arrest you or anything. Come out, it'll be a lot easier for both of us."

Still deadness, still no answer.

Hamlin really didn't want to go in there. He knew instinctively this wasn't normal cop shit. He had been hanging with the kid long enough now to know when the tingle goes up his spine it's Twilight Zone time. With a sigh of the inevitable, he entered the monster's mouth.

The room beyond was darker than the other. There were windows here, but none were broken, so any light that got through was filtered through the murky green of filth and mold. It might have been Hamlin's imagination, but it seemed even his flashlight dimmed the moment he entered.

Part of the roof had caved in, and wood and old roofing material littered the floor. But even that gaping three-foot hole in the ceiling didn't let light into this dark place.

His feet kicked empty spray cans piled on the floor. These walls were also covered with images, but where the other room seemed painted with spray cans like traditional graffiti, this one looked like he had run out of paint and had resorted to a sort of black paste, like charcoal mixed with water.

The wall was even more elaborately drawn than the other room. Images of people bowing or lying on the ground at the feet of three figures. Large, all-black beings were drawn blurry as though even the artist couldn't keep the shape of these things in his own head.

Figures, not blurry, but sharp and focused, were scattered around them alternating between bowing and—not lying, but writhing—on the floor at their feet. The crude images almost seemed to move.

This can't be good, thought Hamlin. He heard a scraping sound and spun, aiming the flashlight at the opposite wall. There, crouched close to the floor was a person, a young man, younger even than Christopher. He wore jeans and a t-shirt with some sort of logo on the back, Hamlin didn't recognize it, but his fashion logo body of knowledge consisted of the Nike swoosh.

He had a cloth backpack at his feet, old spray paint cans sticking out. While the clothes looked new, they were covered in filth as though he had bought them a few days ago and then decided to live in a dumpster or sewer. The fingers of his right hand were black from the piece of charcoal he held. He was hunched over, drawing with the charcoal on the wall close to the floor. The baseball cap on his head tilted forward as though about to fall.

The kid paused when the light hit him. He turned his face slightly and looked back at Hamlin. He smiled but tried to hold it in. A giggle bursting to get out. Laughter sputtered through his lips when he could hold it in no longer. He smiled wide with shiny white teeth. Hamlin could only see him in profile. The kid didn't bother to turn around, he just looked at the detective with the one eye.

"The little girl wants me to kill you," the boy said and then laughed again. "She was pretty."

"Why would she want that?" Hamlin asked. His gun angled slightly down—he wouldn't shoot a defenseless kid—but ready to come up at the slightest threat. The last year had taught him things were not always what they seemed and this 'kid' could turn out to be a monster any second.

"She doesn't like you; the Hunter she said was a bad dude," the boy said. He still hadn't turned around, but drool had started to form on his lips, dripping on his pants.

"But I'm not the Hunter, I'm a cop, a good guy," Hamlin said. "Please don't do anything stupid, this is good just talking. Did she do something to you?"

The boy looked down as though a little uncertain. "She changed me, but now I see things, I understand things. Things she doesn't even know. She was so pretty. So innocent."

"How did she change you?"

"She, she, looked at me then I... twisted. She said to watch for the Hunter. And I did, but I am so hungry."

As soon as the words were out of his mouth drool followed. And a look of intense need washed over his face. The giggling smile was replaced by a toothy sneer. Hamlin was losing him.

"What things did you see?"

The kid glanced, still not moving from his crouched position, at the wall Hamlin had been studying a moment ago. The hand with the charcoal pointed.

"They are coming. Nobody knows, not even the girl that twisted me. Not you. They are coming. I saw this while I waited."

"Who is coming?" Hamlin asked.

The kid's eye glazed over as though he was far away. "Who's coming?" Hamlin asked again. A little louder than he should have, but he was afraid the kid wouldn't remain lucid for long.

"They are empty," the kid said. "The Empty people. They are coming, three I think. And they are very, very angry." The kid shuddered violently. "I don't want to talk about them anymore."

"Why did she want you to wait for me?" Hamlin asked. If the kid thought he was the Hunter, he would play the part. He had to get what he could before it was too late.

"She knew you would come because she took the soul of the girl. Then she changed me, she made me hungry. And now I know," the boy said, standing slowly.

"Know what?"

"What I'm hungry for," the boy said and turned from the wall he had been drawing on.

The entire front of the kid and half his face was black. Coal black. At first, Hamlin thought he had just been pressing up against the wall, rubbing the black dust over himself. But then he could see it, the burnt flesh. His body had been burned so severely it was hardening into bits and flecks of charcoal. He had been peeling parts of himself off to make his drawings. Cracks in his blackened hide oozed blood and pus, like a burn victim who should be dying in a hospital bed, not walking and talking in front of Hamlin.

The kid's face was the worst. One half looked normal, maybe even handsome. But the burnt side was a horrible visage. Lips peeled back, exposing blackened teeth and charred gums in another sneer, this one much more gruesome than the last. His eyelid had burned away, but his eyeball stared back at Hamlin, an undamaged white orb.

Hamlin could see faint wisps of smoke rising from the blackened side of the kid's body. Despite being impossible, he was still burning. The kid must have been in intense pain.

"Jesus kid, let me help you. Let's get you to a hospital."

"No," The kids voice had become deeper, edged with slyness and barely contained desire. "I just need a good meal."

The boy charged forward, a half-normal, half-burned sneering smile on his face. He kicked trash up from in front of him.

Hamlin reacted slower than he should have. He had hoped to talk the kid down, he was just a kid. The sudden charge caught him by surprise. He raised the gun. But the kid, the thing charging him, was faster than he expected, certainly faster than he should be considering he was a walking burning corpse.

Before Hamlin could squeeze the trigger, the kid slammed into him like a wrecking ball, his arms splayed out, knocking the gun from Hamlin's hand. A round went off, punching through the rotting floorboards. Hamlin watched the drooling lips pull back even more, exposing soot-covered teeth. Now his mouth opened wide to take a chunk out of the detective.

Hamlin recovered quickly, but not enough to catch his balance before tripping over the debris on the floor. He brought his arms in and between him and the kid holding those chomping teeth inches from his throat.

He almost lost his grip on the monster as he landed on the ground. Wood and nails from the fallen ceiling raked at his back. Something hard and sharp cut straight through his shirt and gouged his skin.

Despite the impact and cuts, he held the kid at bay, despite its unnatural strength. Here was yet another thing a half-burnt corpse shouldn't be able to do. Whatever the girl had done to this kid, he was more monster than human now. Hamlin could feel the heat pouring off its body. Wherever his hand or arm touched the blackened flesh, he could feel it burning him. Not a severe burn like an open flame would create, but uncomfortable heat like a bad sunburn eating at his skin.

Taking the risk, Hamlin held the monster back with one arm while he quickly released his grip with the other hand to punch it. His fist slammed into the human looking half of its face. The kid's head twisted from the force of the blow and his grip lessened, but held. Hamlin pounded him again and again. Blood flew on the last strike as a cut opened on the creature's face.

But the blows only had a marginal effect. The monster reared back and let loose with his own blows. With the temporary reprieve from the snapping jaws, Hamlin was able to get his hand up to protect his face from the full force. Still, the fist was like a sledgehammer making stars fill Hamlin's vision.

A second blow followed the first, then a third. Blood ran into Hamlin's eye and he knew it was his own. The kid was now straddling his chest, he had the leverage and the angle. It bellowed in some sort of primal victory cry. Another blow and Hamlin would be out, but the monster didn't go for another punch. Instead its head came down for a bite, no doubt thinking Hamlin was stunned. It was expecting a docile meal.

Hamlin was anything but docile.

The head diving at him was a wavering blur made fuzzy by blood, but Hamlin threw his arm up shoving his forearm blindly at the gaping jaw. He caught it by surprise, but then Hamlin felt teeth sinking into the muscle on his arm.

Now Hamlin's own screams joined with the monster's animal grunts as it latched on. Pain, as well as disgust, drove the adrenaline coursing through his veins to a whole new level.

He bucked hard and the monster, for all its viciousness and strength still weighed the same as an emaciated teenage kid. He flew off Hamlin, but with his mouth still attached, he didn't go far.

He landed next to Hamlin, wrenching the detective's arm to the side and setting off even more pain. The floorboard creaked loudly, followed by a crack and suddenly the floor beneath the monster was gone. With a surprised grunt, the kid fell through the hole.

Unfortunately, Hamlin was still attached. He was pulled into the hole, catching himself just as he slid partially over the edge, hanging half in, half out. For a moment, despite the monster hanging from his arm, he thought he might be able to work with this. Then there was another crack.

The floor collapsed beneath Hamlin and they both plunged into the darkness.

The room below was pitch black. During the fall he felt the monster pull away, ripping off part of his skin in the process. But he was no longer attached. Then Hamlin slammed into the concrete floor. His breath was knocked from his body and he was pretty sure that sharp pain in the side of his chest was a rib cracking.

He was surrounded by darkness, the only light coming from the hole above, and that was from his dropped flashlight pointed at a wall. Only the faintest of gray light was down here, but it was enough to see the large mouth-shaped black spot on his forearm. Though he couldn't see it well, the pain was enough to tell him it was bad.

He saw a glowing from the darkness, like angry red cracks. It took him only moments to understand what he was looking at. It was the kid. The flame underneath his charcoal half had flared. The monster now looked like some kind of lava creature.

Hamlin struggled to roll to his feet. His ribs and the rest of his battered body cried out in pain. The sharp stab in his ribs stunned him with its intensity, he sucked air in through his teeth.

The monster moved toward him, limping slowly; it must also be injured from the fall. It moaned a gurgling crackle sound like water on fire. That was all the motivation Hamlin needed to fight through the pain. He staggered to his feet, his hands falling on what felt like a bottle on the floor. Desperate for any weapon, he grasped the neck and came to his feet.

The monster lurched forward swinging at the detective. Hamlin couldn't see anything about the room in the murky dark, but the glowing red fissures crisscrossing the monster's body gave him a nice target. He swung the bottle up, smashing it into the human side of the monster's face.

The glass shattered as the shard still in Hamlin's hand dragged across the creature's face. It screeched and staggered back, its half-blackened hands came up to its face in a reflexive gesture.

Hamlin took advantage of the moment and charged. The darkness made it impossible for him to find a way out of the room quickly; his only option was to take the thing head on. He slammed into it, shoulder down in a brutal tackle reminiscent of his football days.

Of course, when he played football he had been thirty-five years younger and didn't have a cracked rib and bruised body. The sharp stitch of pain in his ribs made him falter, his charge lacked power. His shoulder made contact with the smoldering creature's chest. He felt the burning heat through his shirt and its tough charcoal like skin was like connecting with brittle rock. Chunks fell away from it, and Hamlin pushed it up against a stone wall.

Its arms came down in a massive blow to his back, driving him to his knees. The creature took hold of Hamlin's torso, and with unnatural strength tossed him to the side. Hamlin spun through the air and landed in a heap.

More bruises and cuts and a thousand points of pain. With cold dread, he realized this might be it. He lay on his back in the pile of debris from the room above. He could see the faint light filtering in from the windows above. His eyes must have adjusted to the low light because he could now see some moonlight cutting through, stirred up dust danced through it.

He never thought he would be one of those guys that waxed poetic at the moment of his death. But here he was not even considering getting back up. The monster was just too much.

He could hear it grunt, taking its time to pounce. Maybe it was hurt more than he knew. The thought emboldened him, and he ran his hands through the debris searching for another bottle or piece of wood, anything he could use as a weapon. Then the monster was looming over him.

It gazed down at him with a mix of amusement and hunger. All traces of humanity were gone. It was a monster in the dark, unnatural and as far from a human kid as possible. There was a smile-sneer on its face, but he could see the cuts and blood on its human side. It might think it had won—and truthfully, it might—but it was hurt. Hamlin could at least say he put up a good fight.

Then his flailing hand hit something hard and metallic. It was the butt of his gun. Somehow it had fallen with him. He wrapped his hand around it.

"When she made me, when she showed me a new way, she said the Hunter would be hard, he would be dangerous and I had to be careful to kill him," the monster said. His voice was more stone on stone than human. Then he shrugged. "I think you are not dangerous, you are no Hunter."

"You're half right," Hamlin said. "I'm not the Hunter, but I am dangerous. I'm NYPD motherfucker!"

He pulled the gun from the debris and swung it at the monster. He felt a moment of satisfaction as its eyes went wide for a moment. Then Hamlin was pulling the trigger, and its head slammed back as the round found his forehead. Hamlin kept pulling the trigger, firing round after round into the thing. The first round might have killed it, but Hamlin wasn't taking any chances. The force of the shots knocked it back and as bullet after bullet found its mark, it jerked left and right in a macabre dance.

By the fifth shot, it fell against the far wall. Hamlin kept firing. He heard a cry that built up to a scream nearby before realizing it was him. Then the gun was clicking in his hand, the magazine empty.

The blackened creature sat against the wall, eyes open but unseeing. His body was still giving off smoke where the fire burned.

Hamlin was sitting up, the pain in his body nearly forgotten as he used every ounce of concentration on killing that thing.

Once he was sure it wasn't going to jump up like every bad guy in every horror movie, he holstered the gun and focused on trying to stand. He got to his feet but quickly staggered to a wall to hold himself up. His stomach turned and he wanted to throw up more than he had ever wanted to throw up in his life. Somebody was listening to his inward pleas, and he spilled the half-digested contents of his stomach all over the wall and floor.

He became aware of a strong odor in the air, and there seemed to be more light in the room. The body was brighter now and burning.

Flames licked up and down the unmoving body, consuming the remains of the thing's clothes and human flesh. It burned hot, changing flesh and bone to brittle charcoal. An acrid cloud of smoke formed above the body. In moments the body, now almost burned through, collapsed in on itself. Soon all that was left was a pile of ash.

Well that takes care of trying to dispose of the body, thought Hamlin.

The flames were quickly burning out, but in the dimming light Hamlin saw a doorway. He was able to reach it before everything went dark again. The atmosphere was different now, the darkness less dark and more natural. It was as though killing that thing had lifted some kind of curse. Light from the streetlamps and moon outside found its way in through cracks and holes.

In the faint light, Hamlin was able to find his way out with minimal stumbling and barked shins. His injuries slowed him down and he moved with a careful slowness.

Outside he sat beneath a park light to examine his wounds. He couldn't see the damage to his face, but he could feel it. Ditto with his cracked rib. His arm, however, was another matter. He could see that quite clearly, even if he wished he couldn't. The bite of the thing had ripped away skin and some muscle. His arm and shirt were soaked with blood and he knew anybody who saw him would assume he had just walked through a blender. He needed a doctor.

But first, he called Christopher's cellphone. The call went straight to voicemail.

"This is Hamlin. We were right, it's her. I just had a run in with a little present she had left behind for you. I'm okay, just a little beat up. I assume you talked with your book buddy. Call me when you get this so we can compare notes."

He was in no condition to drive; he would have to make it to the street and call a cab. With what seemed like the greatest effort he had ever had to summon, he stood up and limped—when did he screw up his knee?—down the path. It sucked getting old, but then again it also sucked fighting a soul-twisted monster in an abandoned building.

He pulled out his phone again and called a cab to take him to the hospital. He could have used Uber—he wasn't that old—but he knew New York. The cab drivers here might ask a lot of questions, but they also knew how to keep their mouths shut. They would ask how he got the shit kicked out of him, but whatever he told them wouldn't make it far beyond that ride.

He fell into the backseat when the cab pulled up and told the driver to take him to the nearest hospital. It occurred to him that it was the same one Eris was at. He could stop in and check on her. Demon or not, he liked her. She was a good kid.

Meanwhile, he stared out the window, watching the city go by while he tried to think about what to do about their new problem. It seemed the little girl was growing up—and she was a bitch!

7

It was in pain. The thing is, she didn't care.

The soul floated in the air two feet in front of Grace, eye level. She examined it, head cocked to one side, staring at it the way someone sitting around a campfire stares at the flames, seeing shapes that made sense only to them. But what she saw in the soul was real, in a sense. The images of the life it once had. She was learning to thumb through them with her mind.

They weren't really memories, they were emotional states, dreams, desires. These were more important than simple memories. They told her more about who this poor person had been and what she had experienced than any set of memories, no matter how detailed. No, these weren't memories of events; they were images of how those events made the person feel.

Grace was in the laboratory that also served as her bedroom in the New York apartment. It was her favorite residence. It had all the luxury she had come to appreciate in the last year, mixed with the utility a witch in training needed. The laboratory was an industrial mixture of steel and glass, with quite a few splashes of hot pink. Just to make it pop.

It was at once cold, professional, sterile, and tastefully pretty. Just like Grace herself. A king size bed of pink and gray was pushed up against one wall, along with a matching dresser and vanity. Large, floor to ceiling windows filled another, letting in copious amounts of natural light.

The whole room was immaculate. It had been just recently cleaned top to bottom. The faint smell of cleaning fluids filled the room, but she was used to it. She was not a clean person by nature, but she had a personal maid. She had to use her for something.

The other half of the room was a cross between a science lab and an occult temple. Chemicals, vials, and beakers sat on shelves alongside ancient books and mystical symbols. On one wall hung an old tablet from prehistoric England right next to a picture of Harry Styles.

Several wooden exam tables filled the other half of the room. Crystal jars sat on each. Two of them held glowing souls. A third was empty, its inhabitant floating two feet from Grace's face.

Grace herself was less than basic today. She had on simple jeans and a t-shirt that read "F CK, all I need is U" on the front.

Her maid was currently scrubbing the floor near one of the wooden tables. Grace watched the bent over back of the woman as she worked.

Things change so quickly, she thought. *Once you can be on top of the world, the next, you fuck up and you're scrubbing floors.*

"That's enough, Anabelle. Wait in the corner until I call for you. Face the wall."

Grace's maid, Anabelle, former ranking member of the Alliance of dark souls stood slowly and made her way to the corner where she did as she was told and faced the wall. Gone was the beauty and grace that had framed this woman's life. She had been tortured and beaten, her power weakened by the others in the Alliance to the point where she could no longer hold up the illusions she used to control the minds of men and make her beauty a thing of legend.

Now she was a broken old hag. Wrinkles covered her face, shriveling it up like a raisin. Her hair hung in greasy locks across her face. Her frame was thin and wasted, her arms like toothpicks.

Grace had no sympathy for her. She loved to watch Anabelle suffer and constantly thought of new horrible tasks for her to undertake. Just over a year ago their positions had been reversed. Grace had been held prisoner in Anabelle's basement, herself tortured and beaten by this hag.

"This is hubris," Golyat had told Grace. "Anabelle thought she could step aside from the Alliance and take on the Hunter by herself, thereby taking the leadership for herself. She thought she was better than the rest of her brethren. This is what happens when your loyalty slips, when you think yourself above your betters."

Grace was not an idiot, she knew Golyat meant this as a lesson for Grace: *Don't fuck with me, remember to be loyal or worse will happen to you.*

"Fuck him," thought Grace. But deep down she knew that was hollow. Golyat was... Golyat. You don't fuck with him.

At least not directly. He had a soul for her to work with—a twisted, tortured, hateful soul—but a soul nevertheless, and those were her stock and trade as a soul shaper witch. As she fantasized about what she could do to Golyat's soul, her eyes drifted to the crystal vial on the shelf, the one that contained an exceptional soul, or at least part of one. It was a part of the Hunter's soul that the werehellhound had torn from him and had eventually found its way to her.

It was her prized possession as well as a reminder of her failure. It wasn't unexpected; she was young, untrained, and had no idea how to master a soul. Still, she had been able to hurt the Hunter; in fact, she had almost destroyed him. But then he had found some way to bind that power he has within him to fill the hole left behind by this missing piece. She still didn't understand what he had done.

Her only comfort was that he probably didn't know either. In the limited glimpses she had of him, it was obvious he was working on instinct too. They had that in common. Then she smiled. She was a quick study. Like the trap she had left for the Hunter at the abandoned building. It probably wouldn't stop him, but it would surprise him. Her soul manipulation power was growing faster every day.

And it wasn't just soul-shaping. There was other stuff... things she couldn't quite figure out. But it was power, just beyond her reach, and if she kept stretching every day, eventually it would be hers.

She reached out to the soul in front of her with both her mind and her fingers and slowly plucked at strands she could see woven throughout it. She pulled at one, but it was slippery and slid from her fingers like a wet spaghetti noodle.

She grunted in frustration. Each strand was an experience complete with memory and emotions, all tied together. She wanted to see if she could separate one, remove it, from the complete soul. Take the life experience from the poor pitiful wretch. She had been working on it for weeks, ever since she had discovered the strands.

Wait... wet spaghetti noodle. She had an idea. She reached out again pulling at the strand. She couldn't get a good hold, but she could tease it out, lift it a little way from the whole. She could feel the fear emanating from the soul. Then her head darted forward like a striking snake. She caught the strand in her mouth and then, just like a noodle, she slurped it up.

It was long, but she pulled it into her mouth. The soul spun like a ball of twine as the thread was consumed. She could hear it scream as she pulled the life experience into herself. She could feel its pain, but it was distant as though she was numb to it. And why shouldn't she be? It wasn't her pain.

Besides, she was in ecstasy. The thoughts, the feelings, the emotions—everything coursed through her. She had never had sex, but she had to imagine this was a thousand times better. Every piece of that experience permeated her being.

The lingering smell of saltwater filled her sinuses. She could feel the sand shifting under her feet, flowing up between her toes as she wiggled them. The waves roared and crashed next to her. She fell to the ground landing on a towel. Laughter bubbled over inside her and came out.

It was her first time at the beach. The sun was warm, the air full of scents of the sea and coconut suntan lotion. She was young, not more than ten, her hair long and brown. There were a picnic basket and cooler next to her. She pulled out an ice-cold soda, the chill in contrast to the hot sun sent goosebumps up her arm.

Then it was gone. Grace opened her eyes. She had consumed the thread, the noodle, of experience. But all the memories of that moment, when she was *somewhere* else, when she was *someone* else, were etched in her, just as if she had experienced it. Grace gasped as she tried to process what had happened. All she knew is she felt... fulfilled.

But already she the feeling drained from her, the ecstasy was leaving. The experience was still there, it was hers now, but the euphoria had abated. She had discovered the ultimate drug.

The soul still floated in front of her, and she could feel terror coming from it in waves. She sorted the threads again. It was hard to find distinct ones, and her impatience won out. She grabbed a thread at random, her mouth darted forward, and she caught it in her mouth with a giggle. This was fun. She slurped.

The ecstasy came again, despite the nature of the experience. It was a funeral and it should have been raining, but it wasn't; it was sunny. In the movies it was always raining, and that seemed right. She was twelve now, same long brown hair. No bathing suit this time; she wore a black dress, hastily bought a few days ago. It didn't even feel right. She found herself constantly adjusting it, pulling and tugging. She just wanted to scream.

The preacher droned on and on. He mentioned her mom's name several times, telling everyone how great she had been, what an amazing person her mom had been.

He didn't have to tell her. Wave after wave of sadness washed over her. She wanted to be gone, she wanted to be home under her blankets where no one could see her. No one looked at her while they lowered her mom into a grave.

Again, it was gone, but the memory remained. Grace had fallen to her knees; she slowly got to her feet. Her body thrummed with excitement. She felt as though that experience was hers. That she had been the girl at the funeral. It had been a sad experience, but it made her almost giggle with joy.

She delved into the soul again slurping up experience after experience, thought after thought. The good, the bad, all of it. Every thread thrilled her. This poor girl's life had been downhill after the funeral: drugs, prostitution, living on the streets, disease. All of it had made her soul what it had become. And Grace devoured it.

By the time she was done, she was on the floor rolling around, pleasure coursing through her body. She laughed until she cried. She couldn't stop, it was everything. The girl, Haley, had become her, she had consumed her and everything she had ever known or felt or lived through was now a part of Grace.

She got to her feet and bounced from one to the other. She was full, but she wanted more, like a junkie needed another hit. She had two other souls ready for experiments, but she knew she would not be able to hold back. Think of the experiences they would have, what she could learn from consuming them. Their life would be hers, they would be a part of her. And they were just the beginning. Her mind was racing. She wondered if this was what a meth addict experienced. She could consume many souls, making each one a part of her. Think of the power, the control.

She heard a noise, like a whimper, and spun to Anabelle in the corner. The old hag had turned around and seen everything. Now she quaked in fear. Grace could see it. What was she so afraid of?

Then it occurred to Grace, what if she consumed a dark soul? What if she devoured something of that immense power, pulled from the well of Hell? Was it even possible?

And that's when she understood Anabelle's fear. She probably could take a dark soul that way. They were just souls after all, albeit powerful ones. Grace stared at Anabelle and could feel the smile forming almost of its own will and the giggles emerging from her own throat. Anabelle began to wail, throwing up her hands against Grace although Grace hadn't moved. Yet.

Grace stared at the wailing woman swinging her arms in feeble defense. *Wow*, she thought, *I am so hungry*.

8

Hamlin sat next to Eris' hospital bed staring at her like he could force her awake by sheer force of will. She looked so small and almost as pale as her hospital sheets. Tubes and wires ran from machines to her way emaciated body. The pale institutional light gave her skin a mottled look.

Not that Hamlin looked much better. The doctors in the ER had fixed him up, but it would take a master makeup artist to hide the bruises and swelling, not to mention the bandages over the stitches. Yeah, he didn't really make a pretty picture himself.

After getting stitched up, he had made a detour on his way out to look in on Eris. She was a Jane Doe, so the last thing he wanted to do was draw attention to himself visiting her. There would be questions, especially if they found out he was a detective.

So, he had tried to slip in unseen. Hard to do with bruised ribs and a pronounced limp, but so far, so good.

Without thinking he reached out and brushed back the hair from her forehead. Part girl, part demon, it didn't matter. She was good for them, and she deserved better than this. She was as tough as they come. He only hoped she could be tough enough because they needed her.

More importantly, Christopher needed her. He was changing into something—Hamlin had no idea into what—but it wasn't good. He was a good kid but losing his way. She, demon and all, grounded him. Despite his emotional bankruptcy, even Hamlin could tell she was the only one who could pull Christopher back from whatever dark abyss he stood on the edge of.

He sat down and took her fragile hand in his, the skin so transparent he thought he could see the blood vessels pumping away faintly.

"I'm not sure if you can hear me, but we miss you here. We want you back, we need you back. Rest and heal, but hurry back. You're missed."

He leaned over and gently kissed her hand. Then he thought he would stay a little while longer, just hold her hand for a few minutes more.

9

Apophis stared at the ancient building as a tourist took pictures and wondered aloud with oohs and ahs at the antiquity and history around them. Apophis looked once again at the dusty brown structure. It hadn't even existed when he last walked the earth.

They were in Old Town Cairo, the new capital of this land. In some ways it was familiar. He could smell the cooking from the outdoor market, the spices and scents were a part of his memory.

The sounds too were similar: the sellers hocking their wares, the laughter, the arguments over price or quality. This all invoked his ancient memories. But then there were the differences.

Cell phones ringing, instantly sending messages and voices around the world, vast amounts of information at your fingertips. Kids listening to music with earbuds, lost in their own world as they walked through the real one.

Modern fumes of pollution saturated the place. They were fresh from the ground, so it was particularly pungent to him, while the people of this era had become numb to it.

There was a gritty, grimy texture to this world as though modern excess had left a fine dust on everything. Apophis reached out to touch the old stone and then wiped his hand on his shirt. He could almost taste the modernness of it all.

It tasted of metal and oil. Like a gun barrel.

Yes, they knew what guns were. They also knew what airplanes were, cars, computers, the internet. They were no strangers to technology, innovation, or global politics.

As they lay under the earth, the world slid over them. They were not active, did not have consciousness to form or a physical body to act on the world around, but they absorbed. It's what they did, these hollow beings, it was what they were built for. To learn, observe, understand, then destroy.

While they slumbered, they watched the world turn. They watched the rise of the great pyramids and fall of Egyptian dynasties, they watched the beauty of ancient Greece crumble away and the rise of Rome. They rode the consciousness of the people of these times. They weren't omniscient, they did not know all, but they moved through each age following, learning.

There was no rhyme or rhythm to it, they drifted from country to country, in this dream-like state, but following it all. It might have been what kept them sane through the centuries. Although it could be argued that because of their nature they could not be driven mad. They were made not created like humans. But it didn't really matter. It did not change who and what they were.

And they had a nemesis: The Beast as he was sometimes called, the Hunter of those that had escaped the underworld. His job, to condemn those souls to damnation in that realm. Before anything else, they must destroy him, the who tried to banish Apophis for eternity.

They had followed him when they could, in that dreaming state of undeath. It was not easy to follow one like him, and they would lose track of him for centuries. Then they would catch a glimpse of his power in the world and just like that, he was gone again.

So they had felt the recent transition. The subtle change in the Beast's power had rippled through the realm where they existed, that place between Heaven and Hell.

And now they had seen the rise of this new hero. The one taking over the role of the Hunter, fighting the dark souls like he was a superhero. The internet praised him and his fighting of the monsters and demons that had suddenly been unleashed on the world. Apophis and his brethren had watched as the world debated whether he even existed, whether these things were really monsters or just mass delusions and special effects.

But Apophis knew what was real. He knew that dark souls and monsters were real. He also knew how to get to this new Hunter. It was all too obvious. The weakness of mortals.

Although the sun had just set and the afternoon heat had not started to dissipate, as one they pulled the hoods of their coats over their heads. In uncanny unison they pulled the scarves around their necks up to cover their noses and mouths. Someday they would not need to hide their identity; for now though, it was still a weapon.

They walked along the market, Apophis' eyes sliding from stall to stall looking at the faces around him, looking for something specific. Then he thought he saw it: Courage.

A youth leaned against one wall as his parents, tourists, perused a particularly gaudy stall filled with cheap trinkets and low-quality novelty t-shirts emblazoned with sayings like 'I saw the great pyramids of Giza' and bumper stickers declaring 'My other ride is a camel'.

He wore a black t-shirt with a smear of an image on the front, probably a heavy metal band; his hair hung in his eyes and covered his pale skin like the drapes in a house of the dead. He would do.

Apophis approached the boy. The kid didn't even seem to notice until he stood right in front of him. He looked up out of irritation.

"What the fuck dude?"

American, good. "I will give you fifty dollars to record video of the market for the next three minutes," Apophis said.

"What?" said the kid. "What are you talking about? Record what?"

"I would like you to record what happens in the next three minutes and then upload and share on all the social media. You do have social media accounts, correct?"

"Well yeah, of course. Facebook, Insta, all that shit. Hell, tell you what, I can go live on Facebook. Instant fame dude. But what are you gonna do, rob somebody? I mean with the scarf around your face and all?"

"I am going to give you fifty dollars for a short, simple task. Can you do this?"

"Yeah, sure. Whatever dude."

The kid took out his earbuds and held up his phone. "Okay guy, do whatever. Takes a lot of hits nowadays to get noticed, so whatever it is, it better be good. Impress me."

Apophis spoke directly to the phone.

"This is for the Beast, the Hunter of Souls. You don't know us, but we know you, we know what you are. Witness our power. This is a taste of what is to come if you do not come find us in Cairo. If we have to come find you, we will leave a trail of bodies to your doorstep."

"Wait a minute! Who the fuck are you?" the kid said and lowered the phone. "Are you talking about the guy with the sword?"

"Raise the phone up boy. Remember, as long as you continue recording, you will live. Stop, and you will join the chaos."

The strength of Apophis' voice, the force of will alone was enough to force the kid to raise the phone.

He and his brothers stepped into the crowd. Long, wicked blades appeared from their coats. Then the killing began.

In a blur of whirling long knives and whipping coattails the three brothers plunged into the crowd. Their blades were precise, striking vital points, slicing into arteries and then darting away to find new victims. The brothers moved at inhuman speed, spinning, cutting, striking. Ten were dead in less than a second, nobody had even moved. The cuts so quick, some who had been struck fatal blows didn't even realize it.

Then the blood started flowing and the bodies started falling. The brothers relished their task. Apophis leaped over part of the crowd, clearing twenty feet and cutting down as he passed over, slicing over scalps. No death with that strike, but pain and blood were just as meaningful for this message.

The brothers did not just kill, they also gutted some, again the display of pain and suffering just as valuable. It was a full three seconds after they had begun that the crowd woke up to what was going on and the first screams began.

Apophis leaped again and landed in front of the kid he had tasked with recording everything. The phone had drifted down as the kid realized what was going on. Horror and stark fear were written across his face when Apophis' visage appeared before him. The kid was coming apart.

Apophis had anticipated this, however. He caught the boy's wrist just above the hand holding the phone and lifted it back up.

Behind him his bothers darted through the crowd killing with inhuman speed. Screams formed the background music to the massacre. Most of the crowd had deteriorated into chaos. Nobody knew where to run, so they scattered in all directions, hitting into each other, trampling over one another as they searched for a way out of the killing field. His brothers danced about them and sprang lightly throughout the mass of people like little birds of death.

"Record it all boy," Apophis hissed and forced the kid to aim the phone back at the slaughter. "Record it all boy, every drop of blood, every cut and slice. And you get to live, your family even gets to live. If you don't share with the world, I and mine will find you."

Blood sprayed across the face of the boy; he screamed but Apophis held his arm in place. "Last chance boy," Apophis said into the boy's ear. "Fail and you join the slaughter."

He let go of the boy's arm and straight into the camera. "Come Hunter or Hero, or whatever you call yourself. If you care, you will come."

With that Apophis sprang back into the fray. His long knives whipped by like silver fish in a dark ocean.

It was over in a few more seconds. Some of the humans had escaped, but most lay scattered about and in some cases piled on top of each other. The air smelled of rusty iron and released bowels. The warm spicy scent of the market was replaced by the musky smells of copper and death.

Some of the stalls were in shambles, torn down in desperate attempts to escape the whirling blades. The music had stopped but there were some sounds left. The dripping that sounded like water but was blood spilling from the slit throat of a man hanging half off a table. The shuddering breath and whimper of the boy who still held the camera at arm's length despite his shaking body. The sobs of the boy's mother as she hid under the shield of her husband. His arms wrapped tightly around her.

The father looked from his son to Apophis and back again. There was deep fear there, but also something else. Apophis knew that if he tried to kill the boy, the father would try and stop him. The man couldn't of course, but Apophis had a grudging respect for that.

There were at least thirty dead, maybe a few more who had crawled or ran away before they could bleed out. There were no injuries, not for Apophis and his brethren, just kills.

Apophis caught up the boy's arm again and looked directly into the camera.

"These deaths are on mine and my brother's head. Come find us in Cairo or the next slaughter will be on yours. Come find us."

10

Christopher woke to the sound of his cellphone going off. It occurred to him that one of the greatest decisions of his life was to set a slow blues jam as his generic ringtone. It sure beat waking up to the shrill bleat of his alarm.

His arm flailed out from the covers and he moaned through the stretch of his aching muscles. He had spent the last few hours training for days in the books of the Library. There wasn't a part of him that didn't hurt or feel like it was more bruise than muscle. Even his fast healing was having a hard time keeping up from repairing the pain. He liked to rest in private after such intense training sessions; it was weird to walk around in front of people like he was an old man with no apparent injuries.

A little more carefully he pulled the phone to his ear.

'Yes," he answered.

"I think we have a problem," Juan said, his voice, normally dripping with sarcasm, sounded serious and almost strained. "You need to get to the lair as soon as possible."

"What is it? Another dark soul causing trouble?"

"I don't know, you just need to get here. I already called and left a message with Hamlin."

The seriousness in Juan's voice brought Christopher to full alertness as he shrugged off the last of the sleep fog. Whatever it was, if it was making Juan way too serious, it had to be bad.

"Okay, I'm on my way."

He ended the call and with a groan way too old for his age, pushed back the covers and rolled out of bed.

"Get up Hellcat," he said. "Time to go to work."

Hellcat looked up from where she lay taking up most of the oversized king bed. At first he had banished her back to the shadows at the end of the day, but every morning he would find her curled up in the center of the bed. He, meanwhile, had been shoved to the edge; the first morning he had actually fallen off.

After that, he tried locking her out of his bedroom. Apparently locked doors are only a minor inconvenience for a creature born of shadows. He had awoken to find her in his bed once again.

That had set off a small contest of wills that Christopher ultimately lost when he awoke one morning feeling like he was being crushed and found Hellcat sprawled across his chest. It seemed that, although he was the Lord of Damnation and Hunter of Lost Souls, his authority over Hellcat was limited to letting her do what she wanted. He guessed a cat was a cat regardless of whether it was from Hell or not. He had given in and had a custom bed made that provided both ample room for Hellcat and a little sliver of space for him. He still woke up to find her sprawled on him more often than not.

He threw some clothes on and grabbed a breakfast bar before gathering the shadows to form his uniform. In twenty minutes he was springing from rooftop to rooftop.

He dismissed his coat and hood before getting to the park that housed the entrance to the lair so he could blend in with the crowds of people. It was summertime and the parks were full, which made it a little difficult to sneak into his secret hideout beneath the zoo.

But soon he was through the entrance unseen and in the main room. Juan was there, looking like he hadn't slept in a while, stacks of junk food wrappers piled around him.

"What's going on?" Christopher asked as he plopped down in a chair next to Juan and put his feet up on the computer desk.

Juan looked sick; his normally dark skin had a definite pale sheen to it. But Christopher didn't think it was the flu. "You have to see this video, it's a message meant for you."

"Jesus, Juan. You looked like you saw the most disturbing video in the world. Can it be any worse than what we saw in Mexico?"

"Just watch," Juan said.

Juan clicked on a video and the amateurly recorded video played out in front of him. From the beginning, he could tell it wasn't the U.S.

"Where is this? Some middle eastern country?"

"Cairo, just watch," Juan said.

Christopher watched with growing dread and anguish as the video progressed. He watched the man, face swathed in a scarf to hide his features, call him out. And then he looked on as the man demonstrated the consequences of inaction.

He watched the three brothers tear into the crowd, blades flashing at impossible speeds. These men were not human. No mortal could move that fast, no mortal could jump across the killing field like that. At least a dozen people had their throats cut or vital organs pierced before the first screams began.

The three men... or whatever monsters they might be, were efficient assassins. Precise in all their strikes. Every cut was a killing one —some near instant, others to induce pain and suffering just before death. No one was spared from their whirling blades. The humans stood no chance. They couldn't even leave the market fast enough.

It made Christopher think of a slaughterhouse, except these cows weren't lined up, they were just a mass of fresh meat targets.

It was over in seconds. Christopher guessed only a handful had escaped, most of the crowd slain before they even realized what was happening.

The video ended with the man saying, "Come find us."

Juan drew a shaky breath and Christopher sat back. He had seen a lot of horrible things since becoming the Hunter of Lost Souls. He had seen death and violence on an epic scale; he had seen psychopaths and monsters, but for some reason this mass murder disturbed him the most.

Maybe it was the dispassion in the assassins. He couldn't see their faces, but it seemed to Christopher that they went about their killing like it was just a job, one they were very good at, but all the same, just work.

Or a means to an end, that end being to lure him there.

"But why?" he asked.

"Why? Obviously, they are batshit crazy killers that's why," said Juan.

"No, I mean why call me out? What are they trying to do?"

"Well, obviously they are dark souls that think they can take you. You saw the way they moved, there's no way they're human."

"No not human, I agree. But a dark soul's M.O. is to hide from me as much as possible or try and ambush me, take me by surprise. They are never this blatant. I mean, everybody is going to be looking for them—the police, the Egyptian army. It seems like an unnecessary risk. There's got to be another reason."

"Are you going?" asked Juan.

Christopher looked at him with a frown. "I have to go. We can't let something like that happen again."

"But what if it's a trap?"

"Of course, it's a trap."

They both spun around from the computer desk. Hamlin was standing in the doorway.

"You scared the crap out of me," Christopher said.

"Finally, the tables are turned," said Hamlin.

"You look like shit," Christopher said. And he was right. Hamlin had bandages on parts of his swollen face and when he walked into the room, it was with a pronounced limp and a wince at each step.

Christopher and Juan jumped up from their chairs and rushed forward to help him to the couch.

"What happened?" asked Christopher.

"A little girl is what happened," Hamlin said. "Did you get my voicemail?"

"No, I woke to a call from Juan and rushed right here."

"Get me a drink kid, need to medicate. Hell, I'd still be in the hospital if I hadn't gotten the message from Juan here."

Christopher poured him a whiskey on the rocks and Hamlin downed most of it in one gulp.

He looked from Christopher to Juan, "It's got to be Grace, and she's become much more powerful." Then he grimaced. "Who am I kidding? She's like a child prodigy of evil."

He told them the whole story.

"So, she took some dude, a graffiti artist, and turned him into some sort of servant monster?" asked Juan.

"Yeah. Somehow she was able to fuck him up enough that he would wait for one of us to arrive."

"Like mind control?" Christopher asked thinking of the Anabelle, one of the first dark souls they had encountered, and how she had controlled the werehellhound.

"Not exactly. I mean, it wasn't like he wasn't in control of his actions, more like he was changed fundamentally. Like he truly believed that he had to kill me, like it was just part of who he was. It was his whole purpose in life."

"It was a trap?" asked Juan.

Hamlin nodded and took another big gulp. "Yeah, I think she thought Mr. Hunter here might investigate once the unusual cause of death was discovered."

"I'm sorry Hamlin, I didn't know," Christopher said.

"What are you talking about kid? I'm a fucking cop. I know what I'm getting myself into. You didn't do anything. But if it makes you feel any better, I'll let you get me another drink."

"It looks like rather than one problem to deal with, we have two," said Christopher. He went over to the bar to retrieve the whole bottle. "Obviously I need to go to Cairo as soon as possible."

"But we know it's a trap," Juan said. "The video is all over the internet; that was no personal message, they want everybody to see it. Almost like they were daring you to ignore it."

"Yeah, I get it, but what choice do I have? I can't let them kill a buncha people. That was a slaughter."

"What about the police or the Egyptian military? What are they going to do?" Hamlin suggested.

"Yeah great, get the cops involved. What the fuck are they going to do? Just servants of a corrupt world order," Juan said and then seemed to notice Hamlin's glare. "Present company excluded."

"You had to go and hire an anarchist for tech support, didn't ya kid?" Hamlin growled.

"Better than a Republican," Juan replied.

"You guys both know that there is no police force in the world capable of understanding, let alone stopping beings like this. No, I have to go before more innocents die," said Christopher.

"Isn't that like negotiating with terrorists? I mean if they can call you out that easily what's to stop some other asshole from using a bunch of people for target practice just to get your attention?"

"I don't think that's much of a secret. I think dark souls know how to push this button. Besides, I don't have a choice. I can't ignore this."

"What about our Grace problem?" asked Hamlin.

Christopher shook his head. "I get that she's a problem, but at the moment her kill rate is much lower than the Brothers Grimm over in Cairo. I've got to make her a lower priority. Besides, we don't have a lead on where to find her or what she and Golyat are going to do next."

Hamlin nodded. "If you head to Egypt, I can try to get a lead on what they're up to." He sighed, "I'm not sure how, but I'll think of something."

"Maybe, but you need your rest too. You got beat up pretty bad, and it might be dangerous without me along."

"Kid," Hamlin growled, "as I've said before I might be old, but I've taken care of myself so far. I can manage a few more years at least."

"So, what do I do?" Juan asked.

"The usual. Hold down the fort and be available when called," Christopher said.

"Here? Don't you want me there in Egypt?"

"I think you'd better stay here. Hamlin might need you and I doubt I'll need your help finding these guys in Egypt. I have a feeling they will find me. Besides, you're only a phone call away. What's wrong Hamlin? You look bothered."

Hamlin's frown had moved to a scowl by the time Christopher finished. Hamlin shook his head.

"I'm just worried. I get that we have to split up, but it just feels wrong. The Frises in the hospital, you heading to the middle east, me staying in New York. Up until now we've stuck together and we've won. It just doesn't feel right to split up."

"What would you have us do? I'm not sure what choice we have."

Hamlin nodded. "Yeah, yeah, I said I get it. But I don't have to like it. It just feels like we are at our weakest when we're alone. I'm worried we are playing into their hands. But yeah kid, I don't have an alternative."

"We'll just have to be careful. Hamlin, check in regularly with Juan so we know you're safe. And yeah, I know you're a tough guy, but please try to be careful. Find out what you can, but don't do anything crazy."

Hamlin nodded and waved his hand dismissively. But he couldn't hide the worried look on his face from Christopher.

11

With Cairo spread out in front of him like a life-size Google map, Christopher surveyed the unfamiliar landscape. He was not sure what he expected, but it was not the huge expanse of city that was before him. The towering skyscrapers and buildings looked like they might have been first built during the time of the Pharaohs. It bustled with life as potent as New York, and just as complex a network of neighborhoods and boroughs.

He had no idea where to start. Hunting the ones who had created that video for him would be next to impossible in such a large metropolitan area. Perhaps he should have thought this through a little better when he had been back in the Bronx lair.

But something in his gut told him he didn't have much time. He had gone straight to the cube room, with its mystic doorway to other lairs throughout the world, to get here as fast as he could. There was a lair in Egypt and the cube room brought him here just as it had to the others. This lair, however, turned out to be the oldest so far.

It had been moderately maintained, at least up until the death of his predecessor. In function, it was very much like the other lairs—several rooms, kitchen, computer room, storage, several sleeping areas, and bathrooms. Despite the modern conveniences, it was obviously an ancient site.

The walls were hand carved with ancient symbols that looked nothing like the hieroglyphics he had seen on TV. He wasn't sure what they meant; they might hold some sort of magic, but they might just as easily be the equivalent of modern-day wallpaper.

The most startling aspect of the Egyptian lair was its location: beneath the famous Egyptian Museum. Like the other lairs, multiple hidden entrances led through an underground maze of access tunnels. His predecessor was good at hiding in plain sight, but he was also good at covering his bases. Christopher suspected if he went through all the paperwork of the complex network of businesses the Beast had left him, he would find that he somehow owned or at least controlled part of the museum and the land it sat on. Even government-owned lands hadn't stopped him from ensuring the physical and legal safety of his lairs.

Christopher pulled out his phone and opened Google maps. The only thing he had to go on was the video. The attack had happened in a market, and in some of the images he had seen older buildings. Perhaps some sort of old town.

He then looked at local news. The attack had only happened yesterday, so the media was still covering it. It was generically labeled a terrorist attack, although no credible militant group had come forward yet.

Reading through the news reports he found some street names; they were, indeed, in the older part of the city. This area was full of Mosques, old stone buildings and a small tourist-friendly market. That had to be it.

He leaped from the building, power billowing about him in dark clouds of shadow. Tendrils of shadow reached out as he flew towards the next building, slightly lower. The tendrils took hold of the buildings around him and guided his path. He loved the feeling of flying through the city. It made him feel he was using a combination of the Incredible Hulk's jumping and Spiderman's webs to navigate through cityscapes. It was as close as he could get to flying; Superman was still out of his reach.

He jumped from building to building, using his power tendrils to help guide. The city was quite beautiful. The architecture, when he moved out of downtown was different than anything Christopher had seen. Muslim designs of domed roofs and large gardens blended with modern steel and concrete. In other places Greco-Roman inspired columns held up massive stone structures. Although still impressive, the buildings were smaller the closer he got to the old town area; the skyscrapers were left behind in downtown.

Although late, the smell of dinner filled the air, spoiled only by the occasional wafting of the scent of evil. He mostly ignored these quick, disgusting scents once he determined they weren't a dark soul.

He could feel the Weapon pulling at him, almost demanding that it be fed these souls, any souls, whether dark or not. And Christopher understood why. It had been a long time since they had taken a soul while hunting. Even Christopher was growing to miss it.

He didn't have time, however, for sport. He had a job here and time was of the essence. As much as Christopher sympathized with the Weapon, saving lives was still more important. For the moment anyway. They could feast on damnation later, starting with these brothers.

The sounds, normal big city sounds of traffic and music, the sounds of life in general, died away as he soared closer to the old market area. The crowds were missing. That made sense, he thought. There had just been a killing spree in the area the night before, and it would take time for the market to recover and tourists to feel safe enough to return.

There were police there, stationed at various spots guarding; a handful still seemed to be investigating the crime scene. It had been twenty-four hours, but there had been a lot of bodies to sort. A medical tent nearby was in the process of being taken down. The emergency mostly over, the dead outnumbered the injured, but all had to go through triage.

As he had approached, Christopher had been more careful, dampening his power and making smaller, precise jumps and taking to the ground when he could. The last thing he needed to do was startle anyone before he was ready to make an appearance. Some dark figure flying toward them was the last thing these folks needed to see after last night.

He paused on top of a nearby building, scanning the area with both his eyes and his nose. If the dark souls were in the area he would smell their corruption. Every day it seemed his base sense grew stronger, more attuned to the hunt.

There was nothing.

He could see the auras around the police and officials wrapping up below along with the mix of colors flashing around their souls. For the most part, they had the same shades of light and dark that all humans possessed; nobody was perfect, but nobody was entirely evil either. He knew that if he went down there, if he got close to those police officers, he would be able to see and smell in detail the sins on their souls. But his eyes slid over them looking, searching for his real prey.

Still nothing.

He was nervous, something wasn't right. He was acutely aware that Hellcat was not by his side. Just before he had traveled to Egypt, he had knelt and gave her head a good petting.

"You can't come with me on this one girl. Hamlin is going to be in danger and he won't have me to help protect him. I need you to keep an eye on him, not so that he can see, but from the shadows."

She made a low, warm sound in her throat and pushed against his chest with her head. Christopher smiled, once again marveling that this was a creature born of Hell.

"I know, but I'll be okay, I've dealt with dark souls before. But Hamlin, if they come after him, he doesn't stand a chance. We can't be in two places at once. But you can't let him know you're there. He gets all grumpy when he thinks he's being babysat."

After another minute of aggressive petting, she seemed okay with it. Now here he was. Alone. But this was a simple hunt; he could handle it. He shook off the lonely thoughts.

It was night and the darkness that he pulled about him as his coat shielded him from the humans below. They would see nothing but an empty roof from that distance.

That gave him a thought. He looked higher, scanning the rooftops. That's when he saw him. The man from the video. He was staring at Christopher from atop a squat building about the same height as the one Christopher stood on. It was just across the street.

He stared at him, frowning. Perhaps he expected something different? He couldn't see Christopher's face, but he seemed a little surprised by the sight of him. The man wasn't covering his face this time. He was large, powerfully built and dark-skinned—obviously he was local and of Egyptian descent. His clothes, though somewhat modern, were loose fitting and baggy, reminding Christopher of Bedouins he had seen on TV. He looked both modern and ancient at the same time. Dust covered his coat and clothes, he looked like he had just ridden out of the desert.

He glanced down and smiled. Christopher followed his gaze and found the police and officials. He knew what the man was thinking, but Christopher hesitated. He did not want the police to die, but what did it really matter in the grand scheme of things? What were the lives of these few mortals compared to stopping this murderer and other dark souls? It wasn't his job to protect them, just to stop the dark souls.

Then he could hear Eris' voice in his head. Telling him that *was* his true purpose. Regardless of how his predecessor had done this job, Christopher's strength was that he was human and understood them—their weakness, their strengths. He knew what it was to be human and why it was important to save them from the damned ones. Only he could be their champion.

No more hesitation, it was time for Christopher to make an appearance in all his fury and damnation glory.

Before the man across the street could move, Christopher leaped through the air and landed in the midst of the mortals. He brought out the Weapon as it transformed into a sword of blackest steel laced with arcing bolts of energy. Power surrounded him, radiating from him. Lightening of harsh blues and whites crackled through the shadow darkness that cloaked and obscured him.

He let his aura wash over the police, like a crashing wave of energy. It didn't hurt them, but it allowed them to feel the immense power on display in front of them. He needed their undivided attention if he was to save them.

He brought the Weapon down, and it released a surge of power into the ground. The concrete cracked, and the ground shook with a low grade, localized earthquake.

Several of the police officers cried out in surprise at his sudden appearance, others ran behind cars and other cover. Sudden yells and radio squelches rang out as the officers tried to call in or call out for help. Most of them pulled out their sidearms, several even shot at him, but the swirling mass of power around him obscured him and the bullets went wide.

"LEAVE NOW," Christopher boomed out over the crowd. His words had the power of Hell behind them and the mortals felt it. Some staggered back as though his words were like a physical blow. Others screamed and ran, whether they were taking his advice or running scared shitless didn't matter.

The Weapon in his hand surged with lust for souls. He held it in check, promising it would soon feast. He then lifted it above his head letting power arc from the blade.

It was by far the best light show he had ever put on.

"LEAVE! THOSE MEN HAVE RETURNED, AND YOU ARE ALL IN DANGER."

More gunshots rang out, a bullet nicked his shoulder. Christopher roared in rage and almost gave in to the desire and anger inside the Weapon. But he just let the power flow through him, guiding it differently, not fighting it. He directed it away from the police.

"I HAVE NO WISH TO HARM YOU. THEY, HOWEVER, WILL NOT BE SO RESTRAINED."

"You're that guy. The one from Mexico and New York?" a police officer, Christopher thought he might have been the one in charge, asked. "The one who fights the monsters?"

He spoke in Arabic, but Christopher's new-found powers made him fluent.

"I AM, BUT WE DON'T HAVE TIME TO TALK. I CAN TAKE CARE OF THEM. RUN!"

"They called you out in the video and you came? Why?"

"SOMEBODY HAD TO."

He heard a noise from behind him. The man who had been on top of the building walked downs the middle of the street, strolling through the remnants of the chaos he had made. The bodies were gone of course, but the damage and the rust colored stains remained. He seemed pleased.

It occurred to Christopher that there was something wrong with the man, something not quite right, but he couldn't put his finger on it.

The police were getting into their cars and speeding off, others were simply running on foot as fast as they could. But a few cars and officers had stayed. They were no longer pointing guns at him though. They looked beyond him at the man approaching.

"GO!" Christopher roared again. "YOU WILL DO MORE HARM THAN GOOD HERE."

And it was true. Even if they tried to stand with him, Christopher would have to focus some of his energy on protecting them. He didn't know what he was dealing with, but he didn't need distractions. He was sure the police had seen what these beings were capable off. They, like everyone, had seen the video.

It seemed to sink in. The officer in charge said something and they all started piling into the cars. The lead officer gave Christopher one last look and nodded before ducking down into the vehicle.

That taken care of, Christopher turned to face his adversary.

The man had come closer and stopped just a few feet away from him. He was tall, broad-shouldered. His face, covered in dust and grime, still gave the illusion he had just wandered out of the desert. Christopher thought he might be in his thirties, but deep creases covered his face gave him the look of someone experienced, someone with wisdom.

"You look different," said the man.

"Well I did get a haircut recently," Christopher said. Keep them talking, that's what they did in the movies. Eventually the bad guy gave away too much.

"You are not him."

"Who? I'm the guy you called out in your sick video."

The man shook his head slowly. "No, you are the Hunter, I can see that in you. But you are not the one we know. The one who imprisoned us."

"Ah! You must mean my predecessor, he was killed."

The man's head came up sharply at that. "Killed? By whom? That is not possible. He was a great warrior."

"Um, yeah but I was there. And I'm here now."

The man nodded. "I know, I can see what you are. A pity, but if we can't take vengeance on the one who imprisoned us for thousands of years, we will settle for vengeance against his office."

"Who are you? And why fight me? I haven't done anything to you."

"We are Apophis, we are the first of the blood spillers. Normally we do our work in the dark, in secrets and shadows. But our need to find you was too great. We have no purpose other than death, and that purpose has found you."

Blades flashed out from beneath the man's coat. Daggers large enough to qualify as short swords appeared in the man's hands. Christopher brought the Weapon up, its large blade dwarfing the man's twin daggers. The man moved forward, short swords weaving back and forth looking for an opening to start.

Christopher rapidly ran through his training. He had spent months learning from the greatest warriors to have ever existed and with the time altering effects while working with the teachers, it was more like several years. Even so, he could tell he was dealing with a hardened warrior; his comparatively minuscule amount of training was probably a drop in the bucket against this guy's experience. His only hope was that the guy was rusty—he said he had been trapped for thousands of years after all—or that his own power was enough to carry him through.

The man darted forward, and their blades met. Power raced along Christopher's sword, giving strength to his blow. The man was knocked back, surprised, but he recovered quickly.

He slipped past Christopher's guard, and the long knives found him. One slid across Christopher's stomach as he darted again back out of reach. Christopher felt the lance of pain and stepped back. Luckily it wasn't deep, but he could feel warm blood seeping from it.

The man was on him again, blades cutting up toward Christopher's exposed gut. Then gunshots rang out and bullets ricocheted off the ground near the man. He took a step back, but Christopher thought the move was more out of surprise than real fear of the gun.

On the nearby rooftops several police officers, the Egyptian equivalent of a SWAT team, had taken up position for sniper cover. There were three that Christopher could see, dressed in black and wearing bulletproof vests.

More bullets rained down, concentrated on the man in front of him. He moved quickly and most of the rounds bounced off the street, but one found the man's shoulder. It punctured clean through, but instead of blood splatter, a puff of dust or sand came out of the exit wound. That's when Christopher knew that bullets were only a nuisance to the being.

This was precisely what he didn't want to happen. He had told the cops to get away. They had to know the danger they were in, although a part of him was happy they were concentrating their fire on his adversary. At least he was getting through to somebody that he was the good guy. They had stayed to help him.

The man glared up at the officer who had shot him. Then Christopher saw the others. This man's brothers were darting across rooftops, almost flying, toward the unsuspecting police.

The man in front of him grinned up at the impending slaughter. The sword, the Hellpower inside, the need to harvest souls, all screamed at Christopher to strike now, while this creature was distracted. The bullets had thrown him off. The man was skilled, and this might be Christopher's only chance to win.

All this ran through his head almost instantaneously. He made his decision. Christopher jumped, tendrils of power lanced out and propelled him toward the nearest rooftop.

The police officer stopped firing and watched Christopher arc through the air toward him. The officer was halfway to his feet when Christopher picked him up.

"Run you fool," Christopher roared into his face, putting as much of the Hellpower into his voice as he could. He wanted this man to understand the danger. The man screamed in terror. His approach seemed to be working.

"Run," Christopher repeated as he tossed the officer toward another rooftop. It wasn't too far, but Christopher hoped he didn't break any bones. He didn't have enough time to be considerate.

Even as he released the officer into the air, he felt the blade sink into his back. Christopher fell forward, spinning his sword around. There was no skill in it, just a desperate strike to get some distance. It worked. The cloaked man surrounded by a thin cloud of sand danced backward.

Christopher fell to one knee as the pain from his wound passed through him. It felt like the man had punctured his kidney. Christopher had time to bring up the Weapon before the man came in for a strike again. He barely deflected the knife blades; in fact, one skittered across his sword and sliced into his shoulder.

These beings, for they were no mortal men, were fast, maybe even faster than him and they wielded their weapons with expert skill. He would not be able to fight a battle of attrition with these things.

The wound in his back wouldn't kill him, he could feel it already healing, but if they got too many blows through, eventually he would be cut apart. He slammed the Weapon up and into the thing's face, it flinched back enough for Christopher to buy some time.

Across the street, a third of these beings were approaching another police officer. Christopher ran and jumped, ignoring the pain lancing from his back and shoulder. He cleared the distance and had his sword between the prone police officer and the what would have been a killing blow.

"Get the fuck out of here," Christopher yelled. And the cop immediately took his advice.

Christopher shifted into a fighting stance that he had learned and tried to arrange his training in his mind. Reality was nothing like training. Luckily his teachers had been brutal.

Christopher smashed the hilt of the Weapon into the man's face. Dust and sand flew, but no blood. He didn't have time to celebrate the blow. He felt rather than saw the horizontal slices across his gut. Somehow the man had gotten a cut in even while being struck in the face.

They were so fast! At least Christopher had bought enough time for the officer to get away.

Then the man was backing away, guard up. That made Christopher nervous. Why didn't they come in for the kill?

Something hit against his leg. He looked down at a severed head. It took him only a minute to realize it was the third police sniper. Across the rooftops, he could see Apophis standing over the decapitated corpse. Blood was still spurting from the neck.

The being took three long strides and jumped off the roof. Christopher reacted on instinct and leaped into the air. They shot towards each other weapons drawn. Power, like writhing shadows, whipped around Christopher and the streaks lanced out to the nearby buildings.

They slammed together in midair above the street. Christopher was able to deflect one of the man's blades with the Weapon, but the other cut into his side. They were too close for Apophis to get any power behind the blow, but just because it was shallow didn't make it any less painful.

They were falling fast, but Christopher had another strategy. With his free hand, he had grabbed Apophis' coat. Part of his training was to incorporate his new abilities into his fighting. The power tendril that had found the other roof flexed and pulled. He spun with

Apophis in his grip. The pull of his power was subtle but changed their trajectory toward the side of a stone building.

Christopher added his own strength and at the end of the spin, threw Apophis at the stone wall. The man slammed into the solid wall with a thud, sending a spiderweb of cracks across its surface. Even the stoic face of Apophis registered pain and what might have been surprise.

Christopher landed on the roof above as Apophis slid down the wall. For a moment, Christopher thought he might be able to win this, if he could just find clever ways to use his power.

Then pain exploded in the back of his head. The world grew dark as streaks of pain, like fireworks, lit up his vision. Somebody had hit him in the back of his head, hard.

Dazed, Christopher turned but only had a moment to see it was one of the brothers before a club-like piece of metal—something the brother had found on the rooftop perhaps—slammed into Christopher's face.

His head snapped back and then he was falling. The sky, what he could see through the haze of losing consciousness, spun. The walls of the nearby building stretched toward that spinning abyss, as though he was falling much further than he should be.

The ground hit him like a concrete mattress. He felt bones break and hoped they weren't the ones he needed to get up. Not that getting up was happening soon. He was surprised he had retained consciousness. Dust and dirt puffed up around him from his impact.

He moaned. Then he tried to move. Broken bones protested, battered flesh, heavy like lead, pulled him down. But he managed to roll to his knees just in time for Apophis to appear at his side, dual blades raised.

"This is the right position for you. Do you finally understand?" Apophis said.

Somehow, miraculously, Christopher had held on to the Weapon as he fell. It had transformed back to a pocket knife—its usual disguise—during the fall, maybe to increase its chances to stay in his hand.

He would only have one chance, but he only needed to hook Apophis' soul, it didn't have to be a solid strike. Just a nick would suck his soul away, damn him back to Hell.

Ignoring the pain in his body, Christopher whipped the pocket knife around. It changed in mid-cut into the longsword he needed, energy running along its blade, hungry for violence.

Apophis jumped back. But not far enough. The tip of the Weapon sunk into his stomach. It sliced cleanly, nothing fatal, but deep enough. The tip of the blade cut in and out quickly. And pulled away...nothing.

Christopher stared at the Weapon in shock. It should have wrenched the soul from Apophis' body. But there was nothing.

Nothing but the ache of longing coming from the Weapon. Horror filled him as realization began to dawn: the Weapon's lack of soul lust. The way he had thought there was something off about these brothers. The lack of any sort of soul smell.

The brothers had no souls. He had not seen it, he had been distracted by the police. Or he had just missed it because he was an idiot. How could he use the Weapon against enemies with no souls? Enemies that don't seem to be injured by normal weapons either.

Or apparently didn't even have blood.

Black sand spilled from Apophis' wound, forming a black pool of grit on the ground. So, it wasn't just sand. It was mixed with some sort of liquid to form an oily sludge. As Christopher watched, the thick flow stopped and the skin beneath Apophis' shirt rippled and shifted as the wound closed. The sludge on the ground moved and pulsed, then like a fast-moving slug it crawled up Apophis' leg and disappeared under his clothes.

A fist, wrapped around a pommel, slammed into Christopher's face and his head snapped back. Then it was all darkness.

12

Regular murder investigations were hard enough, let alone when they involved a soul-shaping teenage girl with raging hormones and daddy issues—assuming the Golyat guy is a father figure to her.

Hamlin was at the precinct, staring at the evidence wall. He had been the one to create it, pasting up pictures, maps, and the few scraps of evidence that they had from each scene of the mysterious deaths. No one else was as interested. Sure, cause of death was unknown, but otherwise, they were either at-risk youth, bound for trouble anyway; or elderly, tragic, but with no family they took a lower rung on the priority ladder.

Not that the NYPD wasn't interested in general, it's just that when Hamlin took the case under his wing, nobody was angry about his butting in. In fact, they seemed almost relieved to be rid of it. Nobody liked the weird cases. They always started off interesting, but in the end, it was something simple—the butler did it kind of thing. And by now most of the guys at the precinct knew Hamlin's reputation, Mr. X Files they sometimes called him. Yeah, working with the kid had really helped him get ahead in his career.

"Give Hamlin the case, he likes that creepy shit."

"She says it wasn't her. She says the demons made her do it. Hey Hamlin, seems right up your alley..."

"Hey Hamlin, why don't you get your psychic pal to see if he can't pick up some vibes..."

So now here he was alone at night trying to solve a case nobody else wanted. And just because he knew who was behind the murders, all he really had was a first name. They needed the why, the how. The purpose was most important. What was she up to? Was it just some sort of practice?

He had looked for a Golyat of course, but other than a reference to an old Jewish name, nothing. Golyat was a supervillain name, and Hamlin needed his secret identity.

Supervillain? Great now he was doing it.

He shook his head and rubbed his face to refocus. He looked at the board, trying to get into the head of a teenage girl. Why had he never had kids? It might have made this easier.

Whatever this girl had become she was a kid of sorts, maybe a little Children of the Corn style, but a kid and inexperienced with hiding a crime. Despite her power, she would be sloppy, she would make rookie mistakes.

This Golyat might not be so amateur; given his dark soul status, Hamlin would guess that he was smart and might be guiding the girl. Still, sloppiness was a place to start.

He started with the location the bodies had been found. He briefly visited one other site earlier during daytime—he wasn't going to make the same mistake twice—and had stayed near the scene, not straying to nearby buildings or secluded alleys.

He reviewed the photos of the crime scene. It was the same, no sign of struggle, the body had been found neatly lying on the ground, the way a body would if it had been deliberately laid there. Not splayed like the victim was running or trying to fight off an attacker.

The victims had not been killed at that location. They had been dropped there afterwards.

Great, so where was the murder location?

His cell phone rang. He looked down at the name displayed on the screen and quickly answered.

"Juan, what do you have for me?"

"Nice to hear from you too. No detective, I don't mind being trapped in this concrete bunker doing your job for you. How's your day going?"

Jesus. Hamlin hated kids who had 'problems with authority' and now he had to deal with two of them.

"My day would be going great if I knew where these murders occurred. Please tell me you have something." Hamlin said.

"Well, I did find something interesting."

After a suitable pause Hamlin said, "You gonna tell me or are you waiting for me to go there and demonstrate my version of police brutality?"

"I just saw you. You're in no condition to beat an egg, let alone a young man in the prime of his life."

"Okay, I'm on my way."

Hamlin was about to end the call and head to the lair when Juan seemed to realize Hamlin was serious.

"Hold up five-oh, I'll give you the intel. The girl was a runaway; she matches the description of a runaway from Ohio. I can send you the info, not sure it if will help though. The old man though, he fits the description of a geezer that disappeared from a death home in the city."

"You mean a retirement home, right?" asked Hamlin.

"Nah, those state-run facilities are nothing but death homes. Clearinghouse for the weak and those that *they* think are not worthy."

Well I guess you can take the boy out of the conspiracy but not the conspiracy out of the boy, thought Hamlin. Out loud he said, "Can you send me—"

"Done. Already texted it to you."

Hamlin heard a beep on his phone and grunted. "What about the other body?"

"That one was tricky. No idea who he was. Best guess you guys had was that he was in his early twenties. So, I did some thinking."

"Did you hurt something?"

Juan said something in Spanish that Hamlin didn't understand but could guess it wasn't flattering. "So, I did some thinking," Juan repeated louder. "And I looked at recent missing person reports in the city, and low and behold a young man was reported missing earlier today by his mother."

"Wait a minute. How did you get accesses to our missing persons system?"

"I used your password. Got right in. On a side note, you really shouldn't keep it on your phone, especially since it is your name plus 1234. How the hell you gonna forget that?"

Hamlin put his head in his hand. For a moment he considered that while the kid was right about his body being pretty messed up, he did carry a gun.

"Okay you stole my password, we can discuss that later. But why didn't I find that? I checked the database just today."

"Well it wasn't really a report; it was only partially filled out, not submitted. I don't think the cops take it seriously when a mom reports her adult son missing. Especially with no evidence of foul play. Man, you guys really are lazy. Also, do you guys really say, 'no evidence of foul play', or is that just the movies and reporters?"

Hamlin toyed with the idea of getting a silencer out of the evidence locker.

"Sent you the dude's info also."

Hamlin's phone pinged again with a text. Was it just him or did the ping sound smug?

"Thanks Juan, I'll take a look at it..."

"Oh, I ain't done," Juan interrupted. "What, you think that's all I was able to do? The guy that almost took over a city with his keyboard? The guy that can get into any computer system on the planet?"

"The guy who almost destroyed Mexico City?" Hamlin regretted the words as soon as they were out of his mouth. But he bit his tongue at apologizing, he needed the kid to get to the point.

There was a long silence on the phone.

"Look Juan," Hamlin started.

"No man. You're right, I'll move on, for all my pride I got lots to atone for. So I got to thinking the missing person report doesn't really help, but since I had a name I was able to find some photos on the web. Then I sort of did a reverse image lookup."

"Ah yes, of course," Hamlin said. He had no idea what Juan was talking about.

Juan sighed. "I used the picture to search for any other images, facial recognition stuff, see what else was out there."

Hamlin was impressed. "You can do that with the internet?"

"Yeah, but I didn't search the internet. I searched the NYPD video archive of all the body cameras, dash cams, and city security video cameras."

"What?" Hamlin stood up. "How the hell did you get access to all that? Oh yeah, my fucking password."

"Ha, no. Even you don't have that kind of clearance. I hacked in. Though your password did help, so don't feel left out. Anyway, using some of my homegrown tools and the mega super shit we have here I found him on some footage from a traffic cam outside a club."

"Holy shit. It was that easy?"

"Fuck no, I just make it look easy. There's probably two other guys in the world that could do it that fast. Some respect, detective."

"Okay, okay, yeah cool. Can you send me the—"

His cell went ping.

"You got the video. You'll want to watch it. Better than Game of Thrones."

Hamlin thanked him and hung up. Then he watched the video. It was better quality than some; he could make out faces, not just black and white blurs they usually post on TV and then ask viewers to call in any tips for a reward. Those Crime Stoppers videos looked like anybody, and they got thousands of phone calls, almost all bullshit. This was a new cam much clearer.

It was outside a nightclub. Hamlin didn't recognize it, but then again, he wasn't really the club kid he used to be. There was a line, so it was popular. The date of the video was last Saturday night; that's about right for just before he was murdered. He looked at the cross street printed across the bottom of the video and wrote it down so he could pin the location later.

A man stumbled from the doorway. Hamlin quickly compared it to the photo Juan had sent him. It was the same guy. He looked right at the security camera and the traffic cam caught his other side. The video switched back and forth between the two cameras. Juan had done some editing to give him the best view. Hamlin had to hand it to him, the kid was good.

The man from the photo was looking at something on his phone. Suddenly the video paused and a large arrow with text popped up

HI HAMLIN, HE IS USING UBER TO HAVE A CAR PICK HIM UP. UBER IS A NEW CAB TYPE SERVICE. A CAR IS LIKE A HORSELESS CARRIAGE.

Fucking Juan. The video resumed again and the man stood, unsteady; he had apparently been drinking. A large black SUV, maybe an Escalade or Chevy Tahoe, pulled up to the curb and the man walked over and leaned against the door. The camera changed to the traffic cam to give him a top-down view. From the angle Hamlin couldn't see in the car, but he could see the young man. Unfortunately, none of the angles gave him a clear view of the license plate. After a quick conversation, he got into the back seat.

The video paused again and an arrow with more text appeared. The arrow pointed to the back door the guy just climbed in.

WAIT FOR IT.

The video resumed. Suddenly the door opened and Hamlin saw an arm come out clawing at the roof as though trying to pull himself out of the car. The arm disappeared violently back inside and the door slammed shut. The car pulled away from the curb. Nobody on the sidewalk noticed, no one in line looked up from their phones.

The traffic cam did get a view of the back of the SUV, but the license plate was smeared with dirt. He might be able to get a letter or two but not much. Hamlin noted that the rest of the car had been recently washed.

WE KNOW WHAT HAPPENED BUT KEEP WATCHING JUST

FOR KICKS.

A few minutes later another car pulled up. The driver sat for a moment before getting out and standing on the sidewalk. Another arrow popped up and pointed at the man.

THE REAL UBER DRIVER, ASKING WHERE HIS DUDE AT? POOR UBER DRIVER. HAMLIN YOU MUST FIND JUSTICE FOR THE UBER DRIVER. HE LOST HIS FARE.

Then the screen changed to black and white before the final word appeared on the screen: "fin."

He was really growing to hate Juan.

So, he had been taken from that club. Hamlin had no doubt in his mind that whoever was in that car was working for Golyat and Grace.

Hamlin put a pin in the wall where the retirement home was and then another where the other victim had been taken. When he stepped back and looked at it, a pattern started to emerge. A circle to be exact.

The disappearance and dump sites were clustered around in a very rough circle. Central Park, Upper East Side was at the center. It was a little bit of a jump—there was lots of real estate in the area surrounded by the pins—but Hamlin had a gut feeling it would be in the wealthiest area in town. This group, the Alliance, was very rich and very powerful. They wouldn't slum it.

For a moment Hamlin thought it couldn't be that easy. But if it was Grace they were dealing with and not Golyat, then amateur mistakes would be the rule rather than the exception. She may not realize she was putting a bullseye on their neighborhood. Either way, it was just one more lead to work with.

Of course, he still was a long way off. The Upper East Side had a population of three hundred thousand. Hamlin still had no idea where to start there. He needed to thin it out more.

Seconds later his phone was out and he was calling Juan again.

"Hello chief," Juan answered.

"Could you do that reverse picture search thing again with the photo of the car and maybe a partial license plate? Specifically, images and videos taken in the Upper East Side."

"You mean use your password to illegally hack into a law enforcement server and access some cases, court sealed files, and personal images and videos?"

"I hate you Juan," Hamlin said with a groan.

"I'll take that as a yes. Sure, I'll do it. Good idea by the way. Although how did you narrow it down to the neighborhood?"

Hamlin briefly explained how he narrowed it down and how it was a little sloppy. Then Juan had a good point.

"Careful Hamlin. They could've made a mistake, but it could be a trap. You might not get out of this one," said Juan.

"Yeah, the thought occurred to me. I'll be alert this time. I've seen what Grace is capable of and I don't want to make that mistake again. I'm gonna head over to that area and wait for any info you have. Just want to get a feel for the neighborhood, it's not my usual beat."

He ended the call, and thirty minutes later he was drinking a five dollar cup of joe in the lobby coffee shop of a building full of apartments that were worth more than his entire lifetime salary. On the plus side, the coffee was very good. And the smell, he loved the smell of coffee shops. As far as he was concerned coffee was the food of the gods, and he drank it like he was fucking Zeus.

The shop was full of pretty people wearing the latest fashions. Brand names, real jewelry, inane conversation. These people had cares that were nowhere near his, not including the bit about working with the right hand of Satan. He had nothing against the fashion chasers or the rich folk, it just wasn't his scene. He was a fish out of water in his cheap suit that no matter how hard he tried seemed to be perpetually wrinkled.

It was a hot evening again, so he sipped on an iced coffee. He was nervous and the coffee wasn't helping, but he wanted the caffeine. The aches and pains throughout his body reminded him of what could go wrong when he found himself closing in on Grace.

His phone beeped, indicating he had a text. He glanced at the screen and read the text from Juan.

Juan: *Found it...*

The next text was a picture of the car driving along the street.

Several more images popped up capturing parts of the car as it passed various cameras. None were perfectly clear shots, but he could confirm it did look like the car that picked up the man.

Juan: *Most occurrences of the car between 5th and Park Ave and e 73rd St and e 76th.*

This image lookup was some next level NSA shit. Whatever tools Juan was using he had to convince the kid to let the NYPD use them. Of course, since Juan hated all forms of authority, especially police, that would be an uphill battle. And not one for today.

Hamlin responded.

Hamlin: *Is there any way to look up owners of balls.*

Juan: *This sounds like a personal issue.*

Hamlin: *Fuck. Autocorrect. Buildings, not balls.*

Juan: *Yeah, I assumed. You text like my mom and as slow as my grandma. And she's dead.*

Fucking Juan. Hamlin admitted defeat and called him.

"I'm disappointed, I never took you for a quitter," Juan said when he answered.

"Can you search who the building owners in that area are? Exclude name corporations like, Apple, Amazon, and big banks that we would all recognize."

"Sure, but what are we looking for?"

"I'm not sure. A list of owners is just a start. Look for anything out of the ordinary, any unusual business structures. You know, small companies owned by other small companies."

"Just because I'm good at math doesn't mean I'm a forensic accountant. But I know one."

"You know one?"

"Sure, when you hack at my level you meet all sorts of interesting characters. I've been in contact with him for the last fifteen minutes. I'll put together a list of potential buildings. But what are you going to do with this list?"

"I don't know for sure, but if we can narrow it down it will be a start. Hell, it's the only thing we have to go on. Meanwhile, I'm gonna take a walk and see what I can dig up."

13

At first, there were blobs of cloudy light, then fade to black. At some point, the light splotches stayed and the dark curtain stopped being drawn. The light solidified around Christopher, bringing images into a fuzzy focus. A wall of stone, chipped and old, passed before his eyes like he was being lifted on some sort of elevator.

Then more images became clear. He could see two of the brothers, their shoulders at least, standing at an impossible angle. Then he was aware of the sensation of movement across his back and the sound of something heavy being dragged across the ground.

He realized that sound was coming from him. He wasn't going up, he was being dragged by the Apophis brothers.

His thoughts were still slipping and sliding out of place, but he knew enough to stay quiet. They hadn't seemed to notice he was awake. And he needed time to think this through. The last thing he remembered was fighting them in the streets of Old Town Cairo.

Then it came back to him in a rush. They had no souls. These were not dark souls, they were something altogether different. What were they and was he even equipped to deal with them? Apparently, the answer was no, based on his current situation. His whole shtick kind of revolved around soul taking and damnation.

As his thoughts solidified and he could think somewhat straight, he realized he no longer had the Weapon. He must have dropped it when he was knocked unconscious.

Soulless or not, it was a powerful tool he no longer had. He hoped it wasn't just lying in the street for anybody to pick up. But then again if it had fallen into these guys' hands, the situation would not be any better.

Christopher opened his eyes and tried to get a better look around without alerting his captors. He was being dragged down a narrow tunnel just wide enough for the two brothers carrying him to walk with him in tow. Occasionally he would see pictographs or hieroglyphics on the walls or a small statue tucked away in a nook or carved into a corner.

Where was he? Was it some ancient Egyptian tomb? It looked like something right out of a Discovery Channel special. More importantly though, why was he being dragged through it?

They didn't speak, just wordlessly turned in unison. Their silence was unnerving. They walked in almost lock step, moving together as though they could read each other's mind. Could they read his?

Hey Apophis? Can you hear me? Guess you couldn't take me one on one huh, little bitch?

Nothing. His relief was short-lived as Christopher was suddenly tossed into a room. He tried to roll to his feet, like in the movies, but the aches and pains, coupled with the dizziness brought on by movement, kept him from executing that feat. Instead, he settled for a moan and coming to rest against the far wall.

The stone he sat against was not natural, but only roughly carved. This place didn't have the finished look of most old Egyptian earthworks. He was unsure if that was because of its age or just sloppiness.

The room was small with no carvings or marking of any sort along the walls. He thought all these ancient ruins had carvings. Although it was pitch black, his gifts allowed him to see perfectly in natural darkness. It seemed Apophis and his brothers shared his gift. They stood in the doorway with no lights.

"We wanted to kill you. To destroy your office as revenge for imprisoning us all those centuries ago," Apophis said.

Christopher used the rough wall to pull himself up. If the fight were to continue, he would do it without the Weapon. His power was formidable enough.

"But that would have been too easy. Too much of a mercy."

"I wasn't the one who imprisoned you. I don't even know who you are," Christopher said.

Apophis just shook his head. "It doesn't matter who you were, all that matters is what you are now. We can see that you are not the power that stopped us before. But you have chosen to take on the job of the most hated entity in the world. The insignificant mortal you were before is irrelevant. The power that you are now is deserving of our vengeance."

"So, you wanted to kill me in this cave? Even though I have done nothing to you?"

"No, we don't want to kill you. We will not give you the mercy denied to us. Despite your mortal path, we know that like us, you cannot die—not from nonviolent means that is. As we were trapped for thousands of years, so shall you be. Deep beneath the desert sand, trapped in eternal darkness."

"No," Christopher said, panic was setting in as he realized what they intended.

"I wonder how long your power will protect you from the madness. In that sense we were lucky I guess. My brothers and I lack souls, we don't have true emotions. This protected us from madness."

"You are mad."

"Then perhaps that is the trick. Embrace madness. You will be here a long time, perhaps forever. Whatever that truly means. This place has no real use, a minor tomb that has never been discovered and never will given its unknown and uninteresting location. We were also lucky that the seal of our prison was a stone of powerful forces and of much use to those who understood. Here is nothing but sand and stone."

Christopher started pulling his power from the shadows, it gathered about him in an aura of energy. He had to move now before they could do whatever it was that they planned.

Christopher lunged forward with inhuman speed and power. But Apophis was quicker, as though he had known it was coming. Despite the strength behind Christopher's blow he missed, and he had put too much into it, he was off balance. A fist like a thousand sledgehammers slammed into his gut. A second struck the back of his head when he leaned forward from the first blow.

He tried to block a kick coming for his face only to have pain explode in his side as a different foot slammed into his ribs, cracking them. The brothers worked in perfect unison. If Christopher blocked one blow, two more struck with unerring accuracy as though they intuitively knew where each would strike next. He had fought multiple opponents before, but none had been this in sync.

It's like they shared one mind.

Christopher was soon overwhelmed. He was still injured from the earlier fight, and he was not making out any better in this one.

A fist smashed into his face and his head snapped back with a crack. He felt his feet leave the ground as he flew back toward the rear wall. They were just too fast, too strong when they worked together. His back slammed against the stone wall, his head cracked against it and he fell forward struggling to hold onto consciousness. The room swam around him.

He could hear a rumble, like an earthquake approaching. Then his vision was obscured by dust and sand; it filled his nostrils, coating his throat with a dusky dryness. His body shook in a sudden surge of coughing. It was all around him, a dust storm, thick and rolling like smoke in a burning house.

The intense coughing was bringing the world back into focus. He coughed and hacked, spitting out paste-like snot covered with dirt. He pulled up his hoodie to cover his mouth and help filter out the worst of the crud. He tried to stand as the dust settled, but the best he could do was get to his knees. At least the coughing was going away.

The tunnel that led out of this small room was gone. Instead, there was a pile of rock. There were many small stones, ones he could easily move with the Hellpower fueling his strength, but there were also giant slabs, probably weighing several tons. He was strong, but not Superman strong.

When he tried to lift a stone, his body screamed in protest. It seemed that no matter how strong he was, his bruised and battered body was in no condition for excavation. He would have to rest. He slid down the back wall until he was sitting on his ass.

At least he could breathe and the dust was settling, but for how long? He looked around the room. Nothing. No holes, no other doors, not even a small crack. He knew that he could not die from lack of oxygen, but he could be affected, maybe lose consciousness. He imagined shifting back and forth between consciousness and unconsciousness in some quasi-dream state, suffering but unable to fully grasp his situation. He shuddered and forced himself to turn away from those dark thoughts.

In the distance he heard long rolling growls of thunder. It took him only a moment to realize it wasn't thunder; they were collapsing the entire passage. Even if he could move the giant boulders, it would take him forever to claw his way out. And he would run out of oxygen before then. Once that happened he would be in no state to plan an escape.

When he was feeling a little better, he stood gingerly and slowly, meticulously working his way around the room looking for... anything. A secret passage, a crack, something. But it was smooth cut stone, old and cracked, and nothing that he could use.

He searched his pockets. He had his cell phone, the light flared to life, startlingly bright after he had become so used to the dark. No service. Of course. He was in the middle of nowhere, who knows how far underground. Apophis must have seen the phone, he just knew it didn't matter.

He tried it anyway. Nothing. Dead air. On the plus side, he could play Candy Crush to pass the time. He turned off the phone and put it away.

He sat that way for a while listening to nothing, trying not to think. It was too scary to think. He heard sounds, quiet rumbles that he knew were just the broken ceiling settling into its new home, content to wait for the next few thousand years or few million. It was as though the rock was talking to him, asking how long he would be here. Would anyone miss him up there? Was he just a fleshy time capsule? He stopped that train of thought, that way led to madness.

Time passed, he was not sure how long—hours maybe, minutes? The rocks had stopped talking a long time ago.

Why the hell did he just go charging off? Here he thought he could take care of three dark souls when he could barely take care of one at a time. If he had listened to Hamlin, he wouldn't be here, not alone. At least the detective would have known where he was and could somehow arrange a rescue party. The arrogance, the pride, when did this power become so much to him? No, he shouldn't blame the power; it was his decision. They were right, Hamlin, the Erises: he was becoming something else and it was clouding who he was.

But he was the Hand of Perdition. He determined the damned and judged redemption. He had the right of might. This power was his and his alone, the others had no idea what he went through. They could never understand what was inside of him.

He had stood and power radiated around him, his eyes flared with the heat of anger, hatred. He could feel the power washing over his body. They could never understand what it was to be the Hand of the Devil. Of course, he wasn't sure he had really ever tried to tell them. No, not really. He had let the power win to some extent, maybe. He liked to think that he had held back from them, stayed aloof, to protect them. But maybe it was because he was afraid of what this power would do to them.

He knew what it was doing to him, how it was changing him, tearing him in two. He knew that if he got too close, if he cared for them too much, this power would turn on them somehow and they would be hurt. He had lost a family once before.

He knelt and slammed his fist down on the stone floor; cracks radiated through the stone from the impact. A hollow boom rang through the floor and walls. He had to stop these thoughts. They would get him nowhere. They were the thoughts of the weak, not of the Hunter of Lost Souls, the Lord of Damnation. He would be strong, he had to be. Time to whine when he was out of this place.

If he had just known they weren't even dark souls, he could have done some research, worked with Juan and Hamlin and... He stopped cold.

The Librarian.

He quickly searched through his pockets and pulled out a tiny book of stamps. Even as he removed it from his pocket, it shifted and grew, becoming a pocket size journal. The Book and the gateway to the Library. He didn't know if it would help at this point—what good would it be to know anything about his enemy now that he can't do anything with it—but it was the only chance he had.

He opened the book and looked at the first page.

It read: TOOK YOU LONG ENOUGH

The words began to blur and shake as his journey began.

14

Apophis stood just above the hole in the sand while his brothers finished sealing it up. It was hot despite the early hour, the sun just up over the horizon, but they didn't sweat; the heat did not touch them. Wind whipped through their clothes, cracking the cloth in violent fits. Tiny grits of sand flew at them like the driest of all hail.

Apophis surveyed the hole, now no more than a dent in the sand. This would hold him, maybe forever. If not, he would at least suffer in the darkness for millennia just Apophis had. He would understand what prison really was. Just as he condemned others to the eternal darkness of Hell, this was to be his damnation. Yes, this was more satisfying than a simple death. And they even had a prize.

He reached into his pocket and pulled out the folded knife. He could feel the power inside it even if he couldn't access it. The Weapon of the Hunter, of the Beast, of the Gate Keeper of Hell, the legendary First Weapon. Its power was vast.

He couldn't force it to serve him, not yet anyway, but they had time. Time to test it, to find its weakness, to shape the weapon just for him. All they had was time. The question really was, what to do with all this time?

They were masterless, and this was not right. They needed a master, someone to give them purpose. Their vengeance done, they now craved a purpose. Without one, they were a ship without a rudder.

For the last few days, Apophis had been feeling something. They had ignored it to focus on the vengeance at hand. But now, now he reached out to it, searched it with his mind. He knew he didn't have a soul, they were not weak mortals spewed at random from some woman's thighs. They were lovingly constructed, with purpose, with beauty. They were the First Bleeders and stealers of lives. They had no mortal coil dragging them down.

No, he did not reach out with his soul, but with his mind and he could see it. Far across the sand and mountains, far across the fields of grass waving in the wind, far beyond the great ocean and its crashing waves. He could see it, the only beacon they had in this time of lost purpose and wandering.

It was the rock that had sealed their prison. Someone had taken it. Whoever had unwittingly released them had the stone, and they might know what power it contained. They knew its value, but nothing of the First Bleeders slumbering beyond. This interested Apophis. To know the value of that stone was to know secrets long since dead to the world above. Whoever wanted that stone might be a worthy master.

They could see it there, over the vast distance. They would be drawn to it. Yes, that was their purpose now. Find the stone and its master and decide if he was good enough to be the master of Apophis.

He turned back to the Jeep parked a few hundred feet away. They had stolen it, but it would get them to the airport. This made him smile. For the past one hundred years as they slumbered below and dreamed, as their minds learned the world, Apophis longed the most to fly. To soar through the sky like the birds. Boats he had done a million times, albeit smaller than the grand ones of today, and cars while interesting were just chariots lacking horses.

No, the plane was the work of wonder. He did not feel like

mortals, this he knew, but he did know excitement and this trip to America would be a pleasure he had never experienced.

It would require money to purchase tickets, but he also knew that here, cash could go a long way. While they slumbered and learned of the world, they had studied all its cities, but none so much as Cairo. They knew this place. Its beauty and its sins, its corruption. It would take a day or two at most to steal funds and arrange to be smuggled into America.

His brothers jumped in the back, and he took the driver's seat. There was no argument, no discussion on who would be the driver. It just was this way. It did not matter. In the end, the brothers were all one. They were Apophis.

The Jeep turned abruptly and kicked up sand. Then, as the sun rose higher in the sky, Apophis headed in the direction of the city. Money, travel documents, and his dream of flight came first, then they would seek the one who had taken their tombstone and freed them.

15

"How dare you?" bellowed Golyat as he slammed open the door to Grace's room. The force of his entrance shattered the wood as it slammed up against the wall. Grace jerked up from where she was sitting. Startled, she fell from her seat.

Golyat stood in the doorway. His bulk filled the space, giving her no room for escape, not that she would have even gotten by him. He was dressed in his usual tailored suit, custom because it was the size of a six-man tent—you don't find that at Armani—but also because Golyat would never wear anything but the best of the best and only for him.

He was huge, but not all fat, more like a giant sumo wrestler; outer layer of fat, but still full of muscle. And tall enough to duck his head when he entered most rooms. That's why his homes were always oversized with cathedral ceilings. Even Grace's room was designed to allow him comfort.

He was bald with small, beady eyes, but Grace knew he saw everything. You didn't become head of the Alliance of dark souls by being an idiot. His mouth was normal sized but looked small on the over-sized head crowning his over-sized body. His thick neck ended in a sausage roll at the back of his head. He was anything but slovenly, however. Everything about him was always perfect. Perfect grooming, perfect dress, perfect killer.

Rings adorned his fingers, jewelry that left marks. Grace knew all about that, sometimes it took magic healing to remove the grooves and cuts left by those rings after a beating. Beatings she usually deserved, but not always.

"How dare you," repeated Golyat, his small eyes bulging in anger. "You go too far. You misjudge your value to me."

Grace got slowly to her feet. This was it, this was her chance. She had to be careful, a wrong move here would get her killed. Slow... steady.

Then he was on her. He moved with incredible speed for one so large. His hand struck her face with a backhand slap that spun her around and knocked her to the ground. He held back of course; if he had wanted to, he could have killed her. She was like a fly to his swatter. His strength was legendary. She would be pulp if he willed it.

As it was, she was stunned, unable to get off the ground. She tried to lift herself up with shaking arms. She could feel the blood dripping from her nose and shattered lip, a gouge in her cheek from his ring had almost ripped all the way through to her mouth. She spat teeth.

But it was just pain, he would help her heal. He wouldn't allow her to be less than perfect for too long. She was his prize, his ornament, and needed to fit in with who he was.

He caught her neck and lifted her several feet into the air. His hands were the size of her head, his fingers easily wrapping around her throat. One hand was all it took to cut off the air from her lungs and the blood from her brain. She would black out in seconds if he let her. And for once she was not entirely sure he wouldn't.

Quickly she drew upon the new knowledge she had recently gleaned from Anabelle's soul. She was no master of this new skill; it would take time, and she had to be subtle, too obvious and he would know. Gently she reached out to him with soothing thoughts. Just a little, just enough for him to loosen his crushing hold. As blackness tinged the edges of her vision, his fingers relaxed a little, just enough for the blood to get by. This was so much quicker than twisting a soul.

"I never gave you permission to kill Anabelle and use her for your experiments. She was one of us. Disloyal maybe, I might eventually have judged her ready for death and return to Hell."

For all his violence Golyat remained calm. Despite his earlier outburst, he was calm now. His voice, deep and formal. He held her out at arm's length and looked at her with coldness, like a man studying a disobedient animal and trying to decide if he should put it down.

"But that was the Alliance's decision. Not for a mortal to decide. Not for a child to decide."

He said mortal as though biting off a particularly distasteful piece of tough meat. She reached out again and slipped in the suggestion to loosen his grip. She could breathe again. He still held her, but she had all the proof she needed. She couldn't help thinking how tasty Golyat's soul would be. Would she gain his strength? She had a sudden, frightening thought: would she get fat like him?

"I have given you souls to practice with. Is that not good enough?"

"Yes Golyat," she said, each word a raspy breath filled with burning in her injured throat. The words were slurred because of her split and swelling lip. "I have practiced with them. I am learning every day. But Anabelle...you know I had special anger for that bitch."

Golyat stared at her with those cold, unblinking eyes. She reached out with her mind again and coaxed him, turned his mind just a little bit, and gave him the suggestion that he should understand her. She would have mentally appealed to his sense of mercy, but he had none.

In an instant, Golyat went from coldly studying her to roaring with anger. The next moment, he tossed her across the room. She landed on the bed and slid across before slamming up against the headboard. She pulled herself up to her knees. She'd have some bruises from that, but he had thrown her to the bed; it could have been worse. Her face was a different matter.

"You are never to strike or injure one of my brethren again. Do you understand? As it is, I will have a hard time explaining to the Alliance what you have done. They will want your head if only as a show of solidarity. The Alliance is held together by a thread and I'm the one holding the end of it."

"Like a puppeteer," Grace said although it came out as 'pupuyeer' through her swollen lip.

"Yes, yes, I like that. Yes, like a puppeteer. I am pulling the strings, but they are thin and fragile."

"Who cares what they think?" she continued; her throbbing lip turned her words to mush, but Golyat seemed to understand. "The next time we see them, they won't even remember Anabelle."

Golyat grunted and straightened his jacket and tie. "They will be here in a few days. Perhaps you'd like to be the one to tell them of her demise?"

That stopped Grace cold and a little fear shivered down her spine. She was at best a tool for the Alliance, a puppy that they hoped would eventually grow into an attack dog. In fact, to some of them she was little more than meat. There would be no sympathy with this group. Then a second thought occurred to her; thinking of them all here in the building made her more than a little hungry. What power they had. Her eyes grew wide and she could feel the huge grin on her face. Golyat saw the smile.

"Ha, don't be a fool! They will tear you apart for killing her," he said, misinterpreting her smile. "I will give them some story if they ask. Have you learned anything further in your studies? Did her soul teach you something new?"

For a moment she thought she was busted, that he knew all along what she had done. She stuttered trying to get words out.

"I was impressed by what you were able to do with the wretch at the abandoned cement factory, but it took a lot of time and energy. Have you grown more efficient?"

She let out an audible sigh. He didn't know what she had become.

"Yes, every day I learn more about how to manipulate souls. I am getting faster, and the twists I make are much more effective."

"Good. Because I believe we will have another shot at our friend the Hunter. I have laid a trap for him."

"You mean the twisted soul at the cement factory? I don't think that will work; he's too powerful for that," said Grace.

"No. That was more of a test for you and an annoyance for him if he ever even finds it. He has grown more powerful since our encounter in Mexico. If only we had dealt with him then instead of leaving it to that idiot Bailey, we would be rid of him and more of my brethren would be walking the earth instead of festering back in Hell. But no, I have laid a different sort of trap.

"We are getting close to being done with the gate and will finally be able to remove him as a threat. Just today we received the final stone from Egypt. That is why my brothers and sisters come."

Grace detected something in his voice, saw some slight trickery in his dark soul. "What type of trap?"

"One that will end him once and for all, one that will bring him to our very doorstep where we would all be waiting for him."

"How?"

"Good quality bait," Golyat said. "You."

"Me? As bait?"

"You need souls to work with, to hone your talent. I need a way to draw him to us, a place where we can be ready for him. The bodies will be a path to our door and you."

"But you are the one he really wants, returning your kind to Hell. Besides you should be happy I killed Anabelle then, it's another body for you to place." She regretted the words as soon as they were out of her mouth. She braced herself for another blow and immediately sent soothing thoughts. There was a flash of anger in Golyat's eyes, but no giant hand struck her.

"Remember your place, girl. You live at my whim and as long as I see the promise of your abilities."

She held back a smile. *Golyat, you have no idea.* She reached out again with her mind, gently probing him, opening him up for suggestions. She was not the expert Anabelle had been, but she was getting the hang of it and she knew not to let herself get too cocky.

"Golyat, when the Alliance meets can I be there? I think I could help."

She could tell he opened his mouth to say no, but he hesitated. He didn't look confused, not quite, but as close to it as Golyat had ever been. She forced her will on him just a little bit more, but softly, always softly. In a direct contest of wills, nobody could beat Golyat; but if he never noticed, it might work.

"How would you help in a room full of beings you could never understand?"

Grace stifled a laugh. She had just eaten a dark soul, consumed it and everything that made her Anabelle. She understood everything. Even the dark tortures of Hell Anabelle had endured for years were a part of who Grace was now. One could say she had grown up with that simple meal.

"With my insights into the Hunter's soul and the soul manipulation I have learned, I might be able to share some thoughts."

It was a lame argument, but with the controlling power she had learned from Anabelle she could see him giving in. He nodded. She smiled.

Then he had snatched her by the neck again and brought he close to the tiny face set in his massive head. "Don't you dare embarrass me again. Remember, they would not bat an eye if I killed you in front of them the moment you get out of line."

He tossed her back down on the hard floor. More bruises for her collection. She was reminded once again of how dangerous this line was to walk.

"Use some of the special healing salve I gave you. You look like Hell."

He turned and stormed out through the shattered doorway, leaving a battered—but no longer broken—Grace on the cold wood floor.

16

When the world stopped spinning, the Library shifted into focus around him. He was on the floor, not quite curled up in the fetal position, but close. His body, though healing from the fight, was still sore and the trip to the Library was always less than a Sunday drive. He rolled over onto his back with a moan.

The Librarian stood near his head looking down at him through that hood of darkness.

"So, how's it going out there in the real world? Looks tiring from here," The Librarian said.

"Well it's a long story. Give me a moment and I'll tell you all about it."

"I wager it starts with you running off to get in a fight without first coming to research and learn about your latest enemy. By the looks of you it was either that or it started with you saying, 'here hold my beer."

He turned abruptly and walked into the comfy study area in the middle of the stacks. Christopher got to his feet and followed much more slowly. He slumped onto the first couch he reached.

"I've come to ask for your help," Christopher said.

"Isn't that always why you come to the Library? Besides you don't need my help, you need an excavator or tunnel boring machine."

"So, you know what happened?"

"My view is limited here, but I know we're buried deep beneath the ground in Egypt. I hope you have a plan. Because despite my extensive board game collection, it will get very boring here after a while."

"Yeah well, I guess we're both fucked," Christopher said. He caught the Librarian up, giving him all the details he could remember, starting from Hamlin's discovery of the bodies, though he wasn't sure it was related to their present situation. Christopher told him about the video sent to lure him to Egypt, and the attack on Hamlin by the thing made by Grace. But there was one thing he hesitated to say. He didn't know why—the Librarian probably already knew about the Weapon since he was connected to the Hunter's two primary tools. He was right.

"There's something you're not telling me," the Librarian said.

With a heavy sigh, Christopher spilled the rest, "I lost the Weapon."

"I know," the Librarian said.

"I really screwed up, didn't I?" Christopher said. For the first time in what seemed like months, he felt something other than coldness, other than the hatred that had seeped ever stronger into him when the darkness he had taken into his soul had fused with his being. Something of who he once was, the kid who had taken the weight of the world on his shoulders, was reemerging. Christopher could feel tears just behind his eyes. Then the darkness inside of him rebelled against that weakness, and the tears remained hidden. For now.

"Yes, you did."

Christopher rolled his head backward. "Helpful as ever. I should have been smarter. Maybe watched the area for a while, maybe tried to hunt down this Apophis and his brothers separately. I just thought they were like the other dark souls I had taken. I should have been able to handle this. If only I were stronger."

The Librarian was strangely quiet. He usually used every opportunity to use his sarcasm.

"I suppose I'm stuck here. How long can I last, buried alive? No food or water?" Christopher asked no one in particular.

"Forever, I suppose," the Librarian said.

"What do you mean? I have no food or water. No air either, that can't help. Eventually, I have to die."

"Not necessarily. Your office gives you near immortality. You can heal most wounds, you can't age, and you can't die of thirst or disease. Only massive damage that you are unable to heal quickly enough can kill you...and certain supernatural weapons and magics, of course."

"So, I can live forever?"

"Well normally I would just laugh that off. You are an inexperienced mortal who has, against all the odds, survived this long. You should move to Vegas, your luck is so good. But all luck turns bad eventually, so I just assumed, in a year at most, you'd be slaughtered."

"As always, such a boost to my confidence. I love you too."

"On the plus side now, it looks like you will live forever."

"Trapped here playing cards with you is not my idea of living happily forever after."

"Yes, and then there will be the suffering and torture. Tea?" the Librarian asked. A teapot had appeared from nowhere, but Christopher barely noticed.

"Torture? What torture?"

The Librarian poured him tea in a cup that had appeared from within the folds of his robe. Still no fingers or flesh for Christopher to see.

"Well the power inside of you comes from Hell itself, it gives you all kinds of strength and abilities; you are still just tapping the surface. But as I said it comes from Hell, it does not care for your pain and suffering. That is why every blow hurts as though it will kill you. No, you will not die from lack of food or water, but you will wish you had."

"Jesus," Christopher had sat forward on the couch. "You mean I will feel myself starve and go crazy from thirst?" He took a sip of the tea; it was good, refreshing. "But I just tasted this tea. Can I drink and eat here?"

"No. Remember your body is not here, it is there; this sustenance is not real. It feels real and you could have a glass of refreshing ice water, eat a steak, but that will only last for so long. Your body will continue to deteriorate. Eventually it will win out over your mind. Then no matter what you eat or drink here, it will never be enough."

"How long? How long until I start to feel the effects?"

"Hard to say. Eating and drinking here will trick your mind. It might be several days before you feel your body suffering here."

Christopher stood up and paced the room. "I should have gone after them one at a time or somehow drawn them to me." He was repeating himself. He knew it was the frustration talking...and a little bit of the fear.

"You don't get it do you?" The Librarian asked.

"I do. I fucked up, it was all my fault."

The Librarian stood there impassively, not moving despite the slight raising of his voice. "That's the problem if you want my two cents."

"I'm pretty sure you're going to give it to me whether I want it or not."

"You are an untrained, inexperienced kid, and yes I am considering all that you have done over the past eighteen months or so. You have learned nothing. I thought you would be dead the first time Rath noticed you were there. I thought for sure the werehellhound would have you or any other of the dark souls you have encountered, yet somehow you have always survived.

"You are nothing like your predecessor; he was eternal, skilled, and knew all the tools. He had no need of a Librarian. How is it you have succeeded so far?"

"Ah..." Christopher wasn't sure if he was supposed to answer. The Librarian had never seemed this...well, pissed.

"My only theory is that you have survived because you are nothing like him. That is, until you put the darkness with your soul; now you are more like him every day."

"I don't think..."

"Yes, I've noticed. He was cold and cared only about his work. He had no choice. You have compassion and force yourself to do this to help the world. He loved the anger, the hatred that made him so good at his job, you...you fell in love."

"Whoa. I think we are..."

"He was alone, you are not. You have a team. But here you sit whining all about you, about how *you* could have done better, if only *you* had made better decisions."

Christopher didn't know what to say. Then the darkness rose up and washed over him, anger flared. He was the Hunter of Lost Souls, Lord of Damnation. It was him, it was his decision and his responsibility. He stood and kicked over the coffee table as the anger raged over him.

"I don't have time for a lecture, Librarian. I need out of that hole in the ground. I need ideas, not an analysis of my feelings."

The Librarian stood quietly for a moment. "Very well, let's go over this piece by piece. You need a way out of a sealed room deep beneath the desert in Egypt. Hmm. Nope, can't think of anything."

Christopher started pacing, he wanted to scream. "There has to be something. This is THE Library right? I mean all the knowledge in the world, right? There's got to be something."

"All the knowledge that ever has been or ever will be. Except about your unique circumstance of being a mortal Hunter. What that means for you...that knowledge is not here. But Apophis, that is another matter."

"What do you mean?"

"The name is familiar. I'm sure I can dig something up on it. It is the name of an ancient being, something your predecessor encountered."

"Yes, Apophis did seem to be harboring a grudge against him, that was his whole motivation for going after me. But what good will understanding Apophis do if I can't get out of the tomb? Even if I know their life story and all their weaknesses I'm stuck here."

Christopher instantly regretted the use of the word tomb; it sent a chill up his spine.

"I don't know, but it is a place to start. Besides, I won't be the only one looking for a solution."

"Great, point me in the right direction; I can start looking through the shelves. I might not be as fast as you, honestly I was never good at using the what's-it-called Dewey Decimal system, but I'll give it a shot." The idea of searching through an infinitely large library was too daunting to even think about, but he needed to do something. He needed some sort of hope.

"I was thinking of a more special form of research for you. You searching through this place for such specific information would be futile," said the Librarian.

Then he turned and glided off through the books. Christopher, caught by surprise, chased after him. "What exactly did you have in mind?"

"I can search this body of knowledge; however, only you can search for the answer inside yourself."

"Please don't tell me you have a touchy-feely self-help section you want me to read through. I mean, I suppose they can help some situations, but I don't think reading a copy of *How to Make Friends and Influence People* is the best use of my time right now."

The Librarian stopped and turned back to him. Christopher couldn't see his face, and nothing had changed about his body language, but he was pretty sure the Librarian was angry. When he spoke, however, the words still had that same calm control.

"I'm glad your humor is still going strong even as you look at hundreds, maybe thousands of years of suffering. Not to mention mine at having to deal with you. Frankly, I wish I could die because I would gladly go to hell rather than listen to your whining for eternity."

Christopher put up his hands in a placating gesture. "Whoa there, sorry to set you off. I know full well what's at stake here. I'm the one out there wasting away in a hole in the ground. I've got skin in this game, so you'll pardon me if I use a little humor to get me through it."

"Fine," the Librarian said. "But I am not giving you self-help books. I'm suggesting we advance your training."

They turned a corner and in front of them was one lone book shelf. The books were all different shapes and sizes from different time periods. Some were ancient tomes covered in dust, others glossy paperbacks that could have been found in a bookstore today. It was like a microcosm of the Library itself, modern and ancient at the same time.

"These are like training books I have used before?"

"Yes, in fact some of these are those books. My thought is if you train your body and mind to be stronger perhaps it will give you access to stronger power in yourself, maybe the wisdom to see a way out of your situation."

Christopher looked over the books on the shelf. "So, this is your plan? Train my ass off, learn as much as I can with no guarantee that I will discover anything to save myself? That seems more like desperation than a plan."

"Perhaps, but do you have any ideas? I don't know the extent of your power, but you don't know either. Don't you think it behooves us to learn as much as possible? Besides, if one of us finds a way out of this wouldn't it be useful to become skilled enough to win against this Apophis?"

He had a point, but still, it seemed pointless to Christopher. "But what good is a couple days of training going to accomplish? Like you said, I might not die, but my body is going to deteriorate. I won't last long going through the type of training I have been for the past year or so."

"It won't be a day or two, you have as much time as you want," the Librarian said slowly as though talking to a child.

"But I thought you said..." Then it hit him. "You want me to pull a Bill and Ted's."

The Librarian was silent for a moment as though pondering. "A what?"

"Bill and Ted's Excellent Adventure. Or maybe the sequel. It was a little before my time, but it's kind of timeless."

The Librarian was silent, but Christopher didn't need to see his face to know he was puzzled. "It's a movie about two, let's just say not very bright, teenagers that want to be rock stars. They get a time machine...I won't go into details but at the end they are moments away from having to play a concert and they never learned to play their instruments."

Still silence, he wasn't getting it.

"Just before they have to perform they use the time machine to go spend years learning to play and then return to the exact same time and spot able to shred with the best of them. They had years of experience, but no time had passed for everyone else."

Slowly the Librarian nodded. "Yes, I suppose this is a 'Bill and Ted' thing. Especially the part about not being very bright—"

"Hey."

"—As before no time will pass when you are in these books. You can spend days, weeks, even years in them training and only seconds will have passed in the stone tomb."

"Years? The longest I've ever done a session was a couple of days. And these aren't pleasure cruises. It's like every great warrior is a sadist deep down when it comes to training."

"I didn't say it would be easy. It might be the hardest thing you'll ever have to do. Except for that whole suffering from thirst and starvation for thousands of years thing."

Christopher absentmindedly held one of the books trying to think this through. "I just don't want to waste my energy going through all this for nothing. I mean, will doing this for weeks or even years as you suggest even work? Can my mind handle it? It's not like there have been studies done on this sort of thing."

"Yes, I agree. You will most likely go mad. I think it is a risk worth taking."

"Of course you do; it's not your mind we're talking about."

"Only by pushing yourself physically and mentally will you discover new things about your power. At least that's my theory."

"You have always had a wonderful way of instilling confidence in me. What if I lose myself? What if I go through this training, and it does span years? How will I remember who I am? How will...how... what if I forget about Eris and Hamlin? What if I forget this life?"

"I might have some ideas, but I don't know if it will work. Either way, we don't have much choice," the Librarian said. A little gentler than usual, Christopher thought. Then he went on.

"Similar to the other training you have gone through, this shelf contains great warriors and soldiers, but it is also a selection of philosophers and mystics, everything from eastern esoteric religions to European occultists to kundalini yoga masters. Anything I thought would be useful. I suggest you start with continuing your warrior training. If you get out of here, that will serve you best when you again encounter this Apophis. I will look into your enemy and see what I can discover."

"But if only seconds pass here, will you be able to get any work done before I'm back however many years older?"

"This form is for your benefit. Once I am out of sight I can work much faster; not as fast as you, but I will not be idle for the minutes you are gone. Besides, I believe you will need breaks."

Christopher watched the Librarian disappear back into the stacks. Perhaps it was knowing his body was back in a dark underground room, perhaps it was the vastness of the Library, but he had never felt so alone. Christopher was suddenly thankful that the mysterious and sometimes bluntly honest Librarian was here for him. He had faded from view when Christopher spoke again.

"Thanks, for trying at least."

The voice of the Librarian came from far away. "See, it's already working."

Christopher smiled faintly and looked at the book in his hand.

The title read: Ksitigarbha, the Bodhisattva of Hell Beings.

"Ha," Christopher said out loud as he sat down. "How appropriate."

Then he opened the book and his mind fell in.

17

The building was tall and imposing. It wasn't the largest in the Upper East Side, but it somehow seemed to dominate. Just a little nicer, a little newer than its neighbors. Hamlin had asked around as subtly as he could and the one reoccurring theme regarding it was that the owners were constantly remodeling with the latest in design trends.

When Juan had given Hamlin the list of potential buildings with complex or suspicious ownership corporate structure, narrowed down by Juan's accountant friend, Hamlin had made a point to visit each one over the course of the last day and a half. Just a quick walk by, not enough to raise suspicion. He had even bought a new outfit one that wouldn't scream "cop."

For the most part this had just added to his frustration. Each building had been rich, opulent even, with specialty stores at the retail level, executive style gyms and garages full of cars that each cost at least three times his salary.

This one, however, had one slight difference. Where the others seemed to be a typical splattering of wealth this one seemed almost too perfect. It was more like a museum than an apartment building for the uber rich. Perfectly clean, perfectly ordered.

Still, this might not have stood out except for the complexity of ownership. Several corporations owned it, those in turn were subsidiaries of other even larger corporations. Juan's friend said he had never seen a deal this complex, but as he followed each twist and turn one name kept coming up regularly. Goliath Corp. Most of the companies ultimately were owned by this somewhat unknown mega corporation.

Then Juan had fit the final piece of the puzzle. Golyat was the old Jewish spelling of the name Goliath. It was too obvious to pass up, this had to be the building. Only a handful of tenants lived in the extensive structure, all of them were listed as working for Goliath Corp.

There was only one problem.

"It's too easy," Hamlin said turning away from the van window. Juan was sitting in the back of the van bringing the computers online. The interior was full of screens and whirling servers, as well as an assortment of other equipment whose purpose Hamlin could not even guess. The van was also fitted with a communication array hidden in the roof. Juan had it custom built. When Christopher had given him an astronomical budget to work with, he had been like a kid in a candy shop. Now here Hamlin sat feeling like he was in a Mission Impossible movie.

"There you go with that word again. I told you I just make it look that way. It took some serious data work and financial review from my buddy. This shit was buried."

"And what is the name of your accountant buddy?"

"Warren Buffet."

"I'm telling you this is a trap. The bodies, the financial trail, the obvious name recognition. It was like they were leading us straight here."

"Well of course it's a trap, never said it wasn't. I'm just saying it was not easy."

Hamlin nodded and made sure his pistol was secure. He couldn't help but think this was stupid.

"Have you heard from Chris?" Hamlin asked and a part of him realized he was stalling.

Juan's smile disappeared, "No, not since the day before yesterday," he said.

"Something's wrong, he wouldn't just disappear like that," Hamlin said. "You've been following social media, right? Have you seen anything?"

Juan shook his head. "Nothing, not about Chris and not about the crazy fucks who made the video. They haven't said a peep, it's like they just disappeared. Do you want to back away from this? Sort of regroup, try to find out what happened to him?"

"It is a distraction. I'm worried about the kid and if this silence goes on much longer, I'll be the first on a flight to find him. But the truth is there's not much we can do for him. There is, however, something we could do here. At least while we wait for his return."

"But you're going up against some strong forces. Are you sure you want to do that? I mean I got your back, but I'm a nerd in a box. I can work magic on that building's systems, including security, but when the shit hits the fan and demon monsters start to appear, I'm just as liable to crap my pants than to be able to pull you out. I mean, we don't even have the demoness here for back up."

"I'm just going in for a look around, I'll see how far I can get. I don't plan on taking on a dark soul all by myself. That's the kid's gig. But I'm a cop, I can't just ignore the threat. Goes against who I am."

Juan seemed to study him for a moment as if deciding. "Then take this."

Juan handed him a tiny piece of plastic that looked like it had a USB port on one side and a cell phone charger connection on the other. It was about the size of a small tack.

"What's this?" asked Hamlin.

"That's the silver bullet we need, at least it's what will get us the silver bullet."

Hamlin held it up for inspection. Despite Juan's opinion of his technical ability he knew what USB was. "How does it work?"

"Well, like I said, I can hack into the building systems fairly easy.

They are all on a network exposed to the internet; sure they have firewalls and all sort of protection, but those are the fuckers that tricked me into doing their dirty work so I'm sure I can get in quick."

"So why this thing?"

"That is our key into the real data vault. If you can plug that into a computer inside Golyat's personal network or on the Alliance's network or whatever, I can try to get us access."

"How do we even know he has any sort of network beyond what's exposed to the internet?"

"Because I worked with them. I got a personal look into all the networks and domains I had at my disposal. So I did some poking around. Even when they had me in the false reality, I knew enough to poke around a little. I might have been a company man, but my subconscious was always suspicious."

He sat back in the fancy seat he had installed that could slide from screen to screen in that little van. "I was too out of it to really learn the details, but I remember there was some pretty tricky concealed shit that I got close to. I know it's there, just can't remember the details to get to it."

"And this little plastic thing will get you in?" Hamlin asked doubtfully.

"Yeah, if you get it into a laptop or phone that is in any way connected to this hidden network, it will give me a starting point. From there the world is your oyster."

"How do I know if a phone or computer has access to this invisible network?"

"You won't, just do your best to pick a computer that looks important and we try our luck."

Hamlin slipped it into his pocket. "I think you and I have different ideas on how this is supposed to go. Okay, but I have no idea if I'll even get far enough to stick it in."

"That's what she said," Juan said and then handed him a small box. "Take these too."

Inside the box were two tiny earpieces, so small he wasn't even sure they would stay in his ear. "I *am* on a Mission Impossible movie set."

"What? Those? You can get them on Amazon. I just made a modification that allows them to work across different types of networks. We should be able to stay in contact. Speaking of which, I think you might get further than you think. Check this out."

Hamlin moved over to the screen in front of Juan. On the display was a three-dimensional rendering of the building with tiny red dots moving on all the floors.

"I got into the cell phone networks throughout the building and was able to access the GPS on every phone, tablet, or any other GPS device in the building. They say it's only accurate within five feet, but that's bullshit for the sheep of the masses. They can track that shit to within one foot or closer."

"Damn, and you were able to hack this all right now?" Hamlin said, stunned.

"Oh, hell no! What do you think I've been doing for the past few months, playing video games? I learned a lot in the mind prison they fucked me with. I used that knowledge to preset some hacks to various network infrastructure here in the US of A. This is just the first time I'm actually using it."

"You are a treasure. Now if I could only get you to turn your attention to helping the other good guys—"

"Fuck the police. Besides, what part of any of this could I have done without a warrant? And how do we get a warrant? Tell the judge a monster and his teenage daughter are killing people throughout the city and we have a hunch they are all posh in this Upper East Side penthouse?"

Hamlin groaned again. "Okay, so this lets you see where everybody is and you can give me a heads up whenever I'm about to be discovered?"

"Si, as long as they have a cell phone or other networked device. But everybody has a cell these days, right?"

"Yeah, I guess we will have to test that theory. What about security cameras and sensors?"

"Please. I have all that access, I had those skills when I was twelve. The cameras will only see what I want them to see, the elevator will come when you call even without a card key. All that shit."

"Okay I guess I'm ready," He slipped the earpiece in and opened the door to step out. But he turned around one last time. "I'm pretty sure this is the stupidest thing I have ever done and that's saying a lot considering I've known Chris for well over a year now. Remind me to tell you about the time we fought a hoard of zombies."

"That sounds like a good, yet horrifying story. Be careful in there Hamlin, I want you to live to tell it to me."

"That's the plan," Hamlin said, more to himself than Juan as he stepped onto the curb. A little voice in his head kept telling him this was a bad idea and he kept telling it back they had no choice. But he knew what he was going up against, and with Christopher MIA it made him doubly nervous.

Christopher is fine, he told himself. It was the only way he could put one foot in front of the other. As he approached the building he changed his assessment; it wasn't the tallest, but it was a large building. According to Juan it was mostly residences, but several floors were reserved for business offices, all presumably for this Goliath company.

That made him nervous too. According to the kid this Golyat was a giant of a man. Was he the real Goliath? He couldn't be that old, could he? Of course, he had seen stranger things since hooking up with the kid. This would be par for the course. He was just hoping they were supposed to be David in this story.

"Heads up, the security in the lobby and the lower part of the building are all standard rent-a-cops—a prestigious security company, only the best of the best here, but still civilian. Above the first couple of floors I see a lot of movement that looks like security making rounds, but they aren't accounted for by the same company. My guess is they are private contractors or work directly for Golyat and may not be ethically minded."

"Got it," Hamlin said quietly. "But I don't even know if I'll get out of the lobby."

"Sure, you will. I got you covered."

Hamlin wasn't sure he liked the way that sounded.

The lobby, it turned out, was large and, except for a person at the front desk, completely empty. It was neat to the point of obsession, a glass and metal modern look. It looked like a germaphobe's paradise. Sterile. Even the artwork, while elegant, lacked color and passion.

The man at the front desk was older, perhaps early sixties, and wearing a stylish suit straight out of a fashion magazine. His hair was perfectly trimmed and mustache manicured. Everything was neat, tidy, and aligned with modern styles. It fit in nicely with the little they knew of this Golyat.

When Hamlin stepped into the lobby he nodded briefly to the man, who barely raised an eyebrow, and looked around. There were a set of couches and a coffee table; a couple of chairs with another table between them were up against a wall. None of the furniture looked like it had ever been used.

To the left and behind the lobby desk were two elevators. There would be a stairwell somewhere and that might be a better option for getting to a higher floor. The residential floors would be difficult to get to and it would be hard to explain his purpose if he was caught looking around a home. So that was out of the question. His best bet was a floor set up for the Goliath corp.

He suspected they were little more than a front, just some conference rooms owned by the corporation for the use of the tenants that couldn't be bothered to come to the headquarters. But if he was captured there he could at least use the cop coming to ask some questions routine.

Now the only question was how did he get to one of those floors?

"Can I help you?" the man at the front desk said.

Hamlin was facing one of the pieces of art, trying not to be obvious while sticking out like a sore thumb.

"Better do something quick," Hamlin whispered, hoping Juan heard him, "Because I'm getting the stink-eye pretty hardcore."

"What is stink-eye? Did you fart?" Juan answered through the earpiece. "Don't worry though, I got you covered. Go talk to the man."

"Talk to the man? About what?"

"Sir. Can I help you?" This time the man added a little more emphasis. Hamlin was the hoi polloi.

"No. I'm just looking," Hamlin said. He was not good at improv. He had two thoughts; one, that he hated Juan and two, this would be so much easier if he could just pull out his badge.

The man frowned and was about to say something else when his computer beeped. He glanced down, and his frown deepened.

"Pardon me sir, I will be right back," the desk man said as he walked toward the door behind the desk, his eyes never leaving Hamlin.

"No problem, I think I have the wrong address anyway."

"I set off a fire alarm in the back room," Juan's voice said over the earpiece. "They have an interesting fire alarm system. The lower floor ones are two stages. The first stage is for a slight temperature change, it just alerts the front desk. The second stage is for a major temp change like open flame or activated by the front desk. I gave it an error code for the first stage. It will just look like a glitch."

As soon as the man was through the door, Hamlin whispered to Juan, "He's gone, now what?"

"Elevator. Hurry before he comes back. The cameras are all taken care of."

Hamlin hurried over to the elevator bank and hit the call button. The doors immediately opened. And Hamlin prayed once again this kid never returned to a life of crime.

Once inside the steel and wood elevator the doors shut and the third-floor button lit up. Muzak played quietly over the speaker.

"Any requests?" Juan asked. "For the music I mean."

Hamlin ignored him. "Third floor is part of the business front?"

"Yeah, private conference rooms and offices. There are only a couple of people on this floor, and I don't think they're security."

The door opened and Hamlin stepped into a room that looked like a small lobby. There was no reception and only a couple of chairs and coffee tables. Again, to Hamlin it felt like this room had never been used. This floor might be safe from security, but he suspected that's because there's nothing on it to protect. He said as much to Juan.

"Well you can check for a computer then, maybe they'll have one on that floor," Juan said. "Okay, take the door on the right. But wait."

Hamlin paused with his hand inches from the doorknob.

"I can hear you cursing under your breath Hamlin."

"Good," Hamlin growled.

"There was someone in the hallway beyond, but they're gone now."

Hamlin slipped into the hallway beyond. It was empty and Hamlin let out a breath he hadn't realized he had been holding. The hall had three doors leaving it besides the one he had just come through.

"Is this room clear?"

"Yeah, nobody home on this one or any of the others on this floor."

Hamlin looked in. It was a standard office set up. A desk, chair, some cabinets. It was nice, high-end office setting, but it also felt unused. The magazines were several months old.

"There's a computer, but the office looks completely unused. It's just part of the front. I'm guessing that computer is useless."

"Probably. But put the USB device in and boot it up anyway. Let's just check."

Hamlin inserted the tiny USB drive and booted up the laptop. He had just reached the login screen when the door opened behind him.

The man standing in the doorway looked just as surprised as Hamlin. He was not the standard rent-a-cop. He looked ex-military and ate cereal mixed with steroids for breakfast. He was tall and would fit better on a defensive line than in a suit. His head was shaved down to stubble. Hamlin was a little disappointed he wasn't wearing shades. Seemed like that would have completed the image.

"Shit. Company," Hamlin said.

They both went for their guns, but Hamlin's broken body slowed him down. His bruised ribs twitched with pain as he tried for his shoulder holster. He paused and winced involuntarily. The other man's gun was out before his hand was even on the butt of his pistol.

"Freeze!" The man commanded. "Who the fuck are you and what are you doing here?"

"Cleaning service?" Hamlin offered.

"Shit, fuck, he must not have a cell phone. Who the hell has no cell phone?" said Juan in his ear.

"On the ground now!" shouted the man.

"Look, I'm a cop." Hamlin started raising his hands.

"I don't care who the fuck you are, you got three seconds to tell me what you are doing here before I kill you."

"Didn't you just ask me who the fuck I was?" Hamlin was not sure why even in the face of death his tongue betrayed him. He was pretty sure it was Chris and Juan rubbing off on him, however. There was no way he was taking this guy down even if he didn't have a gun. He was twice Hamlin's size and Hamlin was still aching from the last time he was used as a punching bag.

"Cops have no power in this building. They die like all the rest. One, two..." Hammer pulled back for dramatic effect. "Three."

A roar echoed throughout the room. And Hamlin knew that roar. He would have kissed the kid if he had been there. From the only shadows in the room, the darkness under the desk, burst the giant panther. Hellcat sprang from the shadows in one giant leap. The man never had a chance to move his pistol.

His eyes opened wide in shock and terror. Hellcat's huge muzzle, lined with razor sharp teeth, a jaw that could literally tear your soul from your body, opened wide beneath blazing red eyes. The man screamed briefly, but it was cut off as the massive jaw clamped down on his throat. With a wet tearing sound, Hellcat ripped out his throat.

"That's grisly as fuck! Jesus," Hamlin said. He loved that kitty more than ever now, but feeding time was still a horror show.

"Get the fuck out of there Hamlin, I don't know who heard that noise. Move your ass."

That got Hamlin moving. He started toward the door he had come in.

"Don't forget the USB thing."

Fuck! He spun around and his sore knee raged in protest. He limped back to the desk. They had quickly gone from Mission Impossible to the Three Stooges in a hurry. He reached for the USB but his rib twitched again and he cried out. Fuck it. He snagged the whole laptop. *I'll remove it later when I'm not running for my life.*

He half-limped, half-ran back to the door, but paused just before opening. He looked back at Hellcat. She stood above her kill, watching him with blood dripping from her crimson muzzle.

"Good girl, I'm gonna buy you the biggest bag of catnip I can find. Now back into the shadows where you can be safe."

She almost seemed to nod before diving back under the desk with a meaty growl.

"Is the coast clear?" asked Hamlin.

"Yes. At least I think. There is one camera in the hall that shows clear. No alarms have been sounded that I can see."

"You really need to work on your confidence building kid," Hamlin said and opened the door.

The coast was clear. He ran, favoring his knee, to the elevator. It was waiting for him courtesy of Juan, the door opened and he was inside as quick as he could move.

"Bringing you down now," Juan said.

"No," said Hamlin, "Fuck it. Take me to the penthouse."

This was their only chance. Once they found that body, they would know their security had been breached the building would become Fort Knox. But if he could get this little USB thingy into the right device it would be like winning the lottery. This was their best chance to break open this alliance.

Besides, he was feeling a little more badass with an 800-pound demonic cat watching his back.

18

"No problem, I was gonna take you there anyway," Juan said. "Because I know you're batshit loco."

The elevator started rising.

"You know this is it, our only chance?" asked Hamlin.

"Yeah, and I was just starting to like you, even if you are a cop. Okay, if we're gonna do this here's the intel. There are at least four people up there and limited cameras; I guess the big guy likes his privacy. I can only find them in the entry, dining room, kitchen and a couple of hallways. Basically, the common areas. I've overridden the elevator alert and disabled every alarm or sensor I could find between you and the penthouse. Holy fuck..."

"What?"

"I just saw the big guy in a camera. He's home, so he's got to be one of the cell phones. Are you still sure you want to do this?"

Hamlin sucked in a long breath. "Yeah, there's got to be a computer somewhere that I can get to. Afterward... well, at least you'll be able to access the system. Just keep tabs on everyone and guide me. Is there anybody in the entry?"

"No, the coast is clear. I'm not sure where Golyat went, but it looks like a room in the back of the apartment. No cameras, so I'm not sure what room it is. Wait, it's a smaller room compared to the others, I think he's taking a shit."

"You know there is TMI in intel as well."

The elevator was silent when it opened into the penthouse entry room. No ding announcing his arrival. Video cameras on loops, the kid was good. Although there was a little voice in the back of his brain that said this was a little too easy, he shrugged it off. There was nothing they could do about it now.

The penthouse was stunning. Beautiful artwork lined the walls, probably famous pieces that Hamlin would never be able to recognize. A thick rug covered the center of the floor and helped muffle his footsteps. The ceiling was over twelve feet high here. The entry hall stretched off in either direction, but in front of him right across from the elevators were a set of large double doors thrown open to the living room beyond. Floor to ceiling windows looked out onto the city.

And he thought the kid's swanky home was impressive. It had nothing on this place. Golyat knew how to live in style.

"Quick! Down the hallway to your right. Someone's coming the other way."

Hamlin quickly headed off down the right hallway, trying not to look over his shoulder.

"Take the first hallway on your left," said Juan.

He passed several doors he was tempted to open, but he had to trust Juan. He turned down the hall Juan had said.

"Now first door on your left, hurry."

Hamlin opened the door and ducked in, quietly shutting the door behind him. He was in a powder room. It was about the size of his apartment. That might be a slight exaggeration, but everything about the penthouse seemed oversized. The powder room was bigger than most master baths and the hallways seemed somehow artificially wide. It must have all been custom for Golyat. He still hadn't seen him in person, but he was beginning to get an idea of how massive he really was.

He shifted the laptop to his left hand so he could press his head up against the door and listen. From the other side he could hear movement, one, no two men, talking quietly. He couldn't make out all the words, the door and walls were too thick—also very unlike his own apartment—but it seemed to be a casual conversation. Just two soldiers passing each other on patrol.

What if one of them needed to use the bathroom? Fuck. He spotted a closet and slipped inside. Correction, the powder room closet was bigger than his apartment.

He didn't quite have the door shut when the bathroom door opened. Hamlin paused with the closet door open a crack as the security guard came in. He was dressed in a suit like the one on the man downstairs and he was just as big, but that's where the similarities ended. His head was shaved and covered with sickly-looking molted skin. He looked like a ten-day-old corpse.

I swear to God if these are more zombies I'm going to scream.

But the man seemed too in control to be the variety of the walking dead that Hamlin had encountered. Everywhere it was exposed, his skin was covered in tattoos. Hamlin could only see the black ink on his head and hands, but he had no doubt it covered the man's body beneath that suit. Not street tattoos; Hamlin was familiar with street and prison tats. These were different and seemed to shimmer and move in the light, like living occult symbols shifting on his body. If this was a natural tattoo, the artist was a genius.

The man came in and used the toilet, another good sign he wasn't the living dead, and then adjusted his suit in the mirror. From his hiding place, Hamlin could see his reflection. His eyes flashed a blue-silver briefly before he turned and left the bathroom, shutting the door behind him.

Hamlin let out a long breath before leaving the closet.

"See, no problem. I got your back," Juan said.

"Just tell me when they are clear. I'm so tense I feel like I'm gonna jump out of my fucking skin."

"It's clear. Leave the bathroom and turn left."

Hamlin stepped out cautiously, Juan had been wrong before. The coast was clear. He walked down the hall but stopped in front of a door. "Is this room clear?"

"Yes, but I have no idea what's in it."

Hamlin opened it. It was a guest room. No computer. "It's a bust, guest room."

"There's a set of stairs just around the corner from you, not the main staircase, more like a service one. It'll get you to the second floor of the penthouse."

"This fucking thing is two stories?"

"Three. When you got money you go big or go home. Just thinking the second floor might be more interesting. The third floor is a blank for me, no floor plan registered that I could find. But I do see stairs going up."

Hamlin left the guest room and found the small stairs heading up. He slipped up them as quietly as he could. Once up there he checked three more rooms. One was storage, one another guest room, and the third an attached bathroom.

Twice Juan had Hamlin duck behind a door to avoid detection. Hamlin's nerves were as raw as his steaks.

"At this rate, they're going to find me before I find a TV remote, let alone a computer."

"Yeah, the longer you're there, the harder it will be to avoid detection. Eventually, they're going to figure out what I've done to the cameras and alarms. Maybe we should get you out of there, call it a bust?"

"Just one more room," Hamlin said. This one looked promising, large double doors dominated the wall. Whatever was behind it was more important than a guest room.

"Shit, Hamlin the big guy is heading up the main stairs. You got to hide."

Hamlin made a decision. He went into the room, shutting the double doors behind him as quietly as he could.

"Hamlin, he's heading in that direction; he might be coming to that room. What is it?"

Good question. Hamlin turned to see where he was taking refuge.

This was the first room that had a look of age. Most of the walls were covered with intricately carved bookshelves and cabinets. To one side a large leather couch and chair sat near a massive fireplace that looked like it had been stolen from a medieval castle. Old rugs covered the hardwood floor; they looked antique as did most of the furniture in the room, including the oversized desk in front of the window with a sweeping view of the city.

On that desk was a monitor and a keyboard that looked like it was designed for hands twice the size of his.

"Bingo," Hamlin whispered. "I think we found his study."

"Tell me there's a computer?"

"Big and beautiful," Hamlin said. He walked behind the desk and set down the laptop. There it was, a black box just humming along in the dark beneath the desk.

"Oh fuck, Golyat had stopped at another room, but now he is coming there. He's moving fast, and he's not alone."

Hamlin stood up, looking for another exit. On the edge of his peripheral vision, he saw something. There mounted on the corner was a small camera.

"I thought you said no cameras in this room," Hamlin said.

"I don't see it on any network; it must be a separate private system. Fuck, there could be all sorts of alarms. Run!"

Hamlin didn't need to be told twice. There was one other door out of the room, he made for it as fast as his bruised body would let him. His hand was on the handle twisting the knob when the door flew open. It slammed into him with unnatural force knocking him back. He stumbled over the chair behind him, his injuries making him too slow to catch himself. He tumbled over it and to the ground, scrambling for his pistol.

One of the mystically tattooed guards came through the door. This one was shirtless, his heavily muscled skin shimmering with the writhing ink. He was grinning. Hamlin had his gun out and brought it up. Then the tattooed man was on him, moving faster than Hamlin thought possible. He wrenched the pistol from Hamlin's hands before he even had a chance to squeeze the trigger.

A blurred shadow shot from the darkness behind the desk and slammed into the tattooed man. With a roar, Hellcat raked her claws across the man's face and chest, disrupting the flow of the tattoos. He cried out and tried to fight off the massive beast with his bare hands. It was like playing mercy with a food processor. There was no doubt that man had supernatural strength, but it was no match for the demon cat.

Hamlin crawled to his gun just as the large double doors flew open. Golyat stood in the doorway, filling the entire frame with his bulk, calmly assessing the situation. His eyes flicked from where Hamlin lay on the floor to the massive panther mauling his soldier. Then he strode over to Hellcat and with both meaty hands grabbed her by the scruff and tossed her across the room as though she weighed no more than a fur coat.

She hit the ground on all fours like any respectable cat, but the momentum sent her slamming into the fireplace. Hamlin could do the math. As powerful as she was, she was no match for Golyat one on one. Of course, she was of another opinion. Hellcat roared and prepared for another leap. Golyat stood calmly waiting for the attack. It would be suicide and it would be because of him.

Ignoring the pain, he sat up enough to wrap his arms around her neck and whispered fiercely into her ear. "No! You must find Chris."

She seemed to be ignoring him, her eyes on Golyat, but she didn't lunge.

"You come into my house, into my world. You grow too bold, and don't think you won't pay the price. Where is the Hunter?" Golyat said. He was taking off his suit coat and folding it neatly on a chair next to him. Then he calmly rolled up a sleeve. Hellcat watched him warily, a low growl in her throat.

"Go, find the kid. I can get out of this. You have to help protect him," Hamlin whispered in her ear. She looked at him one last time and licked his face. Despite all that had happened, he smiled.

She roared as loud as he had ever heard her in a mighty challenge, then she dove into the shadows and was gone.

And just like that it was over. Hamlin debated even trying for his gun, it would be useless against this dark soul. He had failed, at best they would kill him; at worst, try to use him as bait. For a moment he toyed with the idea of grabbing his gun and killing himself. At least then Golyat wouldn't have a bargaining chip.

The tattooed guard was faster. He stepped over Hamlin to retrieve the gun. He was bleeding from a dozen deep claw marks across his face and chest, but he seemed unfazed as he picked it up and grinned down at him. He wasn't weak from blood loss. From his crazed grin it was almost as though he enjoyed the gore, even if it was his own.

Then a thick rough hand wrapped around his throat and he was lifted into the air like a ragdoll. Golyat held him at eye level and glared at him. His giant hand tightened around his neck and made it hard to breathe. Hamlin pulled at it out of reflex. It was like clawing at stone.

This was the first time Hamlin had seen Golyat face to face, and he realized he was staring straight into the face of a monster. Golyat's eyes were filled with red lines and bulged slightly as though anger raged just behind his calm exterior straining to get out. Heat radiated from his body as though some sort of furnace of hatred burned inside of him. Still, his outside image radiated coldness. Hamlin realized it was only iron discipline keeping that monster in check. Just one slip and he'd be fucking Godzilla in the city.

"You can't be alone? Who would be that stupid?" Golyat pulled him closer and Hamlin could smell the rot on his breath. "You are that police detective that he uses right? You were supposed to lead him into my trap, not trip it yourself."

He laughed a mirthless laugh devoid of all joy. "Is he such a coward? Does he trust you so much?"

Hamlin didn't say anything; he was too busy trying to suck in air through this tightening throat

"What have you caught Golyat?" asked a voice from behind him.

Over the giant's shoulder Hamlin saw a teenage girl, maybe fourteen or fifteen. Her face had dark splotches that Hamlin realized were fading bruises. She was wearing pink pajama pants and a t-shirt that said 'I'm not always a bitch! Sometimes I'm a psycho!'

This must be Grace.

"What are you doing down here, Grace?" Golyat asked. "You should be in your room."

"What, I'm being confined to my room now? That's so not cool. I heard the private alarm and came to check it out."

Hamlin saw irritation flash across Golyat's face. Hamlin almost laughed; apparently being an evil escapee soul from Hell with immense power and wealth didn't exempt you from teenage attitude.

"We've had a visit from our friend's associate. Looks like he couldn't be bothered to come himself, so he has sent an expendable."

Several other tattooed guards were coming into the room. Hamlin was amazed he had made it as far as he had. Juan had led him skillfully.

Juan! Hamlin realized he wasn't hearing him. Now he could feel the earpiece was no longer in his ear. Hamlin had a small moment of panic. It must have fallen out when he fell over the chair. If they found it, they would know he wasn't alone and would start looking for whoever was on the other end.

Despite suddenly being very alone, falling out was probably the best thing to happen. They would have found it when they searched him, but they won't find a device as tiny as a speck on the carpet.

"What are you going to do with him?" Grace asked.

"Eventually kill him, but we'll question him first. Learn what we can about this new Hunter and this small..." he paused as though searching for the right word, "Pathetic team. If they even can be called that."

Hamlin was able to squeeze some air through his throat. "This pathetic team stopped your Days of Chaos and returned a lot of you people back to Hell."

He used a lot of air, but he felt it was worth it. The fire behind Golyat's eyes seemed to burn brighter for a moment. With a sound of disgust, he threw Hamlin to the hard ground. It was a casual gesture, but Hamlin felt like he had been struck by a bus. Golyat was above him. Hamlin felt like a kick was coming, one that would crush him into a pulp.

"Let me take him Golyat," Grace said softly, her voice suddenly dripping with honey rather than sarcasm. Her eyes flicked up and down Hamlin like she was inspecting a bug. Despite that, her words calmed him. Suddenly everything was going to be all right.

Golyat frowned and turned partway toward Grace. "Why? What can you do that my doctors cannot?"

Hamlin didn't like the way he said doctors; he was pretty sure they weren't your usual Hippocratic oath taking type of doctors.

"I can practice." She stepped closer to Hamlin still looking at him with those piercing eyes. But the voice, it made him warm. She was just a kid, she was no harm. He hoped Golyat would give him to her.

Wait! What the fuck was he saying?

A small change passed over Golyat and his frown softened. "You could use the practice I suppose. But no killing him. We might need him as bait."

It was worst case, torture and then bait. He hadn't even completed his mission. They had nothing on what Golyat was up to. He had failed.

One of the tattoo guards picked up the laptop from the desk. "He brought this computer with him."

"Well then, maybe it won't be just torture that gives us information," Golyat said and gestured aimlessly to the other half of the penthouse. "Take it to the security room, run some scans and see what you can find on it. Meanwhile, take the detective to Grace's lab and secure him however she wants. Remember Grace, have some fun and get what you can from him, but don't accidentally kill him."

19

Juan held the earphones close to his head as he listened. He had heard the earpiece fall from Hamlin, but it was sensitive enough to pick up the general conversation in the room if he turned it up enough. He was able to make out the sound of Hellcat arriving and attacking as well as the thump of her being thrown to the ground. He listened through the scuffle and the conversation, trying to pick up on every little detail.

He breathed a sigh of relief when he figured out they weren't going to be killing Hamlin on the spot. And again when he realized they didn't see the earpiece. He knew he should leave, it would make sense for them to search for an accomplice even if they thought Hamlin acted alone. But he had to watch as long as he could.

He could follow where they were taking Hamlin. They had taken his cell phone of course, but he noted which ones were the guards and could track their movement if he stayed at the computer. If he could pinpoint where Hamlin was kept, Chris could use this information. If he could get ahold of Chris.

He glanced up through the tinted windshield at the front of the van. Men in suits like executive bodyguards, were coming out of the main doors. Several had tattoos covering bald heads. These stood apart from the other security guards; they were working together, but it was obvious who was in charge. They were spreading out from the building.

Fuck!

Juan turned back to the computer, the guards holding Hamlin were still walking, slowly which meant they must be holding him.

"Hurry the fuck up!" Juan growled. He glanced out the window again. The guards were coming closer. They were at the end of the block. One of the tattooed guards had spotted the van. He called to the others and they all focused on the vehicle.

There were people on the streets, but it wasn't crowded. What few people got in the way they gently shoved to the side. There were three of them, and as Juan watched they reached under their jackets, for guns no doubt.

He turned back to the screen. They had taken Hamlin to the top floor. He didn't have a complete floor plan, but it was going to have to be good enough. Time to get out of here.

He slid into the driver's seat and turned the ignition at the same time glancing out of the window. The guards were gone. That caused Juan to pause for a moment. Where did they go? They didn't just disappear.

Tap, tap.

Outside the passenger window, a tattoo guard smiled at him and waved. Then he punched through the glass. The heavy, reinforced, bulletproof glass Juan had installed. Juan screamed as the guard ripped the door off. Now the guard grinned at him from the open door.

Juan hit the gas and the engine revved, but he went nowhere, the van was still in park.

"Fuck!" Juan yelled as he scrambled the gear shift. He was used to the shifter being on the floor and with a psychopath about to jump in the car, he wasn't thinking too clearly. His hands flailed for a moment looking for the nonexistent shifter.

The tattooed guard lunched forward hands outstretched, coming for Juan's throat. But then the man stopped abruptly mid-lunge. His eyes went wide in a combination of surprise and terror. Then he screamed.

With a growling rumble around her mouthful, he was yanked out of the van violently by Hellcat.

"Yeah motherfucker! What a good kitty!" Juan yelled through a huge grin.

Hellcat pulled the tattooed man from the passenger seat and whipped him toward the curb. The man's face skidded across the cement and smashed into the concrete with a sickening thunk. A chunk of the man's thigh also came off, ripped away by Hellcat's vice-like jaw.

"Woohoo!" Juan yelled like an overexcited cheerleader.

Then the window shattered behind his head and a tattooed arm as thick as a python snaked around his throat. He was yanked back and almost out the window, but managed to grab an exposed metal support strip inside the roof of the van and temporarily stopped his backward trajectory.

Unfortunately, that meant the arm could cinch up easier. Abruptly the air to his lungs and the blood flow to his brain was cut off. Instantly the world started going black. He would pass out in seconds, already his grip was loosening on the metal rail.

Then he saw dents forming on the roof and heard the steel groaning in protest as something large and heavy strode across it. Claws pierced the the steel as she crossed.

There was a cry from behind him and the arm loosened. Then a roar followed by a sickening crunch just behind his ear. The arm went slack as the body fell away, missing a head.

Juan spun around in the chair until he was once again facing forward. Two more men, one a tattoo guard staring defiantly at the gigantic black panther on top of the van, the other a mortal security guard eyes wide in terror as he brought his assault rifle to bear on Hellcat.

He opened fire as Hellcat leaped at them. A hand full of rounds hit her, but Juan was pretty sure they would have little effect on a creature made of shadow and Hell. At least that's what he hoped.

She slammed into both, her rear claws tearing into the man's chest, spraying blood on the cars slamming to a halt in the street. Her front claws raked against the tattooed guard's chest, but he had moved with much faster reflexes than the mortal and instead of being torn open, he was sent spinning onto the curb.

It was time to leave, this was his chance. Juan gunned the van and drove up on the sidewalk to avoid the suddenly stopped traffic on the road. Pedestrians dove out of the way. Luckily the foot traffic was light around here today, and between his driving and their jumping, he managed to not hit anyone.

He banged his hand against the door panel as he passed Hellcat, who was warily watching the tattooed man get slowly to his feet.

"Come on girl," Juan called. When she glanced at him he tapped the roof. "Come on, time to go before the police show or more of those tattooed freaks." With what seemed like a reluctant growl she turned from the recovering man and leaped onto the roof of the moving van.

Her claws dug into the thickened metal. And he gunned it. As soon as he cleared the traffic jam of parked cars he careened back onto the street. He heard Hellcat skitter a little as he made some violent twists and turns, but she held on, although he was certain she was shredding the roof like it was the arm of a couch.

Juan raced down the street with the giant panther on the roof. So much for not attracting attention. Once he was a few blocks away from the building, he pulled over and opened the rear doors.

"Get in here girl," Juan said making sure no one could see him.

He hadn't seen any cameras yet, but that doesn't mean they won't pop up. Hellcat had her own kind of internet fame. There was even a Kickstarter for stuffed animal versions of her. What the hell was the world coming too? But it did make him wonder about setting up a Kickstarter for an action hero figure version of himself. You know, just in case.

Hellcat bounded into the van and faded into the shadows.

"I owe you one, Hellcat. Or should I call you Katy Purry? Get it? What about that one?"

There was a menacing growl from the shadows. "Okay, okay. Got it. Stay with Hellcat... for now."

He got back in the driver's seat and started off again. He took the long way home, making as many turns as he could and searching for signs of pursuit. When he was confident they weren't being followed, he headed back to the lair.

Everything had gone wrong. Hamlin was trapped and who knows what they were going to do? He barely got away with his life. If they tortured Hamlin they might be able to find where the lair is. He knew Hamlin would never rat them out, but he was in the hands of some powerful people. It was probably only a matter of time. He needed to find Chris soon or they would all be dead.

20

Apophis stood in the window of the apartment gazing at the window across the street. It was the top floor, and he had a clear view of the large windows across from him.

The brothers stood next to him, one watched the ground noting the comings and goings of people into the building across. The other gazed at the entrance to their own building. That was just a precaution, they did not expect anyone to come for them.

After obtaining documents and leaving no witnesses, they had changed into clothing more appropriate for America. Jeans, t-shirt, jacket—it didn't matter, they just had to fit in. Gone was the desert, now was the urban decay.

The room smelled of the familiar scent of blood and death; the owner lay slaughtered on the bed. He had been asleep, it had been nothing to end him. And the space was just temporary, a stakeout location in this giant city for them to watch this new player.

They did not talk, for they thought as one. These shared thoughts were their only need for conversation.

The city was a wonder. Though in their sleep they had spied on the world, had seen it evolve, it was still a surprise that it had grown so in their imprisonment. Even the sight of Cairo and its urban sprawl, as magnificent as it was, did not compare to this city of giants. He loved to think about this new world and all the death they could bring to it.

There was movement across the street. The long curtains blocking out the room moved and Apophis could see her once again. She stood for a moment looking out over the city, lost in thought. She was beautiful. She could not see them, he was sure, for they were far across the street and the lights were out. They were safe from her notice. He was glad they chose caution rather than force.

When they had come yesterday, when they had found this place, they had been drawn by the stone. The power it held had called to them, and now they knew why. He had chosen wisely. It wasn't the stone they were meant to find. It was her. She was their destiny.

They had watched with caution. They had seen the large man arrive and knew him for what he was: his power was immense. They did not fear him, but they were not stupid. He was the master here. They had to avoid him until they could be reunited with their queen.

They had seen the girl and they knew her for what she was. They could see it in her—the power, the skill. Just like their first mistress, their first queen. She would be their purpose in this new world. She had power to change everything, to rule once again. And they would be by her side.

She turned from the window and spoke to somebody. Beyond he could see a man being hoisted on a rope, perhaps from a beam. He did not know what this man had done, but the man was in pain. It was obvious that their new mistress shared some of their tastes.

It was time to go to her.

21

His time away was long and trying. Christopher first stepped in the book and onto a mountainside. Cold winds blasted against his unprepared body. He stood in knee deep snow, and a blizzard whipped about him, surrounding him in a cold, white blanket. Through scattered breaks in the whiteout he could see craggy peaks in all directions.

Another blast of wind knocked him to his knees in the snow. Already he could feel numbness seeping into his feet and hands. The wind was so icy it felt like a million needles hailing down on him. He needed shelter fast or he would have to open the book and return to the Library. He had no idea which direction to go. He could barely see two feet in front of his face. If he was high in mountains, he could step off the edge of a cliff and never know it.

His face burned from the harsh wind and he was about to give up and just go back when he saw a light ahead. It was faint and for a moment Christopher thought he might have imagined it. Then, during a pause in the wind, he saw it again. Still clutching the book that was both his entrance and exit to this world, he got to his feet and made his way to the light.

It was further than he had thought. Trudging through the thick snow held him back like molasses. He had none of his power here it seemed. No Hell-powered stamina or strength. He could still feel it inside, but in these training worlds things worked by a different set of rules.

He fell more than once and the snow was little protection from the jagged rocks sticking up from the ground. It was drudgery struggling through the freezing wind and whiteout. Every step seeped more energy from him.

His mind began to focus on one thought: just one more step. Always just one more step. At first, he had refused to give up, knowing what waited for him back in the real world. He may not be sure what type of chance this was, but it was a chance and the only one he had.

Then, as his entire world became about walking, about that one more step, he simply started forgetting everything else. He held the book, forgotten in his frozen hands. He lost track of time, it felt like hours or even days, his mind was slipping from him. He was pretty sure his toes were frozen, his ears and nose just frostbitten, dead flesh now.

He lost himself on that mountain. All he was became forward momentum. Just one more step.

Then he was there. Abruptly he stepped out of the blizzard and into a cave. A wonderfully warm cave. The shock of the sudden change startled him, and he fell face first onto the stone surface. He was vaguely aware of the crackle of a fire and the smell of smoke. But it was the warmth that pulled him.

Just one more step. He crawled on what might have been dead hands, frozen fingers. Every movement was agony. If felt as though his nerves had been frozen and now came awake as the heat thawed them. Every joint ached, a confusing jumble of numbness and deep pain.

But the fire was there. He crawled closer and other things came into focus. There were thick blankets and furs around the fire, crudely built wooden shelves leaned against the rock walls. Here and there carved niches held assorted items, but Christopher was too disinterested to guess what they were.

A pot sat near the fire, hot and steaming. He also became aware of another smell hidden under the smoke of the fire. An herbal smell, fragrant and earthy. He crawled until he was on top of the fur and blankets. He felt the warmth seeping in, but he could also feel the dead spots on his appendages. His skin was dry and rough. Open sores from the touches of frostbite were forming.

As he warmed up, he gradually became aware that he was not alone. The cave was coming more into focus, and as his need for survival faded away he noticed it wasn't just a cave, it was a home. A simple one, but a home. Several pots and clay cups sat on a shelf. Other cooking utensils hung from hooks in the wall by the fire. Also nearby was a large pile of firewood. It looked like it could last a year.

Then he saw the man across the fire from him. He was a little man, thin enough that Christopher thought a strong breeze would have carried him away. His hair was long and his beard thick and unruly. He sat on the other blanket, legs crossed. His eyes were closed and he held a steaming cup in his hands. He looked like a cross between a wise old mystic and Charles Manson.

Christopher hoped he was more mystic than Manson.

"That wasn't even the beginning of where you are going, that wasn't the least of what you have yet to experience," the man said.

"What happened?" Christopher said in a voice little more than a croak. "How long was I in that blizzard? Who are you?"

"You got cold. Most of the night. Your first teacher."

It took Christopher a moment to understand that his host was giving answers to his questions. The man opened his eyes and held out the cup of tea. "Drink this, then we begin."

Christopher snapped awake at the offer of tea; he had been falling asleep. "What now? I've lost my fingers to frostbite and I'm exhausted. I won't be able to think straight."

"That is a good start. And you don't need your fingers or toes to go where we are going."

It turned out Christopher hadn't lost his fingers after all; he came close but they remained attached. In a few weeks he had the feeling back in them.

Christopher learned quickly that his new teacher was not one for long speeches. He wouldn't even tell Christopher his name. The monk had told him names were not important. Most of his days were spent in meditation.

They would wake before dawn and did a few chores to prepare for the day. This consisted of cleaning the cave, including flushing out the bathroom with melted snow. To call it a bathroom was probably a stretch. It was a smaller cave off the main one with a hole in the ground. He never asked where the hole went, but it seemed bottomless.

After chores they sat and meditated for at least an hour. The monk never explained anything to him, just instruction on how to breathe, how to empty his mind.

Then a simple breakfast of rice porridge and vegetables stored in a cooler portion of the cave or even frozen outside. After breakfast was morning exercises. This consisted of a series of slow movements like tai chi with some yoga poses thrown in.

The afternoon was more meditation and any evening chores that needed doing. After dinner was still more exercises. These were a separate set of movements. Christopher had no idea what the difference was or why it was important, and the monk never told him.

The first few days were the worst. The weather forced them inside. Christopher couldn't concentrate and sitting still for hours drove him crazy. No matter how much he 'breathed' no matter how much he tried to 'still his mind' all he could think about was the world waiting for him outside.

He thought of his body wasting away, albeit very slowly now. He thought about how he had his ass handed to him by Apophis. He thought about Hamlin and Juan and how they were getting along without him.

In those first few days sitting still was the enemy. He would jump up, pace, trying to think through everything all at once. He had thought this was supposed to be training him to be stronger, to go back fighting. He had no patience to sit on a cold stone floor, ignorant of what was going at home.

He raged against the monk those first few days. The third day there he screamed in the monk's face. The hatred of the Hellpower raged up in him despite its usual distance. He came close to striking the little man before calming himself.

Through it all the little man had said nothing besides the instructions to sit and breath and still the mind. Christopher discovered that the book was gone, his passage back to reality was missing. He suspected the monk had taken it. Though he looked through the cavern every chance he got, it was nowhere to be found.

Christopher suspected it was a conspiracy, like an intervention. Somehow the monk and the Librarian had ganged up on him. They were forcing him to do this.

Several times he had left the cave, running through the makeshift cave door. Perhaps he could throw himself from a cliff and the shock of impact would kick him out of the book. He knew dying was not possible in this world. But he also feared laying at the foot of a cliff, his body broken in a million pieces but unable to move or die.

Suffice to say that thought and the incredible cold drove him back to the cave and that horrible little monk who sat calmly and did nothing.

After the futile rage and the runaway attempts, he had nothing left but tears and finally he gave in. He sat there calmly trying to breathe as the monk had told him, trying to still the mind.

After a week he thought it might be working, in some ways it was as simple as forgetting. The more he tried, the more the rage and hatred of the Hellpower calmed and settled. Still, there was one thing left that he could not stop, one thought that was always there always running through his head.

"I can't stop thinking about her," Christopher said one day, more than three weeks after he had first fallen into the monk's cave. He looked over at his teacher who had closed his eyes, but Christopher knew him well enough to know the man was not asleep. "I know, I know clear the mind. Stop thinking about anything. I get it."

"You are making progress," the monk said.

This made Christopher slip out of whatever semi-meditative state he was in. Making progress? Why? Because he wasn't screaming and yelling at the monk anymore. He would call that remembering his manners, not 'progress.'

"It doesn't feel like it," was all Christopher said. "I just wish I knew if Eris was okay. I left her there in that hospital. I felt like I should have focused on her, sat with her. Fuck being recognized. But this stupid power, this stupid job. I let it control me, I let it help me forget. I think part of me just felt she had died."

"Despite what many think, despite what you think...love, not hatred is the hardest to let go of. You are making progress."

A few days later, towards the end of their morning meditation, for a moment...just a moment...he was thinking of nothing. It was all gone. No anger, no hatred, only peace. Of course, as soon as he felt it all thought rushed back in. When he opened his eyes, the monk was staring at him.

"And now we can really start," the monk said.

After that it really did. It started with expanding the silence, the calming of his mind while sitting still, and then it was while they were doing the movements that Christopher referred to as Tai Chi 2.0. Over the next few months he strove to bring this calmness, this empty mind to everything he did. He cultivated what the monk called *perfect state*. Christopher called it the Jedi mind trick.

Spring came and they worked outside on the mountain tops then down a little way amongst the flowers in the valley, hiking, sometimes running up and down the mountain. He was in the best shape of his life; too bad it was in this dream world. They would pause every once in a while, and the monk would point out some animal or how the wind moved through the trees. He just pointed these things out, never giving a lesson just pointing the way. But by now Christopher knew there was a lesson in everything he did.

At some point, towards late summer he realized he could not feel the darkness inside of him. The Hellpower and the part that was fused to his soul, filling the gap was still there, but its control over him was less. It had retreated so far, he had to look for it. That's when he realized the purpose of this, why he needed this training. It was bringing control back to him.

They spent less and less time in seated meditation, more time focused on the exercises. The movements became faster, flowing from one to the next. Eight months after his arrival, late in the summer, Christopher took up his position to begin the pattern when the monk faced him.

Christopher's moment of confusion disappeared when the monk attacked. He shot forward striking but not striking, kicking but not kicking. Christopher hesitated, but quickly recovered, his body automatically falling into the familiar movements. His mind, after recovering from the surprise, fell back into that state of no-mind.

This was the next stage of his training, meditation through combat. Over the next few months the fighting got faster, longer. Blows became more solid when they landed, defenses became stronger. Christopher found himself slipping in other techniques that he had learned in his past trainings.

He didn't think, it just came to him. It was the only time he detected a smile trying to break through the monk's stony face. He did not plan his attacks, he flowed from one to the other.

Exactly one year after he had come to this mountaintop, he stood on a ledge just outside the cave. It was a beautiful night, no storm this time. Just clear skies and jagged rocks covered with snow. The moon was full and caused the long stretches of snow and glaciers to flash brightly. He wished he had some skis.

He heard the monk approach, the soft crunching of snow under hide boots. It occurred to Christopher that he had learned many skills this past year, the still mind was just the most important. He had also learned to live in the mountains, basic survival tasks. He almost laughed, this year had been the most enlightening of his life.

He turned to face the monk as he approached. The monk shoved the book into his chest.

"Time to go," the monk said.

"What? Wait, I'm not done. There's no way you've taught me

everything," Christopher said and for all his stoic training he could still hear an edge of panic in his voice.

The monk laughed, at least Christopher thought he did. He had never heard him laugh before.

"For all that I have taught you, you have a million things more to learn. But not by me."

"But..." Christopher started.

"This, all of this, is just the beginning. This was merely the foundation. You have a journey of many more books, more pieces of knowledge. But know this: for all of that, in the end, it all comes back to knowing nothing. To be of no-mind. Never stop practicing."

The monk went back into the cave and shut the crude wooden door behind him. It had a finality to it. He knew he was not meant to open it again.

He took one last look around at the beauty. He absorbed it all at once with his no-mind. Then he opened the book and was gone.

22

He found himself seated on a rug in the Library the closed book in his hand. For a moment he wasn't sure where he was. Memories from the real world, only an hour old, collided with the memory of the year he had just spent on the mountaintop.

The room spun like vertigo and his stomach lurched. Was yesterday, yesterday? Or was it last week? A year ago? He felt reality slipping away.

He slid from the chair to the floor. Images of Eris and Hamlin swirled through his head. His family, only two years dead, or was it three years—he wasn't sure—were there. As was the memory of monstrous dark souls he had sent to Hell. It was a horror show of monsters and pain blended with the good memories of his friends and family. Eris in the hospital bed... Hamlin beat up, broken.

But it was all confused, he felt his mind slipping. Where was he again? What day was it?

Instinct took over, he began the process of stilling his mind. One by one he calmed his thoughts by focusing on his breath. The techniques were in him, natural. He didn't have to think as he methodically silenced his mind. It wasn't easy. The side effect of spending a year in that other world while only seconds passed in the Library and the real world was debilitating. His mind couldn't process it all at once.

Slowly he got it under control. He started with no-mind and then let the memories and thoughts come to him naturally, one by one. The mind is an incredible thing and handled it now that he had calmed the mad flow. Until now he had never spent more than a day or two in training. With such short stays the memory disruption was minimal. Christopher was pretty sure that if he had not spent that year learning what he did, he would have gone mad. It was the foundation of his training in more ways than one.

An hour later he found himself seated with his feet folded under him. He looked around at the Library with new eyes. It had been a year since he had laid eyes on it, a year for him, only a moment for here.

A thought of homesickness rose up in his head. He acknowledged it, he wanted to go home. Christopher wanted to sleep in his own bed, he wanted this more than anything. Well, almost more than anything. He wanted to see Eris, to stand by her and just touch her, let her know that he was there and wanted her back.

He couldn't do any of that trapped in a hole in the ground. He glanced back at the bookshelf. He had to select a new book, a next step, but he wasn't ready yet. His mind was still fragile.

The Librarian was gone, but then it had only been minutes since Christopher had left. His memory was still a little askew, but he remembered the Librarian was off learning what he could about Apophis.

Christopher spent a few hours there thinking and not thinking. He would never have been able to sit so silent and still a year ago...or a moment ago, depending on which timeline you used. More than once anxiety reared up as he thought about pulling another book. Each time he steadied himself with his new skill. It was a great gift.

Eventually, it was time for him to move on. He didn't have a method to get out of the cave yet. His mission wasn't done. He selected another book and opened it. And this time he was gone for a very long time.

He came back briefly several times. Pausing to regain his calm. Sometimes he arrived after years away. The memories washing over him every time threatening to drive him mad. Each time he breathed, he stilled his mind, he became focused by letting it all go. Sometimes he would drink water or eat a little food while he prepared himself for the next book. Even though it was not real, his mind took the refreshment.

He was living adventures now, each book of knowledge a new learning, a new test. He fought on battlefields alongside barbarian hordes, he studied with the greatest Asian and European mystics, he climbed mountains. He stormed the beach at Normandy along with a great warrior, doing his time as a simple soldier. He sailed seas and found battles ship to ship.

Each book was a land of dreams. He had fought in worlds dreamed up by his teachers. In some, he used his Hellpower. He learned not just how to use weapons, but also how to use them in harmony with his other power. His speed and dexterity were far beyond what they had been when he first started this journey.

He trained in a half-dozen fighting styles, taking what worked and fusing it with other techniques. His body was covered with a thousand different scars that remained on his mind and soul if not his body. He didn't stay long enough with each teacher to master any one training. But as he progressed through from master to mystic to honored soldier to warrior to occultist and beyond he understood that the underlying skill, power, and learning were the same. He had been told that a master of an art shows mastery in his every action.

In the years he was gone, he lived enough adventures to fill many books.

And then it was time to return.

When he came home that final time he was standing. The books he had lived scattered about him in a semi-circle. He still had vertigo at the rush of memories, but he stilled his mind out of habit and slowly, one by one, processed the memories. They were distant now, but Hamlin and Juan were still there; he even remembered Courtney and Jeremy. And of course, there was Eris. That thought hurt along with a pang of guilt.

But they were distant memories. Although in the real world only a day or two had passed and the memories were right there at his fingertips, they were fuzzy.

"It is because you are a different person." The Librarian had arrived from the shadows as he finished his meditation. Christopher had known he was there, had sensed him; he was no longer startled by the Librarian's sudden appearance.

"What was that Librarian?" Christopher said. "It has been a long time since I have seen you."

"Yes, quite," the Librarian responded. "Did you find what you were seeking?"

"Yes. I believe so. I have learned so much, I have mastered so much. The person I was before, the child, the newborn is gone. I have understood real power and I am the master of it. I have learned the workings of the world, I see the ebb and flow of energy."

"And your memories?" the Librarian asked. "Do you remember your friends? How they help you?"

"They are there, but distant. That is for the best. At this point I am someone different, someone better. The darkness, the Hellpower inside me is now my servant, my control is complete—"

"Yes, that is great," the Librarian interrupted. "I just have one last book for you to use."

He held out a book with a solid black cover. There was no title on the front or the spine. Christopher took it and flipped it over in his hands.

"What is this?" Christopher asked. "I don't need another book, Librarian. Not now. I have to save my body and return to my job hunting dark souls."

"You'll have to trust me. This is important. It is the greatest teacher you could have. He will take everything you have learned until now to the next level."

Christopher looked at the book doubtfully. What teacher could this be who could do all that? Then he asked, "Who is it?"

"It is best if you just trust me," the Librarian said. "Have I ever led you astray?"

"Not astray, but you have failed to tell me a few things."

"All important omissions for your growth."

"Sure Librarian. Okay, but I can't spend long on whatever training is there for me. My body wastes away even as we speak."

"It won't take long," he said.

Christopher looked down at the ominous black book, hesitating for a moment. Something about it made him nervous. He had other plans, a world that only he could save. He shrugged it off. This would just take a moment. He could leave this new teacher anytime.

He opened the book, but instead of falling in, it all fell out and into him. Like a fire hose of power, energy shot out of the pages and washed over him head to toe. Memories deep and rich came back to him.

His family long before the horrible day he returned from school. His sister and mother smiling as they played in the yard, went camping, and of course their trips to Disneyland. These memories were old but strong. Mostly it was the good times, but a few sad and profound moments blossomed fresh in his mind.

Like watching a movie, the memories moved forward, becoming stronger the closer they came to the present. He experienced his high school days a second time, not just the good times, but the bad and embarrassing ones as well.

The book wasn't so much giving him these memories; instead the power seemed to be moving through his head awakening the old thoughts. It was moving faster and faster.

Then his college days sped by; the classes he loved as well as the ones he hated but made him think. And there was Courtney. His first love and first heartbreak. It had taught him a lot.

That was it. It was hard to focus on putting logical thoughts together as he went through this memory onslaught, but his subconscious was getting a grip on what was happening and let it slip into his consciousness trying to process the flaring memories. These were the key moments that made him who he was, all memories made him the person he was, but these moments were the true shapers.

The memories were more vibrant as he passed through the time after he had encountered the Beast. He saw all his missteps, all his foolish mistakes yet somehow, he survived.

He remembered how Hamlin had been there from the beginning and then there were the Erises: dark Eris the demon fighting by his side, saving him when needed, and Eris there for him to talk to and show him the compassionate way. Followed quickly by Juan, rescued from a deep mind fuck, who just wanted to help. And he was an anarchist. He thought of the team because that is what they were. Not just his support staff.

Then he remembered the gang member in Mexico and the true extent of what he had done at that moment came to him. The one who had brutalized his family deserved his damnation, but the other one, that one still had a chance, but Christopher had taken that chance from him the moment he judged the kid and sent him to Hell.

In his arrogance he had condemned a poor kid to an eternity of suffering. Anguish bent his body in two and he wailed. He could blame it on the darkness that had been growing in him, that Grace had manipulated him with her power. But he had opened the door to it, then he had opened it wider when he used the Hellpower to try and help heal his soul.

In the end it was him, it was his mistakes; he was the one who let the darkness in. He was the one who had let the balance slip in favor of hatred.

The Hellpower in him flared up, stoked by the darkness tied to his soul, as though angered by the memories, rebelling against anything that showed compassion or reliance. Anything that showed weakness.

His training was still there, however, and came to him in a reflex and he channeled that anger away, letting the memories thrum through his head.

When it was done Christopher found himself on his knees. He

heard crying and as the rush of memories faded he realized it was just him.

"It was me," he finally said, whispering it. "It was my book."

"Yes. I had to special order it," the Librarian replied. "After that many years away, living that other life, I knew you would need something to bring you back to now, to who you are. This seemed like the best way."

"You mean, creating an emotionally fragile wreck before sending me out to do battle with the monsters?"

It might have worked. His two lives fused together, but in reverse. His years spent training were in the background, not forgotten. He felt as if all he had experienced was at his fingertips, it was just put into perspective, so to speak. It was all very confusing.

"Ah trained with a psychologist, did we? You were experiencing a wealth of philosophy and martial skill. You were learning ten lifetimes of knowledge and skill in a handful of years. Before you left, the darkness inside of you was making you arrogant with power. I suspected when you returned you would be insufferable. I was right."

"You thought this would help?"

"It did help," the Librarian said, somewhat smugly, Christopher thought. "At least that is the theory. I guess we will have to see how it all plays out. You do seem somewhat less arrogant than you were a moment ago."

"Great." Christopher wasn't convinced. He did feel better than he had in a year. He was exhausted physically and mentally and emotionally. His life away had taken its place in his memories. It was there but not dominant. Still, he could feel the darkness simmering just below the surface like it was just waiting to break free and start shaping him again.

And that need, that hunger to claim souls for hell was still there stronger than ever. In fact, it flared as he thought of it. Although, part of that might have been the physical hunger his body was going through.

"I need to get back. How long has it been?" he was tired and drained, his brain fuzzy from it all. It felt like his mind had been pulled from his body and flayed. It hurt and was numb all at the same time.

"Three days I believe," the Librarian said.

Christopher smiled, only three days. He didn't think he'd be right in the head for a long time. He wiped the tears from his eyes. He pulled from his training and calmed himself. "I have to get back, I have to get out of that cave and stop Apophis."

He stood up, a little unsteady. The room spun a little.

"You should rest a moment at least. Drink something, it won't help long term but psychologically it might help while I tell you the rest."

"The rest? That doesn't sound good. Please don't tell me you're going to give one of your famous pep talks."

"No, I have found the origin of Apophis, you will not find him in your hunter's journal. But if you want a pep talk, I can say he will probably kill you quickly if you encounter him. None of this stuck in the ground stuff."

"Thanks, I'm glad I can always count on you to have my back."

"Quite. Apophis is a bit of a challenge you see. He, I mean they, are not living."

"Tell that to the guys who kicked my ass a few years...um, I mean days ago." This was going to take some getting used too.

"They appear living, but they are not mortal nor living, and definitely not a dark soul."

"Are they like a beast then, some sort of monster?" Christopher asked.

"Not exactly, they are not living things, but not undead either. They were created thousands of years ago by a powerful witch queen. Golem is the technical term. They were shaped from an ancient substance much like clay and enchanted. They look human but have no true humanity."

"They're like some sort of ancient android?"

A glass of water had appeared on the table next to him. As he sipped on it, he suddenly became insanely thirsty. He could taste the refreshing water, and moments later his thirst was the same.

"More or less. The ancient witch queen created the amorphous substance that is their essence and enchanted it then, she gave it purpose."

"And what is the purpose of these particular golems?"

"The name Apophis is a legendary name. It is the Greek pronunciation of an Egyptian god. It means Lord of Chaos."

"That is an appropriate name. They sure created a shit ton of chaos. At least for me."

"The Egyptian god was equated with the god of evil and the enemy of life itself, and he was blamed for all the evils that befell the ancient world. However, I think it was more specific than that. The witch created them with one purpose only, to kill her enemies."

"Like her personal soldiers?"

"Not exactly. Although many people killed for money, some say Apophis was the first assassin. At least the first true one to openly serve royalty. The witch who created them was a queen of chaos herself, always keeping her land off balance to maintain order. The paranoid type who regularly cleaned house, killing her lieutenants and counselors. From what I understand she was keen to kill innocents, support the guilty. Her small kingdom along the Nile, long before the great Egyptian dynasties came along, was just this side of Hell."

"What happened? How were they trapped?" Christopher asked, his mind had stopped spinning and he was able to follow along for the most part.

"That part was unclear. The queen eventually died, slain in a revolution of her closest allies. Three of her generals and several of the most powerful merchants. They killed her when Apophis was away on some errand for the witch queen and her own bodyguards were overcome."

"I assume that didn't sit well with Apophis?" Christopher asked. "I already get they are the vengeful type."

"Yes, over the next two days the generals were found dead, as well as the merchants who had supported them and their closest servants."

"Well that does sound like—"

"Then the merchant's families, everyone including the smallest grandchild. Then the entire palace staff was slaughtered in one night, next it was the five hundred soldiers who had followed the generals that night. All killed. In the span of a few days."

Christopher was sobering up quickly. "You're saying they're good at killing?"

"They are the best. From what I could find, after their vengeance was complete, they wandered, looking for purpose but finding only death. They hired themselves out to the highest bidder. But they never served another like the witch queen, they never found someone to give them purpose."

"And somewhere along the line, they crossed paths with my predecessor."

"Yes, though that part is unclear. They must have interfered with his retrieval of a dark soul. That is my only guess."

"He was able to defeat them. But why just lock them up? Why not kill them permanently?"

Christopher caught the minute movement of a shrug under the Librarian's robes. "I don't know. Perhaps they are unkillable?"

"Well that's just great. Not only do they not possess a soul for me to dispatch with my trusty blade, but I also may not be able to kill them? What am I supposed to do? Put them in prison again?"

"Well, that would be a type of solution. However, if I might speculate, while they may not be able to die, they might be destroyable."

"Hmm, aren't those the same?"

"To use your android reference, they may not be killed by a mortal blow or even a dozen mortal blows, nor do they have a soul to take; but you might, for example, be able to melt them in a crucible of liquid metal."

"That was a cyborg, not an android," said Christopher. The Librarian remained silent in judgment. "But I get what you mean. So, all I need is a giant pot of melted steel?"

"It seems that last book was too effective, you are truly your old self. No, not a vat of steel, just enough destruction that they cannot self-heal, then somehow dispose of the parts."

"Got it, cut the ancient enchanted super-assassins into little bits and then flush them down the toilet."

The Librarian sighed and seemed to look disappointedly at the shelves of books Christopher had just trained through. "The Beast was able to capture them and imprison them. My only guess is that he used a type of canopic jar to store their malleable essence after he was able to destroy the bodies they inhabit." He apparently recognized Christopher's blank stare, because he continued. "A canopic jar is what ancient Egyptian embalmers used to store the organs of the bodies they interred. If you could capture this essence in a similar container, they might be trapped until you find a vat of molten metal, or a volcano, or a large enough toilet."

"I have to go," Christopher said standing slowly. "None of this matters if I can't get out of that room. And then figure out a way to get my Weapon back if I can find it."

"That will be the easier task. It will call to you. Follow your instincts and you will find it. As for who you must take it away from, that could be a problem. But I'm sure you'll figure it out."

A door had appeared in the wall between two shelves.

"Just remember, when you step through that door and arrive in your body you will feel all the suffering that it is currently going through. Hunger and thirst like you never imagined."

"That's what I like about you, Librarian, I can always count on your parting words of motivation and inspiration. If I still can't make this work, I'll be back for good."

With that, Christopher stepped back into the real world.

23

The first thing that hit Christopher, even before the fading darkness of his journey from the Library, was a thirst like no other. It surpassed the hunger he felt for souls when he was hunting. It was down deep inside of him; when he returned to his body he doubled over and retched. It was all dry, nothing there.

His throat and eyes burned. A headache came on in full force and almost drained all thought from his mind. His life was suddenly pain and longing. His body ached all over, his skin felt dry and brittle. At that moment he would have given anything for a drink of water, he would have traded any soul.

Even Eris'?

For a moment he teetered on madness, but that thought pulled him together just a little. It was the training in his subconscious coming through.

Even Hamlin's?

He sat up with those thoughts, his legs subconsciously folded under him. Instantly he calmed his mind and began meditating. He fell back on the first and most basic of what he had learned. He strove to still his mind over the raging thirst.

After the first three breaths he had steadied his mind. Pangs of thirst and pain came to him. He acknowledged them and then dismissed them; they were still there but the desire could be compartmentalized. They were just another fact of his existence. Soon he could become dispassionate about it.

When he had the madness at bay, he focused his thoughts on his dilemma. The room was still wrapped in darkness so thick it was like he swam in an inky sea. That could also be the lack of oxygen talking. He was finding it harder to breathe. He didn't have much time left.

At first, Christopher considered brute force. He might be able to summon up enough strength and energy to try and rip a hole through the ceiling or the collapsed tunnel. But what if he couldn't bring that much power to bear? Until now he had only channeled infernal energy through himself and his Weapon. He wasn't sure he could project that with enough force to make a difference, and if he did Christopher was just as likely to bring the ceiling and tons of rock and sand down on his head.

No, that was too dangerous, he was still too new to his power.

He seized upon the only advantage he had—darkness, the natural home of his power. The hellfire born power inside flared to life. The darkness was his home now, not just here but out there out in the real world. The night was his hunting time, the shadows his cloak and armor. And it was someone else's too. Hellcat.

How could he use this? It was time to explore his power, time to work with some of the thoughts he had formed over the last ten years of his training. But the core of the idea came from a different source something that might be just as good a teacher as all that he had learned. Star Wars.

He sent his thoughts out through the shadows. Starting with the darkness that surrounded him, he let his awareness spread out, seeking the limit of this room. At first, the darkness stopped at the walls and he could feel the shape of the room with his mind, letting himself fill every corner. Then he tested it. The chamber was sealed physically, but he discovered something. There were little pathways, hidden and obscure in the dark, not physical pathways of course, ones that only his mind, fueled by the Hellpower, could find.

Controlling it like a spigot, he let the power flow through him, propelling his awareness onto these pathways. Instantly he recognized these dark shadow paths as a labyrinth. It would be easy to get lost in such a place.

He started slowly searching down paths seeing where they led. He was too inexperienced to know where exactly he was going. But he tested the waters so to speak. He did know that his awareness could stretch out and just maybe seek others.

There were other entities there, moving just beyond him. He could sense they were malevolent, hateful things. He stayed away from them, not ready to do battle with the denizens of the shadows. This was a new discovery; there would be time to explore the path of shadows another time.

After testing for a few hours, learning the feel and movement along these dark paths, he pulled back and rested a moment. He spent another hour just honing his strength and focus. This escape would not be a quick thing. Then the thirst dug into him again and he changed his mind. It was now or never.

This time he reached out relying on his newly honed Hunter instincts. He flew through the shadow paths, searching. He would touch upon alien beings so strange it made him question how they could exist so close to the real world. Perhaps there were worse things than those that had escaped Hell.

He stretched out his awareness and cast it wide. He called to Hellcat. At least that was what he thought he was doing. He reached out like it was the Force and he was Luke, sending his call as far as he could. It worked in the movies, so why not?

He was at it for hours, casting his mental net into the vast ocean of shadows before he felt something. Something he recognized. He focused in on it in desperation and pulled in closer. He thought it recognized him in return.

And then Hellcat was there, touching his awareness.

Come to me, he thought to her. Then he realized he was weakening. He could feel himself slipping back towards this body. The thirst and hunger were winning. Eventually he lost the connection he had made as the distance between his mind and the shadow network grew.

"Help," he cried in the physical world as well as this shadow one.

And then she was there chasing after him. She whipped along the shadows paths as he retreated.

That's my girl, he thought even as he felt himself weaken further. His awareness, his hold on the shadows was dwindling. *Save me girl.*

He was going to lose her. It was going to be all over. Then he saw her, a black physical manifestation in front of him. This is her world, as physical to her as the real one was to him. She lunged forward, biting into his awareness.

He was almost startled enough to snap back into his body. But the jaws clamped down on him. It was an odd sensation, her powerful jaws clamping down on his insubstantial presence. Then again, she was created to bite into the souls of mortals.

It didn't hurt, at least not enough to detract from the insane thirst that was crippling his body. But he felt it physically as though the jaw had sunk into his shoulder, awakening memories of the old wound. Then she pulled.

She was both in the shadow realm and in the room with him. Pulling him deeper and deeper into the dark paths. With a final pull, his physical body followed his awareness into the dark with a wet sucking sound that made Christopher think of the moment of birth played backward.

He must have lost consciousness for a moment because the next thing he was aware of was a coldness. It was seeping into him, but the hellfire inside seemed to welcome it and warm him. He knew he was in the shadow world now and he had the sensation of movement. He looked up and there was Hellcat dragging him by his shoulder. He could hear the noises she made and the quiet hissing sound of his body being dragged across the ground. But it was muted, like the darkness around him absorbed most of it.

The shape of Hellcat shifted and moved as though here in shadow it could not find a permanent form. It blurred too, the darkness did something to his vision. Like she was going in and out of focus. It could have been the dehydration, but he thought it had something to do with this shadow realm.

He was tired, so tired and he felt his strength draining away. He could do little but hold onto consciousness as Hellcat pulled him through. Eventually even that was too much and he faded into unconsciousness.

He awoke in brightness and heat. Thankfully he was in the shade of a large rock. He lifted himself up onto his elbows and rolled over until he leaned on the large boulder. It was part of a pile of sand and rock. He thought it might have been the rubble that sealed his tomb, at least that's what it looked like from the outside.

The outside!

He had a sudden burst of energy at the thought. He was outside! They had made it. Next to him sat Hellcat quietly cleaning herself in the shade. She had done it, she had pulled him through the shadow paths, it had almost killed him, but she had saved him.

Then the thirst rolled over him ten times stronger perhaps because of the insane heat out here in the desert. He moaned and Hellcat looked at him. He wanted to thank her, but his throat was as dry as the sand around him. Where ever *here* was. The world stretched away in a beige rock and sand blur.

He needed to find water, or he was going to lose it. His new strength of mind would only go so far. Even now he was pushing beyond any mortal limits. Christopher reached out to Hellcat and gripping her fur, slowly pulled himself upon her back. It was his only choice. He couldn't get to his feet, let alone walk out of this place.

He pulled himself forward so he could lie on her broad back. Into her ear he was able to croak, "Water," Before passing out. He didn't know how much time had passed before he opened his eyes again. But it seemed to be later in the day, the sun was low on the horizon. He didn't think about that, he couldn't think about that. He needed water.

He was even hallucinating. He could hear children paying and the voices of people talking. Why would there be people in the middle of the desert? Why would children be playing in a hell hole like this? They would die of thirst. Then the voices rose in alarm, the kids suddenly stopped their laughter and started yelling.

The commotion was too detailed to be a hallucination. Christopher used the last of his strength to turn his head toward the sounds. Through the haze of dehydration and exhaustion even as he felt himself slipping from Hellcat's, back he could see small brown structures with tents mixed in. It looked like a small village. His last thought before fading again was that they probably had really, really good water.

24

Christopher awoke to the sensation of cold water flooding his mouth. It might have been the greatest feeling in the world. He found himself lifting to meet the source of water.

"No, no, slowly at first. Otherwise, you will just be sick. It does no good all over the floor of my house and not in your belly." The speaker was an old man leaning over him. He had dark, leathery skin and spoke in some form of Arabic. Christopher could understand him clearly with the gift of his power, but he had no idea what language they were conversing in.

"Thank you," Christopher said. He voice was still a croak, but a little better than before. "Can I have just a little more please?"

He hoped the man said yes because he was not sure he could keep from taking the water if the man said no, and that would be no way to thank his host. The man just smiled and poured a little more into Christopher's mouth. He drank deeply, relishing the water.

The room he was in was plain, dirt floor stone walls; a think rug and some pillows made the bed he was laying in. He could smell food cooking and while he wasn't sure what it was, he was positive he could eat all of it.

There was one door to the room and several windows. A crude

shelf ran along part of one wall with a radio and some other odds and ends on it.

"Where is my cat?" Christopher asked. Hellcat was nowhere to be found.

"You mean that giant beast you rode in on? I don't know. After you fell off its back it stood over you briefly. We could see you were sick, but none of us would get close. It was terrifying. Then it ran off. Then we could come check on you."

"Where am I?"

"The village of Al-Bul not too far from Cairo."

"I have to go, I need to get to Cairo," He started to get up, but he was still weak. He sunk back down.

"Not so fast my friend. We are still stunned that you are even alive. In fact, I would not believe someone so dehydrated out of the desert would still be alive. You are a miracle, from Allah himself."

Christopher did not bother to tell him how far off he was.

"Besides, it is late," the man continued. "You need to at least drink some more and eat. Cairo will still be there in the morning."

He was already feeling better as the fluids and his fast healing did their work on him. But then a thought occurred to him.

"Did you see three men come through here? Strangers?"

The man sat back on his heels and studied Christopher. "A few days ago, three men came through. Men that were no men, they had the stink of death about them. The passed through only to take some water from the well. We kept away from them. Are they with you?"

Christopher could tell by the tone of the man he had to be very careful how he answered. "They are my enemies, they left me to die, but now I hunt them."

The man continued to look at him suspiciously as though deciding, then his look suddenly softened. "Then I am glad I helped you. I don't know who they are or who you are, but they are up to no good. You will rest tonight and then tomorrow I will take you to Cairo. I have a jeep."

He said that last part with a measure of pride, and Christopher couldn't help but smile. Then a woman came in from the back; she wore a simple dress and a scarf on her head. Christopher was not sure if it was technically a hijab or not, but her face was not covered. Her clothing quickly became irrelevant, however; she had food in her hands and that was all Christopher had eyes for.

She handed him the plate. He had no idea what he was eating, but it was the better than any five-star restaurant in New York.

25

Despite his imminent death, Hamlin couldn't help but laugh at how much this was like a movie. Of course, he was only laughing on the inside.

The tattooed men had hung him by the wrists from a beam in what must have been the most psychotic teenage girl's room ever. All metal, glass and wood, old books and jars on every shelf. With a splash of pink and silver and what looked like a stuffed unicorn. He couldn't help but feel a little sorry for Grace. This is what Anabelle and Golyat had done to her. A twisted and monstrous witch, with a little girl trying to come out.

But all this was secondary. Waves of pain washed over him as they hung him up, his bruised muscles and ribs pulled and stretched. He winced and grunted but was able to keep from crying out.

"You should go," Grace commanded the guards once they had positioned him. They looked at her, hesitating. Obviously they thought leaving her alone was a bad idea. They were probably right. Hamlin felt sorry for her, but if he had the chance he would escape, even if that meant going through her. "I am not asking. Go."

There was something in her voice Hamlin thought, something odd, but he couldn't place it. He just knew that, if he were able, he would have left at that moment. Her voice compelled him. The guards seemed to agree and left the room rather quickly. Hamlin looked back at Grace only to find her staring up at him.

"This will be cool. So far, every specimen I have had to work with died immediately as I extracted the soul. But you are a challenge. I've been told I need to keep you alive, at least for the moment. It will be a challenge deciding how to manipulate your soul from the outside. But I think it will involve a lot of pain."

A flash of light over Grace's shoulder caught Hamlin's attention. A glass container with a shimmering substance writhing in it sat on the shelf. Grace followed his gaze and smiled.

"Ah, you recognize your master? That's my little trophy. It is the Hunter's soul shard."

It was small Hamlin thought. If he could find a way to escape, it would be easy to grab it and bring it back for the kid. He needed it.

"I like it and it has taught me a lot. Like how to twist the essence of a person into something more useful," then she sighed. "But it's not a whole soul, so it has its limitations. I had trouble gleaning information from it. It will however, serve me well when the Hunter comes to try and retrieve it."

"He won't," came a dry, grating voice from the back of the room, darkened by shadows. Hamlin was not the only one surprised by the sound. Grace spun and backed almost close enough that Hamlin could have kicked her if his broken body would have let him. But it didn't matter, she didn't get close enough.

Three men stepped out from the shadow. They were dark skinned, Arabic perhaps? Hamlin saw the way they stood, calm and in control, but ready to explode into violence; he recognized the hardness in their eyes. These were cold-blooded killers. And there was something else. They seemed familiar.

"Who are you? And how did you get into my room?" asked Grace. She raised her hand and curled it into a claw. The table nearest the men slide across the floor blocking their path to Grace.

Now that is new, thought Hamlin. *Her power isn't just about souls.*

"Peace, mistress. I have no desire to harm you in any way. On the contrary, I wish to serve you. My name is Apophis."

"You did not answer my question. How did you get in here? If you come any closer I will have guards here instantly."

"Mistress, I can tell you how I came to be here; getting in and out of places like this are trivial for my skills, but it is a long story and not the most important one. For now, know that I have chosen you to be my mistress. I wish to serve you."

"Ha, so just like that you show up in my bedroom and tell me you want to serve? And I'm supposed to be all like, I got three more random guards working for me? Why should I believe you? Why shouldn't I, like, call the guards? It makes no sense."

"I am no random guard. Look at me. Really look at me with your witch eyes."

Grace was quiet for a moment, then she gasped and leaned forward. "You have no souls," she whispered. "But how are you not mindless zombies? Wait."

She moved closer, no longer concerned about the danger. "You are not alive, but not dead either. What are you?"

"These bodies are convenient shells for me, but that is all they are—shells of flesh that will someday rot and fade away. I, however, will never fade."

Grace moved even closer as though the thought of danger had completely left her mind.

Apophis continued. "I was created by one like you, a queen with great gifts. I recognize the same gifts in you and have come to serve. I request only that you give me purpose."

"That is all pretty language, but how do I know you are telling the truth? You could be waiting for me to turn my back so you can kill me," Grace said.

Despite her words, Hamlin could see the man's words were having an effect on her. She seemed to be a sucker for flattery.

Apophis thought for a moment. "I don't have proof, and I have no soul for you to read, but I offer evidence. The Hunter is your enemy, correct? He is no longer a threat."

"You lie," hissed Hamlin.

Apophis glanced at him as though seeing him for the first time. "And who are you?" he asked.

"That's one of the Hunter's minions," Grace said. "We caught him snooping around where he didn't belong."

"Despite what the hanging man says mistress, we assure you he will not bother you again. He owed me vengeance and I collected."

Then Hamlin recognized them. The last time he had seen them, they had been wearing scarves across their faces, slaughtering innocents as bait in a trap for Chris.

"You killed him?" She glanced and the glowing soul shard on the shelf. "I think not."

"No, that would be too easy. We did what his predecessor had done to us. We buried him in the sand, beneath tons of rock that not even he could escape."

"So, he is *not* dead," she said. "It's sounding kind of shady to me."

"Worse than death, mistress," Apophis continued and moved a little closer, but not threatening. If anything, he seemed subservient. "He suffers immeasurably. He has been trapped for days starving and dying of thirst, but unable to die. By now he must be mad. I doubt he can do more than lie on the ground. No mistress, his fate is far worse than death."

"You son of a bitch," Hamlin cried out. He struggled against the bindings on his hands and swayed back and forth in his bonds. "It's bullshit! There's no way you defeated him."

Apophis ignored him and continued to stare at the ground just in front of Grace, keeping his eyes averted.

"How do I know you tell the truth?" Grace asked,

"Has the Hunter come? You have his man, I know the power you have here in the building. Certainly he would have come himself? Wouldn't he come to at least snatch his man from you? Or kill him to keep him from talking to you?"

"You do have a point," She looked back at Hamlin. "Why would he send this loser in his place? So, you were able to defeat the Hunter in a fight?"

"Of course, mistress, we are the best, the first of the Bleeders. We will kill all those who stand against you, simply give us the word. And I offer proof."

Apophis held out his hand. In it rested a small pocket knife. It even had the swiss army knife emblem on it. Hamlin recognized it instantly and his heart sank. Was it all true?

"This is weird, but if it's true, it's awesome. Always wanted my own henchmen so I didn't have to rely on Golyat's all the time. What are the names of your friends?"

"I am Apophis."

"Yeah, I get that, but who are the two dudes behind you?"

"They are me. I am Apophis. It is just best if you address me when I'm around."

Hamlin was only half listening to the conversation. Could the kid really be dead? Well, not dead if he believed this Apophis. Just suffering, starving for eternity? He had to get out of here, somehow; he had to find Chris. Apophis said sand? Was he buried in Egypt?

"Come with me, I want to introduce you to Golyat. He is the one giving the orders around here and he is lame as hell, but we have to make nice with him. If he doesn't like you, he'll kill you on the spot, so I hope you aren't playing a game."

"He will not kill us. I have told you, we are the First Bleeders. We are unstoppable."

"Didn't you just say you were trapped for thousands of years by the first Hunter? You sound fucking stoppable to me," said Hamlin with a toothy grin.

Grace stepped up to Hamlin, made claw shape with her hand, and thrust her fingers into his gut. They sunk into his skin like ghost fingers, not touching him physically. But he could feel her cold touch all over his being. Like she had found his central nervous system and poked at it with an ice pick. Pain, like electricity shot through his body, only he knew it wasn't his body. It was striking at his soul. It was the most painful experience of his life.

His body convulsed, shaking the rafter above. His eyes bulged out and without warning vomit spewed from his mouth, splattering to the floor. Grace jumped back and, thankfully, removed her fingers from him.

"Ew, that is so gross. Why did you have to do a thing like that?" She looked down at the foul-smelling liquid and held her nose. Then she put her head back and made a little moan while she stamped her foot. "And I lost my maid today. That's just great. Come on Apophis let's go meet Golyat. I'll just make some guard clean this up."

Hamlin knew they left, but it was hard to focus after that last assault. His body had finally had enough and his brain was shutting down. Unconsciousness beckoned. He tried to fight it, he needed to find a way to escape and save Chris. That was his last thought as everything went black.

26

Christopher stepped into the main room of the Brooklyn Lair from the cube room and he knew he had come home. It was a dark bunker of a building, but he had never been so happy to see the place. The book the Librarian had given him had refreshed his memory, brought him to the here and now, but some things seemed distant. He still had the sense that he had been gone a long time.

"Juan," Christopher said.

Juan was sitting slumped over the computer desk, head in hands. He looked defeated. His hair was messed like he hadn't washed it in a while his clothes looked like he had slept in them. Something was wrong.

"Juan," Christopher said again.

Juan raised his head but did not look at Christopher. As though he wasn't sure if he had heard anything. Then he looked over and his eyes widened.

"Chris!" he said as he jumped up from the chair. His face was red and his eyes swollen. Something was definitely wrong. "Jesus where have you been? Everything is screwed up."

Juan was speaking Spanish and the words were running together. But he suddenly stopped and ran over and hugged Chris. Christopher smiled as he hugged him back. Hellcat faded in from the shadows and rubbed up against them.

"I was wondering where you disappeared to Hellcat," then to Christopher he said, "Thank god you're here. I thought you were gone for good."

"No, I was trapped and it's a long story. Let's call Hamlin so I can just tell the story once. We have a new enemy out there we must figure out how to... what? Did something happen to Hamlin? Is Eris still in the hospital?"

"The Eris' are okay at least as far as I know. Hamlin though, he's been captured."

Christopher could feel the familiar anger building up inside of him.

"Tell me everything. Start from the moment I left."

Juan told him everything. From the discovery of the building to stakeout followed by Hamlin being a stupid as hell and walking in the front door.

"What were you thinking? I told you guys to not make a move. Just watch and observe."

"Technically we *were* watching and observing, just really close up. Besides we had no idea where you were or what was going on. For all we knew you were dead."

"We have to go get him," said Christopher.

"Of course, but it's obviously a trap. It was meant for you in the first place."

"You said you had a schematic of the building? You know the layout?"

"Yeah, but you'll never get past the front door. They will have extra security, I don't know what, but they know it will be you that's coming, they'll have something that can give you a run for your money. Something that can stand against your Weapon."

He must have seen something in Christopher's eyes. "You do still have the Weapon?"

"I don't have time for the whole story, but at one point I was unconscious and they took the Weapon. But I can work on getting that back later, right now we need to get Hamlin out of there. Besides, I don't plan on going through the front door."

"But without the Weapon you don't stand a chance. I mean your tough and all, but without a weapon how are you supposed to damn their souls?"

"I don't know. Maybe I don't. Maybe all we do it get out of there with Hamlin and our lives. It doesn't matter. Hunting down the Weapon will take too much time. Time that Hamlin doesn't have. He is a tool for them and you throw away tools when they are no longer useful."

Juan leaned back thinking. "It might be a suicide mission, but I'm in. If you're sure. There will be an army waiting for us, regular guards, those tattooed freaks and at least one powerful dark soul. Plus, whatever surprises Golyat had planned for this trap."

"Will you be able to hack into the security camera's again?"

"I doubt it. I bet the moment they found Hamlin they started hardening their security, and there was that secondary security network that I hadn't even detected."

"Is that a no or a maybe but it will be hard?"

Juan stared at Christopher intently for a moment before breaking into a smile. "Well it's only been a few hours, so I think I have a chance they couldn't have plugged every hole in the system. But I can't be sure there isn't some other layer of security that I can't find. That's what happened to Hamlin. That along with the reinforced guards, will make sneaking in impossible."

"I wasn't planning on sneaking in," said Christopher.

"A man of action, I like it. Let's go,"

"I need to make a quick stop before we go," said Christopher. "Also, do we have any small sealable containers of some sort?"

Juan gave him a questioning look, "You mean like Tupperware?"

"No something more durable, metal if possible."

"Well, I have some small metal jars I've been using to store some small repair items. They're about four inches tall and a couple inches in diameter. Will that work?"

"I hope so," Christopher said. He had no idea what size canopic jars should be.

An hour later Christopher entered the hospital room where the Eris' rested. He was in plain clothes as he slipped through the corridors hood and baseball cap obscuring most of his face. It was a risk, but one he had to take.

He had avoided signing in at the visitor's desk and had only been given suspicious look by the security guard. Luckily the guard seemed more interested in some game on his phone than trying to figure out what he was up to.

Months ago the hall and waiting room might have been filled with reporters wanting to talk to the girl that was saved by the mysterious new hero. But when she didn't wake and the hero never turned up to answer questions the story faded away as all news stories do over time.

Christopher was alone with the Eris'. She looked the same as when he had gazed at her from outside the window. But now, closer, able to reach out and touch her, it was different. He saw the touches of life still in her. The small bit of color that had been missing from outside the glass was still there on her cheeks.

He came close to her bed, gently taking her hand in his. Tubes and wires were attached to her body, but she was still beautiful. He knew that now. His memories of her were at once recent and old. To him, it was like he had known her all his life.

"I'm sorry I didn't come to your side earlier," Christopher said. "I told myself it was because I was afraid of being recognized. That if I came to you they would have me on camera and nobody would ever leave you in peace. So I stood outside the window. That glass, that distance separating us.

"But that wasn't what I was afraid of. I was afraid that whatever was between us was making me weak, that fear of losing you would become a weakness. I was afraid that being too close to you would make me weak."

Christopher reached up and brushed back her hair gently, not a normal gesture for the Lord of Damnation, but totally in character for Christopher Sawyer. And that was the point.

"I've changed a lot in just the last few days. I've lived a lot of adventures and I've grown in a lot of ways. But you were always there it gave me strength in ways I couldn't have had if I had never met you. I was afraid of what was between us, between all of us for that matter, but really you are a strength I can't fathom."

He leaned over and gently kissed her brow. "I need you to live, I need you to help me live."

He kissed her one more time before stepping back. "I don't know if you can hear me, but I hope you can, at least a little. I have to go now, saving the world and all that shit, but I will be back to be by your side. As you always were by mine."

With one last squeeze of her hand he left the room. It never occurred to him to question that there were two Eris' in that body and he had been speaking to both.

27

The meeting room was large but cloaked in shadow. Nobody was hiding their face purposefully, but they all lived in a world of mistrust and the darkness helped them maintain their poker faces. The ceiling was high and the room wide. Golyat was the largest dark soul, but many were large, some close to his size. Having a large room made everyone comfortable.

Four members of the alliance sat around the grand table, carefully seated as far from each other as possible. They each knew that one would turn on the other in a heartbeat if it meant they could seize an advantage. The Alliance had formed of necessity, not any real desire to work together. Each member had his or her own goals since escaping Hell; working with other dark souls was just a means to an end.

The alliance was larger than the four that sat here around the table, but they never all met at the same time. Too many in one place risked chaos and violence. They only gathered in numbers large enough to make decisions with enough checks and balances in power present to assure no one of them overstepped.

The room had recently been cleaned, but Grace could smell the sour stench of corruption. No matter how much these dark souls washed, some could never get the stink of Hell off.

Grace stood off to the side, near the bar set into the wall. She was not allowed a place at the table, nor were her new henchmen. Golyat had made them stand to the side also. He eyed them suspiciously while Grace fed him calming thoughts with her stolen mind techniques.

In just this brief time she had learned a lot of control but could not bring the power to bear in a direct assault on his mind. She didn't have the finesse for that and he would certainly kill her if he realized what she was doing. Despite what he had said, she did not overestimate her value to him.

"Why the girl, Golyat? Why is she here with her pets?" the one called Draug asked. "This is no place for her kind."

She did not mind the disgust in his voice. She expected no less, she merely looked over them one by one, wondering which one she would be able to consume first. Which ones had powers and experiences she would want to feel?

There was Draug, Eastern European by his accent. He was a dark, powerfully built man whose eyes glowed with a vicious animal shine, as if a pack of man-eating dogs hid inside him struggling to get out.

There was Andre Lavolier, the Alligator King. He was swathed in hooded robes that covered him from head to toe, but Grace could see the reptilian fingers as they snaked out of his robes to lift his drink. From inside his dark hood, she could see the glassy flashing of his large eyes. It was unsettling.

And then there was Michael. He was cute, Grace thought. She liked him. He was a young one and, in some ways, the male version of Anabelle. Model handsome and charming when he wanted to be. He was like the bad boy of the group, and he was the one who seemed the most at ease. He even smiled and winked at Grace.

Oh yeah, she was crushing hard. She had no idea what his abilities and talents were, but she knew she would save his soul for last. It would be the sweetest of desserts.

"She is here at my request," Golyat paused for a moment as

though confused as to why he would request her presence. "And her pets are..."

"They are my guards," Grace jumped in. "I don't have the natural gifts as you have, I have to rely on special soldiers to guard me." She patted Apophis on the arm.

"Little miss, you seem much more confident than the last time we met," Andre said, his voice more hiss than human.

"I have learned and grown strong."

"Enough," said Draug. "Why are we here Golyat? You said you had an update on the project? I hope so. Have you stopped the stability problem?"

"Yes, the final piece of the puzzle has just been delivered from Egypt. With it we can finish the project. But that is not the only reason I have brought you together. I had wanted to share with you a trap I had laid for the Hunter. I planned to lure him here to this location where we could all dispatch him at once."

"You what?" Andre had slid his chair back and stood. He was not as tall as Golyat, but he dwarfed all the others in the room. "Are you crazy, Golyat?"

The others did not jump, but it was obvious they had become nervous. They tensed up as though expecting an attack at any moment. Draug looked to the window as though gauging it for escape. Grace almost laughed at their fear.

"Sit down, Andre. That *was* my plan. Between having my personal guards here, Grace bending his soul, and the four of us he would not stand a chance. However, it seems there is no need."

He gestured to Apophis standing against the wall.

"It seems my ward's new bodyguards have brought us a present. The Hunter is imprisoned."

"Imprisoned? How? These mortals dispatched the Hunter of Lost Souls?" Andre asked. Golyat simply nodded to Apophis.

"We fought him in Cairo, surely you heard about the massacre in Egypt? It went viral as they say now," Apophis said.

"That was you?" Michael asked. "The slaughter in the market?"

"So, not mere mortals then," Andre said.

"No, not mortal at all," Apophis continued with a shrug. "We drew him out, it was easy really. Then we defeated him but chose not to kill him. Instead, we trapped him underground where he will remain for eternity. Even as we speak he is shriveled from lack of water and food, and he has several tons of rock above his head. There is no way for even him to escape."

"And what proof do you have, or do you expect us to just take your word?"

"There is this," Golyat said and dropped the pocket knife on the table.

Grace watched their faces as they moved from confusion to recognition.

"Is this what I think it is?" Michael asked.

"The Weapon, yes," Golyat said with only a hint of the irritation Grace knew he felt towards the handsome man. "These three gentlemen took it as a trophy."

They were quiet a moment, staring at the Weapon, then Andre spoke. "Well then, I suppose you were right all along. The great Hunter was just a child with luck on his side." He laughed a deep laugh that contained not a little bit of relief. "The great and powerful Lord of Damnation we all feared is a myth, the last vestige of a time long past. A last hurrah, so to speak."

An alarm suddenly sounded; everyone looked up at Golyat, who was scowling. He reached down and pressed something on the touch-screen resting on the table. "What is going on? Why is there a perimeter alarm?"

"Sir, it's the Hunter; he's here," said the voice on the other end.

Golyat returned the cold stares of the dark souls around him.

"So, it seems you have fooled us all once again. Just when we think you are not a failure, you prove us wrong," Draug growled.

Golyat glared at Apophis, "Can you explain this?"

Apophis shrugged. "If it is him, then obviously he escaped. I can defeat him again."

The other dark souls were standing and moving toward a side door, looking for a quick escape Grace suspected.

"Wait!" Golyat roared. "This not a problem, we just fall back on my original plan. If that is the Hunter, then surely our combined strength can easily stop him."

"Sorry Golyat, we can't risk you being wrong again. Not with our freedom on the line. I won't go back to Hell," Michael said. "I would advise you to do the same."

"I want him stopped at the lobby. Bring all available firepower to bear," Golyat roared at guard through the speaker on the desk.

"Um...sir," came the slightly concerned voice on the other end. "He isn't coming through the lobby."

In the distance they heard a thud and crashing sound. It sounded like it was on this same floor. Grace looked at Apophis and nodded to the Weapon on the table. One of his brothers stepped and slipped it into his pocket while Golyat was distracted by his departing fellow dark souls.

"I defeated him once mistress, I can do so again," Apophis said.

"Yes go," she said and then just as they turned to leave. "And Apophis? No mercy, no capturing. Just fucking kill him."

28

"Can you hear me?"

The voice of Juan came over the earpiece. It was just one of the new cool pieces of tech Juan had picked up. The souped-up tech van, parked several blocks away, was another. But then, Christopher had given him a huge budget and no oversight.

"Yes, loud and clear," Christopher replied.

Juan had not wanted to come any closer than a few blocks away. That was probably a good idea considering what had happened to him last time.

Christopher stood on top of a building directly across from Golyat's. He was wrapped in the shadows of his uniform like a familiar blanket. Dark power simmered around him, distorting the air. Next to him Hellcat growled impatiently.

"Soon girl, soon," Christopher said. He felt the same impatience. If Hamlin were not at risk, he would have spent some time at the Library reading up on this particular dark soul. He knew next to nothing about the dark soul that was the ringleader of the alliance. It was a dangerous risk, but every moment he was in there, Hamlin was closer to being dead, if he wasn't already.

Christopher also knew, although he was not proud his mind went there, that the longer they had him in their possession, the more information they could get out of him. He could be forced to give away secrets, like the location of the Lairs. The might not be able to enter them easily, but given enough time who knows? They had to move fast, at least to rescue Hamlin.

"Are sure you're up for this?" asked Juan. "I mean you just went through a lot, you even said yourself you feel like your mind is a little tender and your body might not have fully recovered."

"I am up for this, I have to be. Were you able to get back into the video system?"

"Yeah, they haven't really had time to find all the holes I discovered earlier. I have control of the primary video, but the secondary security network is still invisible to me, so I have my blind spots."

"Can you tell me where Hamlin or Golyat are?"

Hamlin I can't see, but I think he's still in the penthouse; that was where they took him. Golyat though, I saw him moving around, kind of hard to miss someone of that size. He's also on the penthouse level. He and Grace entered a room with large double doors; they had three others with them. I would say they're guards, but they weren't dressed like the rest. I have no video access in the actual room. Anybody could be in there."

Christopher centered his mind, stilling stray thoughts in preparation for the battle ahead. Then he leaped from the building. Power radiated out from him, shooting tendrils of darkness to nearby buildings and propelling him forward. He flew over the street below, it was late but that doesn't slow down New York. The streets were filled with people, and if any of them had looked up they would have seen the dark form surrounded by shadows and crackling energy soar across the sky like a demon riding lightning.

He smashed through the window of the penthouse, rolling to his feet. Furniture flew away from the blast of his entry. He had landed in the main living room, the windows surrounding the room shattered in their frames as the aura of power rippled through the walls.

The living room was multiple stories tall with arched ceilings. Plenty of room for a fight. There was no use in being quiet, he couldn't sneak around here. It was best to confront this trap head on. He picked up a couch and threw it through a wall.

He heard a commotion down the hall and turned to face it. Three men emerged from the darkness. Christopher braced himself. He had no weapon, but he was far from helpless. The hunger to kill and take souls was still in him, rearing up in anger and hatred. Then he saw who had come.

"Apophis?" Christopher asked, for a moment he couldn't believe it. "You work with the Alliance?"

"It seems I do for the moment," he said. "I don't know how you got out of your little hole, but the next one you go into will be permanent."

Apophis' brothers spread out along the wall as though trying to surround Christopher. For a moment fear froze Christopher. He was not ready for this, confronting the being who had just so handily defeated him. But then the training came back, the lives he spent learning about himself, how to control what he had become.

"Interesting," Christopher said a grin spreading across his face. "It took you a few thousand years to escape, right? It only took me a couple of days."

For a being that seemed to lack most emotions, that seemed to really piss it off. Long knives slide out of the sheaths hidden under Apophis' jacket, and the two brothers on either side charged.

But Christopher was ready. He had to move against them one by one rather than allow them to all attack at once. They were closing with inhuman speed, but he was just as fast. His foot shot out and kicked a large chair at the brother approaching from his left. It smashed into him, sending the golem falling back. Christopher never saw any of this though, he was already moving toward the other brother with blistering speed.

The second brother was caught by surprise at Christopher's abrupt attack. He brought his knife up in a hurried attempt to slice at Christopher, who nimbly dodged the striking knife, letting it cut the air where he had just stood. Then his fist shot out, not going for the brother's face—too obvious, and slammed into the nerve center of the outstretched arm that held the knife.

The blow, powered by the fires of Hell, did more than strike a nerve. The arm shattered where he had hit it, skin ripping open. Dry sand puffed from the wound and black sludge, like sand mixed with oil, spewed from the opening.

A follow-up punch to the brother's gut sent him back a few feet, doubled over. The first brother had regained his feet and was charging at him. But in the moment before they started exchanging blows, Christopher felt something, a stirring of his power. It distracted him for a fraction of a second, and that was long enough for the first brother to take advantage of it.

His long knife flashed towards Christopher's face. Christopher pulled back in time to avoid a deep cut, but the tip caught his cheek and split it open. Then the brother reversed his cut and slammed the hilt into Christopher's temple.

Christopher fell back, stunned, but remembered his training. It was coming to him out of instinct and it should, he spent ten years fighting for his life. Sensing his opponent's weakness, the first brother followed up his blow with a thrust at Christopher's gut.

Though his head was still fuzzy, Christopher stepped aside and allowed his assailant's own momentum to pull him forward, then caught his arm and pulled with just enough force to set him off balance and stretched out before him.

Christopher brought his foot up into the brother's midsection in a kick strong enough to send the golem off the ground and into the cavernous ceiling above. Plaster and dust rained down on them as he came crashing down onto a glass coffee table.

Christopher felt another tug at the seed of Hell inside him. He had the strange feeling something was trying to get his attention.

Then he felt a sharp pain in his back. He was distracted again, and the second brother struck him from behind. The blade pierced his gut, before it was wrenched out. Instantly Christopher was in a state of no-mind. He acknowledged the pain but then pushed aside as he spun around, bringing the back of his fist across the second brother's face.

The second brother's face ripped open in a burst of sand and black sludge for blood. His arm, however, had already started healing, reforming as the black sludge pulled the muscle and tendon back into alignment.

Christopher stumbled, the deep wound in his gut could be ignored to some extent with his new skills, but the damage was still damage and his accelerating healing was not instantaneous.

The question is; where was big brother? The Apophis that did all the talking? He had disappeared from the scene.

The first brother was already on his feet and lunging, but Christopher did not move. He knew something the first brother didn't. With a glass shattering roar, Hellcat slammed into the brother.

Christopher felt another annoying tug on his power. The first brother was squaring up on him again. Again, the power tugged at him, more urgent. He glanced at the brother's jacket. There was something inside the pocket. Christopher thought he knew what it was. But could it be that easy?

Blades came darting in at Christopher from the first brother, though his face was shattered and oozing sandy tar and puffs of dust. Christopher dodged the blows, letting them pass through the air. The last time he had fought Apophis he had been outmatched; now he held his own. He could see the surprise on the brother's face.

Behind him, he heard the roars and crunching sound of Hellcat battling with the other brother. He couldn't take his eyes away from this combat, but he was pretty sure she could take care of herself.

Then the first brother made a mistake. He overextended one of his strikes. The old Christopher wouldn't have even noticed, but the new Christopher did—and he took advantage. He struck the eyes, gouging at them. With a mortal he would have gone for the throat, but lack of air would not have stopped this sand golem. No eyes though, that could cause it problems.

He ripped the eye from the socket and crushed it in his hands.

Black sludge oozed out of it. The first brother cried out and grasped at his empty socket, black sand spilling out like an hourglass.

With more blind luck—literally—than skill the brother swiped the remaining long knife at Christopher, catching his shoulder; he felt the knife blade drag across bone and blood arced from the deep cut. New training or not, that hurt and Christopher cried out.

Anger rose up inside of him and power billowed out in shadow clouds arced with lighting. He jumped over the first brother, who struggled to see in the new shadows and light flashes Christopher had created. The ceiling was so high Christopher easily cleared the man and his frantically weaving blade.

Christopher landed behind him and before the man could turn to him, grabbed hold of his head and twisted. Christopher wasn't sure there were any bones in there, or just sand sludge, but he did hear a pop as he would have expected while breaking a neck.

He snaked his arm around the golem's neck and, drawing on the infinite Hellpower inside of him, he squeezed and pulled at the same time. The golem's head gave up under all that pressure and came away from the body.

The Librarian had said he needed to inflict as much destruction as he could on the bodies to get to the mailable essence inside.

Now comes the gross part, Christopher thought. With one hand he clasped the wildly swinging wrist holding the knife. Losing its head did nothing to curb the creature's enthusiasm.

Christopher shoved his other hand down the golem's exposed throat. The golem's free hand struck at his back with powerful, but un-aimed punches. Christopher tried to ignore them while he rooted around in the brother's torso.

Black sludge and sand sprayed from the gaping neck hole as Christopher tore out pieces of the golem's insides. The stench of rot and what only could be described as a cesspool surrounded him as he dug into its chest.

Then his fingers hit something a little firmer than the rest of its insides—like a slug of clay. Malleable. He wrapped his fingers around it even as it wiggled to stay out of his grasp. With one last yank, he ripped it up and out through the open neck.

He held a pulsating slug of black clay in his hands. It was slick and trying to squirm away. With his other hand Christopher reached into his shadow coat and pulled out a steel canister. It was just big enough to fit the slug in. He shoved it in and screwed the seal on as his hands, slick with the clay-like material, slid over the lid; but he was able to get it on tight.

Hellcat had the other brother pinned to the ground and was about to tear off his face when the golem put his feet under her and pushed upward, throwing her back and tossing the giant cat like she was a kitten. But he had taken a lot of damage. She had a few cuts, bleeding streams of shadow, but if Christopher had to guess, the cat was winning.

"Hunter!"

The cry came from above. It was so loud and startling that even Hellcat and the last brother stopped fighting to look. Christopher looked up to the balcony above the room. Golyat was there, looking dapper as ever in his suit. Next to him was Grace glaring down at him. A cruel smile slid across her face. She wore a pink t-shirt that said 'Killing it' across the front. Next to her was Apophis. He stood calmly as though seeing his brother defeated in front of him meant nothing.

"You have learned some new tricks since we last met. But some things never change. As I remember, last time you were groveling at my feet," said Golyat.

"Why don't you come down here and I'll show you groveling," said Christopher. He knelt and without moving his eyes from Golyat reached into the dead brother's pocket.

"Perhaps, but I like the view from up here. Did you know for example, that a friend of yours is just in back here?"

"Yeah, just hanging out," Grace said and then giggled.

"If you let him go, I'll let you walk out of here and give you a full day before I start my hunt," Christopher said.

"A full day, you say. How generous, but I think not. What are you doing? Are you so hard up you would steal money from the pockets of a dead man?"

Christopher's fingers brushed against the pocket knife and instantly the power flowed through him. It was the Weapon and he had it back.

With a roar of triumph, he pulled out the Weapon and it transformed into a blazing long sword of steel and energy. Power ran in and waved up and down its length, arcing through the air and joining with the power radiating from him. He finally felt complete again.

But nothing felt as good as the shocked expression on Golyat's face.

"How?" he said, confusion on his face. He patted at his own pockets like he expected to find the knife on him rather than in the hands of his mortal enemy.

"I thought," Grace began and Golyat turned to her, his face flaring red. "I thought that Apophis could use it. I mean, it seemed cool at the time for the brothers to use his own weapon against him."

"You thought it seemed cool? Cool? The Weapon only works for the Lord of Damnation. It is the gateway to Hell."

"Okay, but how was I supposed to know that? I mean you don't even let me into your meetings."

"Speaking of gateways to Hell. Time to send *you* back," Christopher said.

He jumped, leaping through the air towards the balcony. Power shot from him in waves, shaking the building as he moved, like thunder before the rain.

His blade was a blur of power, pulsing with hunger and need to taste Golyat's dark soul. It had a thirst and would not stop until slaked. Even Christopher with his new control couldn't fight the hunger. It radiated through him. He longed to rend Golyat soul and put an end to him.

Golyat didn't move as Christopher shot through the air at him. Only his eyes betrayed fear as they widened just a bit. The blade hummed as it swung through the air, straight for Golyat's giant head.

Inches before it was going to sink into that dark soul flesh, there was a blinding flash and another blade was there, blocking Christopher's blow. The Weapon was stopped dead like it had hit a brick wall, not just another sword.

Then there was a force pushing Christopher back. He had reached the edge of the balcony, but now was thrown back, the blade pushed back against him. He fell to the floor, smashing into an end table and bruising several ribs.

He tried to roll to his feet quickly, but the injuries he had just taken and the stress of his body not quite recovered from dehydration made him move slower than he would have wished. He staggered to his feet just as Apophis jumped down, landing with a resounding thud, causing the floor to shake.

In his hand he held a large, hooked sword. The Christopher of old would have had no clue what it was, but now he could recognize it as a khopesh, and ancient Egyptian sword shaped like a sickle. It shimmered with a silver glow as though it amplified and reflected all light that hit it.

Golyat chuckled.

"It's called a Relic, and you won't be able to survive the wounds it gives you," Golyat said."

Instantly Christopher went cold. He was caught off guard; fear seeped into his armored mind. Apophis raised the khopesh. For a being lacking true emotion, he was doing an excellent job of looking menacing.

"I don't suppose you recognize that weapon," Golyat said. "It is the very same sword that gutted your predecessor."

29

When Hamlin faded back into consciousness the room was empty. Grace and Apophis were gone, but he had no idea how long he had blacked-out. He suspected it wasn't too long because his wrists were still throbbing with pain from hanging. If he had hung for too long he wouldn't have felt anything at all.

He felt unconsciousness trying to pull him back, and shook his head trying to wake himself up. It worked; it was hard to focus, but it was a start.

He had to do something. His body was in a lot of pain, but if what they had said was true, he had to find his way out of here and get help for the kid.

None of the tables, with their various tools, were close enough for him to snag with his foot. His pockets had been emptied and the contents on another shelf across the room, so no pocket knife.

He looked up at his hands. They were bound at either end of a short cord that looped up and over the wooden beam above him. It was not the best way to secure a prisoner, but the tattooed guards had struck him as some sort of supernatural henchmen, not professionals.

The knots were tight and efficient though. His own weight and struggles caused them to cinch up tighter. He would not be able to work his way out of the bindings while hanging. They were just too tight.

He looked up at the beam and silently moaned. He didn't have a choice. This was going to be painful.

He lifted himself higher with his arms. The sore muscles cried in protest, but he pushed through. Then the hard part, he lifted his legs up to his chest.

The bruised ribs and various lacerations tried to tell him how bad of an idea this was, but he gritted his teeth and allowed himself only a few grunts as he brought his legs up over his head. Just when he thought his muscles would give out, he hooked his leg over the beam.

His body was shaking from the pain and exertion, but the worst part was over. His other leg hooked the beam, and he took a few seconds to rest before he moved on to phase two.

With more grunts and a soft cry of pain, he was able to get his arm around the beam also and pull himself up until he was straddling it. He lay there a little longer, resting on the narrow beam.

Now that the tension was gone, blood and sensation were rushing back into his hands like spiteful fire. He stayed as quiet as he could, imagining that the quiet whimper was not him as the nerves in his hand came back alive.

His hands now hung off either side of his wooden platform, connected by a rope that now hung loosely below the beam. As soon as he had enough feeling back in his hands, he started working at the knots.

They were tight and well tied, but any knot can be worked loose if you have enough time and easy access. With the rope slack between them Hamlin found plenty of room to work. A minute later he had one of his hands free.

Later he planned on telling the kid how he had nimbly jumped down from the beam, but the reality was that he was more like a sack of potatoes dropping to the ground.

He landed to more bruises and the loudest moan yet. He lay on the ground only long enough to confirm he hadn't broken anything else before coming to his feet as fast as he could.

There was a crash from below that shook the whole building. Hamlin didn't have time to worry about that; he was sure he would discover whatever it was soon enough. He needed to get out. The question was, how?

Then his eyes caught the glow from the shelf. He couldn't leave without that prize. He snatched the crystal container holding the shard of Christopher's soul.

Next to it, hanging from the shelf on a leather strap was a small pink purse with an inordinate number of rhinestones. But it looked in good condition. He pulled on the purse so that the strap ran across his body and slipped the soul shard right in. Tight, but secure. If it weren't pink and sparkly, he would have an Indiana Jones vibe going.

There was another building-shaking rumble. Something was going on, something causing considerable damage. He wondered if Hellcat was back.

Then the bedroom door was opened violently. Without thinking Hamlin dove behind another shelf unit.

Grace stormed into the room grumbling.

"Some help your henchmen are Grace... why don't you go get the soul shard Grace... save the day again Grace. Fuck you Goly—" she abruptly stopped when she noticed the lack of a body hanging from the wooden beam. "Fuck!"

She immediately spun to where she kept the soul shard.

"Fuck!"

She ran over to the empty space on the shelf where her prize trophy once sat. Hamlin slid deeper behind the shelf unit. He stayed low, crawling on his stomach.

"Fuckinggoddamnit!" she screamed and spun, searching the room. She started toward the shelf he was hiding behind. A large steel table was just behind him. He wished it was better cover, but it was the best he had. He rolled under it.

He lifted his legs to the brace running between two table legs. He grabbed a cross beam support of the table and lifted, doing what amounted to the hardest pull up of his life.

Her footsteps approached and then paused. He had no idea if she was bending over to look or just scanning the room. For a long moment that felt like hours, he held himself suspended above the ground.

His body was once again close to failure. The damage he had taken over the last few days had taken its toll. Sweat formed on his brow and ran down the side of his face. Muscles groaned but he held them flexed. His body shook so hard he worried it might start moving the table.

Then she was walking again, her footsteps retreating to the door.

"Fuck! Goddamn," she yelled. "Guards!"

More footsteps—heavy like large men—they stopped near the doorway.

"He's gone!" She screamed.

"But, that's impossible—" one guard started.

"Are you calling me a liar? Look! Do you see the piece of meat hanging anymore? He's gone. Escaped, you fucking losers! Now, go find him before he can help the Hunter. Can you manage that simple task?"

The kid was here? That would explain her panic and the building shaking. Maybe he wasn't trapped? Had he escaped? Was it a lie?

"Yes, Grace," the guard said.

"Wait," there was a long pause as though she was thinking. "Call me Your Majesty."

"Um. Okay, I guess. Your Majesty," he said it more like a question than a statement. Even the guard suspected she was a little off her rocker.

Then they were gone, and the room was silent for a moment before another thud shook the floor. The vibration was just too much; his muscles gave out and he dropped to the floor. Luckily, from what he could see of the door, he was alone.

He paused for a moment, letting his body rest. Every part of him ached and his body begged him not to move. He knew that if he lay there a moment longer his body would win, and he would drift back into unconsciousness. All he had to work with was his rapidly dwindling supply of adrenaline.

He rolled out from under the table and used the nearby shelf to help him get to his feet. He was a mess; it would be next to impossible for him to get out of this place alive. Not with a building full of those tattooed guards. But he could find the kid. Hell, Chris was probably here to rescue him.

With his next step outlined, no matter how vaguely, he poked his head out of Grace's laboratory-bedroom. The hallway was empty for now. Out here the sounds of fighting were much louder. They seemed to be coming from one floor down, although it was hard to be sure.

He made a call. He needed to head to the battle; the kid needed him. He made his way down the stairs as fast as his broken body would let him.

30

"That doesn't sound good," Juan said through his earpiece.

"This will be a short fight with Captain Obvious whispering in my ear," Christopher said quietly.

"Good news, Hamlin's out. I saw him on the security cams. I think he's heading your way," Juan said.

"What?" Christopher said a little too loudly. "Wait."

"I don't think so," said Apophis.

He leaped at Christopher, and the wicked-looking blade carved a bright arc flashing through the air.

Distracted, Christopher brought up his blade just in time. The Relic and Weapon collided again, this time with force behind both sides. Energy surged around them. Bright light flashed from the Relic, darkness laced with an evil red glow radiated from the Weapon as the two powers connected. The few remaining windows exploded outward at the display.

The force of the concussion traveled back through the blades and Apophis looked as surprised as Christopher felt. They both stepped back a few feet, knocked off balance.

Anger whipped through the Weapon, drawing on the Hellpower inside of Christopher. He could feel the hatred of the thing. Normally it only did this when the soul hunger was strong in it, but this was almost like it was angry that something was challenging it.

Wind ripped through the broken windows of the penthouse, tearing at their clothes. Christopher drew upon the experience of his recent year's training. He emptied his mind even as the Weapon raged for him. The sounds of the violent wind faded into the background, even the raging Weapon was distant.

Behind him Hellcat was ripping at the last remaining brother, tearing its sludge filled arm off. The brother did not scream, but he looked to Apophis in obvious pain. There was nothing he could do; the cat was destroying him.

Then Apophis was on him, his sword striking quick. Christopher flowed, letting his blade counter every attack. He allowed himself to feel everything around him, and soon he was moving with the wind, swaying with the building, and strong like the blade he carried.

Apophis was doing the same, Christopher could tell. He attacked viciously, but with perfect control of his khopesh. The Weapon met the Relic at every turn. Energy radiated down the blades each time they struck. Billowing darkness formed around Christopher as the intensity of the colliding powers grew.

Their skills were almost equal. Almost.

The Relic sliced in toward Christopher's mid-section; reflexively Christopher brought the Weapon to meet it, but it wasn't there. It had been a feint. At the last minute, Apophis reversed the blade strike so fast it was as though the Relic was weightless. Christopher realized his mistake too late. He was off balance but able to partially catch the reversed cut. The khopesh skittered along the Weapon sending off fiery sparks of power.

He almost made it, but the Relic glanced off his shoulder, trailing a shallow cut behind it. Christopher's arm felt like it was suddenly on fire. Though the cut was small, it felt as if his arm had been split open.

He cried out and fell back, a feeling panic rising in him despite his training. The Hellpower inside of him screamed in anger but did not reach out to heal this new wound.

Apophis smiled and nodded in satisfaction.

"So, not quite the same warrior as your predecessor," Apophis said.

Christopher lifted the Weapon. His arm hurt but he dismissed the pain. It hurt worse than any wound he had ever felt, but it became background noise once again. And he tried to focus.

Apophis fought in an efficient but ancient style, the khopesh was designed to hook a shield or opponent's weapon beneath the curve of its blade where it straightened out near the handle. Perhaps it was time to give it something to hook onto.

Apophis came at him, the Relic darting forward. Christopher let it come just close enough that he could almost feel Apophis' sense of triumph. The Weapon slid past the curved part of the blade. Christopher turned his body just enough for the thrusting tip to miss his side. Then the Weapon shifted.

It became a battle-ax with its own curved hook, Christopher nagged the curved part of the khopesh and pulled the Relic even closer along his side, but this time he put the strength of Hell behind it.

Apophis' eyes widened in surprise as the ax locked with the khopesh and he flew forward off balance. But Christopher did stop there. Apophis and the Relic continued forward as Christopher threw him toward the largest piece of furniture in the room, the large wood and glass bar against one wall.

The golem smashed through it, raining wood and glass down on him as the bar disintegrated on impact. The glass top and shelves beyond dropped on top of him, slicing him in a multitude of cuts and lacerations. This wouldn't stop Apophis, Christopher knew that, but it slowed him down.

"You've got company coming," Juan said through the earpiece. "Large group of guards coming through the main hall."

Christopher ran over to the large couch and picked it up just as the group of tattooed guards came bursting into the room, guns up and ready. He threw it straight at the front line. It was a large couch made of steel as well as wood. It had cushions but was built more for looks than comfort.

It smashed into the front line with enough force to continue through like the world's largest bowling ball, and they were unlucky bowling pins. Guns went off randomly as they went down. Some rounds hit their own men. There were cries of surprise and pain. But the pain for them had just begun.

Christopher leaped into the fray. His single battle ax became two; they began to spin in his hand like saw blades. He carved into the group, killing before they could even get to their feet. A few bullets hit him, but out of luck, not careful aim. He ignored them as the hunger for souls flowed from the Weapon and through him.

Like a starved man, the Weapon drank its fill. These guards were men, magically enhanced men, but they had souls and the Weapon was a glutton. It ripped souls from bodies with childish glee, as the souls peeled away from their hosts like stringy cheese, screaming in mortal terror. As fast as he could kill, however, others were recovering from the blow of the couch. They would be able to do quite a bit of damage with their firearms if given time.

"Good news, Hamlin found a toy," Juan said, and Christopher could hear the smile in his voice.

As the remaining guards got to their feet, automatic fire rang out from behind them down the hallway.

"Get out of the way kid," yelled a familiar voice. Hamlin *had* found a toy.

Christopher dove to the ground and rolled out of the way as bullets riddle the guards in front of him. Some turned to return fire, but they had no cover and were out in the open. Christopher couldn't see Hamlin, but he had a feeling Hamlin was a little more prepared for the ambush.

"You idiots!" Came a roar from the balcony. It seemed Golyat was not happy his plans were being foiled by a kid and a beat-up cop. "Kill the Hunter, nobody cares about the mortal!"

Apparently, the guards did care about the guy with a fully automatic weapon shooting at their backs because only a few turned away from the firefight. Christopher was on them instantly, severing limbs and damning souls.

Then Hellcat was with him, laying into the guards with claw and tooth.

"Behind you!" came a cry from Juan.

Christopher spun, leaving Hellcat to deal with the remaining guards. Apophis, covered in hundreds of little cuts leaking sand and blackness, was swinging the Relic straight at his head. Christopher dropped without thinking and the Weapon, reacting to his almost unconscious command, shifted from dual battle axes into two short blades.

One blade came up to defend against the khopesh, the other he drove into Apophis' gut—wrenching it sideways at the last minute. For a mortal, the blow would have spilled his guts all over the floor. With the golem, however, sand and the black sludge spilled out.

Apophis screamed, more in frustration than pain, and backed away holding his stomach together. In his weakened state he tripped over a broken piece of furniture and fell backward. He looked up from the ground at Christopher, covered in his own blackness and sand.

"That is a nice weapon you have. It is just full of tricks. It is not something I remember from fighting the one who came before you. I can promise you, I will be ready for it the next time we meet."

"There won't be a—" Christopher started.

"Jesus, he's fast. Behind you!" came another cry from the Juan.

But this time Christopher wasn't fast enough. He had only turned halfway and didn't even have the Weapon raised when Golyat's fist slammed into his side like a wrecking ball. He felt and heard his ribs snap and crackle as his feet lifted off the ground.

And then he was moving sideways, slamming through the window frame and out into the night air. Pain rippled through his whole body as the concussion wrecked its way through him. The sheer strength was unimaginable. Like a rag doll, he flew across the street.

He held onto consciousness out of force of will he had developed in his training. Then he was smashing through the window of the building across the street. The window frame collapsed inward and glass shattered. His consciousness wavered and for a moment he blacked out. Then the darkness faded, and he found himself staring at the ceiling.

"This world will be mine!" he heard Golyat scream from across the street, his powerful voice bouncing off buildings. "You are nothing! You are weak. You will not defeat me!"

With a groan, Christopher turned his head. It looked like he was in the living room of a very expensive apartment. A man with bed head in a disheveled robe held a large fireplace poker above his shoulder like a baseball bat. He looked like he was ready to hit Christopher at any moment. His eyes flickered between the broken window and Christopher.

A woman, presumably his wife, stood just behind him; she was also in a robe, her eyes were wide in terror and surprise. She was pointing at him and trying to speak at the same time.

Christopher still held the cloak of shadows around him concealing his identity. This was good because just behind the woman a boy of about ten stood in his underwear holding a cell phone. He was recording.

"Cool," the boy said.

"Anthony, get back to your room immediately," his mother yelled but did not turn her head.

"Don't move," the man said. "Who are you and what the hell is going on over there?"

"That's the Demon Slayer dad, the Hunter of Lost Souls, right? You used to be called the Hero of the Bronx?" the boy asked.

"What the hell are you doing on the floor of my home?" the man said, ignoring his son.

"He's saving the world, right sir?"

"Are you okay?" Juan asked over the earpiece. "Please say you're still alive, that was an amazing punch."

"I'm alive," Christopher croaked out. All his focus was on breathing, calming all the warning signs his body was giving him at the catastrophic damage to his bones and organs. He calmly let the Hellpower flare up inside and heal the damage as fast as it could.

"I know you're alive," the man said. "The question is how?"

"I told you dad, he is the Hunter; he can't die!"

The Weapon had become a knife again and lay at his side. Christopher was amazed he had even been able to hold onto it. He grabbed it now and it flared to life as a large broadsword radiating power.

The man yelled and struck with the poker. The Weapon leaped to meet the attack and shattered the poker into pieces. Christopher had not even moved from the floor. The man had backed away and seemed to be dialing 911 on his phone.

Christopher had to think. Golyat wasn't pursuing. Why? He could not stand a blow like that again. Golyat had to know that. The power of Golyat was immense.

Christopher could not match that much raw energy. But maybe he didn't have to, at least not yet. In his training Christopher had learned that it was not always strength or power that won, sometimes it was simply the appearance of strength and power.

He might have a greater weapon. Fear.

Golyat was afraid of him at some level. He had had several chances to engage Christopher directly but had always left it to someone else. Like all the other dark souls, beneath his bravado, Golyat was afraid of Christopher and what he could potentially do.

He represented Golyat's—no all the Alliance's—biggest fears. No matter how outmatched he might appear, there was always the chance that Christopher could take his soul and send him back to his deepest darkest Hell. And that was the only thing that scared Golyat.

Christopher knew he could run now, well crawl away anyway. He could go back to the lair and heal, but Hamlin was still back in that apartment and Golyat would think he had won. Hamlin would be dead, no longer used as bait. He had to go back, and he had to bluff the hell out of the situation.

"Ha! Are you dead, Hunter?" Golyat yelled. "I see no movement.

Was it really that easy or are you just running in fear? I will find your mortal pet, he is in here somewhere. Show yourself!"

Christopher slowly rolled to his feet, but only got as far as his knee before the pain became too much and he had to pause. He could feel blood running from his mouth and his left arm was numb, the bones shattered. If he pulled this off, he wanted an Oscar.

The man and the woman were kneeling by their child holding him close, terror on their faces.

"I will not hurt you; no matter what you see, I will not hurt you," Christopher said to the family. "It might look scary, but understand I mean you no harm. And please stop filming me kid."

The boy nodded, and the dad snatched the phone out of his hands. Christopher got to his feet, barely. It felt like his spine was out of whack. His healing was fast, but he was a mess. It would take time. Time he did not have.

He needed to focus. He took a moment to breathe, though his ribs were in agony with each breath. He let his thoughts come and go before finding his no-mind. He reached out to the darkness around him, his familiar home. And he pulled it close like a blanket.

The man gasped as the room darkened. Dark power surrounded Christopher, spreading out like a shroud of hatred. He stoked the Hellpower inside him until his body radiated energy, arcs of power leaped from the Weapon and up his arm. It screamed at him to take the souls of the family, to taste their essence. But Christopher dismissed the errant desire like he did all the other thoughts that clouded his mind, and the Weapon's roar became background noise.

"Golyat!" Christopher roared, using the Hellpower to project his voice across the street. It echoed even louder off the walls of the buildings. Below traffic was at a standstill as people stopped in the street to look up at the battle above. The explosions had caught their attention. "You will not be rid of me so easily."

The window he had flown through was almost floor to ceiling. He stood there, Weapon at his side. Bands of power leaped from him and spread out across the building. Even then he still pulled power to him, stoking the fires of Hell inside of him more than ever before.

"I've come for you Golyat and am ready to drag you back to Hell."

Golyat stepped into the hole Christopher had left through the window and bottom half of the wall. Christopher could see him quite clearly, his sense augmented by the Hunter powers Hell had given him. Golyat no longer looked so sure of himself.

"I've learned a few tricks, Golyat. Stuff even my predecessor did not know."

"That's impossible," Golyat said quieter, but Christopher could hear him over the wind blowing between them. "You are just a kid."

"Your guards could not stand against me. Your trap was sprung, and I still stand. Who will stand with you now? Your errand boy, Apophis, could not even defeat me."

Golyat looked at something in the room as though considering. The Weapon shifted in Christopher's hand, becoming a large war hammer.

"Even my companion waits in the shadow with tooth and claw to rend. She too has a taste for souls."

Then like a move stolen from a Thor Marvel movie he smashed the hammer into the wall next to him. Energy arced from the darkness outside meeting the Weapon as it crashed into the wall shattering a large section. The brick and mortar exploded away from the impact.

Golyat was gone from the window. The lights had gone out across the street, but the darkness hid nothing from Christopher. He searched through the windows but couldn't see any movement.

It was time to test his bluff. It was also going to be the hardest part. His body was still racked with pain, but he had stalled long enough. He jumped, thrusting out tendrils of power to help propel him across the space between buildings. He struggled to look as graceful as he could; he could not show weakness. His body protested as his body flexed into the jump. It was all he could do to not cry out. But that was nothing compared to the landing.

He landed with a thud back in Golyat's living room. His landing shook the building and at the last moment, as his body gave out, broken bones and torn muscle no longer able to fully support him.

He used his one good arm to slam the Weapon down and he went to one knee. The ground cracked, and power flashed like lighting. Dark clouds rolled away from him, bathing the room in an even deeper darkness.

He hoped the fireworks display covered the fact that he couldn't even stand.

"Damn Chris, even I'm a little shaken up," Juan said in his ear.

Across the darkened room Golyat stood in the entrance to the main hallway. Behind him Christopher could see Grace retreating, pulling a wounded Apophis behind along with her. Before leaving, Apophis looked at Christopher with a mix of coldness and something like begrudging respect.

Already the sand was seeping back into his broken skin, and his many cuts were sealing back up. The gut wound would take longer. Christopher was betting he wouldn't risk continuing the fight for now.

"Watch yourself, Hunter. I will come for my brothers." Then he disappeared with Grace down the hall.

Golyat studied him for a moment. "You are different. I don't know what happened, but you are more of an unknown quantity now. The force I put into that blow should have crushed you. However, you might be weaker than you look. I suspect that if Apophis blew on you hard, you would fall over. You are lucky Grace has commanded him away, that I have chosen not to make that gamble. But mark my words Hunter, when we meet again you will be destroyed."

Golyat turned and left through the hallway, stepping over the bodies of his dead soldiers as though they were mud puddles he had to avoid. Then he was gone. But Christopher had to be sure.

"Is he gone?" he whispered to Juan.

"Yeah, they left in the elevator," said Juan.

With a whimper, Christopher slid to the ground. He heard a door slam and Hamlin was running toward him.

"Jesus, kid! Are you okay?" Hamlin asked.

"No. No, I don't think so. I need a minute. But we need to get out of here."

"Yeah, but we aren't going through the lobby downstairs. Any remaining guards will be in a firefight soon with the police. Even if we made it, we would have to somehow explain all of this to the cops. And I'm not even sure I believe all of it."

"We have to go by rooftop. I can carry you. Help me up."

Hamlin gently helped Christopher to his feet. "Shit kid, you are in no condition to go rooftop skipping on your own, let alone haul my fat ass."

"Things have changed. I have changed. You'd be surprised at what I'm...what we...are capable of now."

Hamlin looked at him as though deciding. "Yeah, there is something new about you. Come on, let's get out of here and then you can tell me all about it."

Hellcat faded out of the shadows near the ruined body of the brother she had torn apart and gave a small roar.

"There's something we have to do before we go. Help me over to the body," Christopher said.

He put his good arm across Hamlin's shoulder and hobbled over. It helped with walking, but any movement sent agony through his broken body. His bones felt like they were being held together through sheer willpower.

The brother's body was slowly reforming. The process was taking time from all the visceral damaged Hellcat had done, but if they left him he would be whole again in a few minutes.

"Hamlin, I need you to cut open its chest. There is something inside it that we have to put in this canister."

"What something?"

"Just take this." Christopher handed Hamlin the Weapon, which had reverted to its more docile pocket knife form when Christopher had collapsed.

For a moment Hamlin looked like he was going to refuse, terror flashing across his face. "I...I can't... I mean it's not for me; it's yours."

"It won't hurt you, for you it will just be a really sharp knife. And Hamlin, I am its wielder, but it is not mine. The Weapon is all of ours, it's for the team."

Hamlin nodded and took the knife, gingerly at first. Then when nothing happened he held it a little more firmly.

"Now dig inside its sandy guts for a putrid, hardened lump," Christopher said. "You'll know it when you find it."

"I'm sure I will," Hamlin said quietly.

Less than a minute later Hamlin was shoving the metal canister into the pink purse with a sludge-covered hand.

"Nice purse by the way," Christopher said.

"Thanks, I got it on sale. We better get the hell out of here."

Christopher grimaced. He had stalled long enough, trying to give his body as much time to heal as possible.

"Hold on tight, I only have one good arm and I think it's going to be a bumpy ride," Christopher said.

Hamlin awkwardly wrapped his arms around Christopher. "I'm not much of a hugger. We shall never speak of this."

"Sure," Christopher said with a grin and held him with his good arm.

"Hey guys," Juan said in Christopher's ear, "Look up at the security camera in the corner. Say Cheese. Perfect, got it all, including Hamlin's very flattering and very sparkly purse."

"What? Is Juan talking to you? Do you have an earpiece?"

"Yes, Juan was just talking to me. He just said he's glad we are still alive."

Before Hamlin could respond Christopher jumped out into the night, speeding toward the rooftop across the street. Hamlin screamed the whole way.

31

Christopher made it a half-dozen blocks before collapsing on the roof of a building. He told Juan where they were so he could bring a van around to pick them up. Hamlin was able to break the lock on the roof access door and when Juan arrived they could limp their way down the stairs and out onto the street.

Juan threw open the door and helped haul Christopher into the van; once inside, Hamlin promptly collapsed too.

"That was one hell of a gamble kid," Hamlin said.

"You saw through my bluff?"

"Ha. I suspected when you were making all that ruckus; I mean I saw that blow you took, that would have killed an elephant. But now it's obvious if Golyat had decided to stay and fight, you wouldn't have stood a chance. Hell, Grace could have taken you out. What made you take that kind of risk?"

"Yeah," Juan said. "What made you think you could pull it off?"

"You mean besides having no other choice? Fear. I know how I was when Golyat last saw me. I was inexperienced, slow, untrained and yet he still had someone else deal with me. No matter how strong he is, he is afraid of what I represent."

Christopher pulled himself up against the side of the van. He was feeling a little better, but it would take some time to heal fully from everything that had happened in the last few days, or maybe the last ten years.

"He won't risk confronting me directly unless he has a clear advantage that I could not possibly overcome. He was expecting the kid he had seen last time, the fresh-faced rookie Hunter. I showed what I had become. I hoped he would realize he did not have quite the advantage he thought he had."

Hamlin was staring at him intently. "And what have you become, Chris? You were fighting in ways I have never seen you before, you were fighting the Apophis with year and years of experience like an equal."

Christopher sighed and leaned his head back. "I'll tell you everything, I promise; for now suffice to say that I did a lot of soul searching when I was trapped. I learned enough for several lifetimes."

Hamlin simply nodded and leaned his own head back. "Okay, we are both exhausted kid, I get it, but after we rest I want to know everything. It's just so messed up."

"What is?" Juan asked.

"All the trouble, all that fighting, and we are no closer to tracking down this Alliance. Sure, we flushed him out of one of his homes. But we still know nothing about how they're organized, what they are planning or how to stop them. For all that pain and we know absolutely nothing."

"Oh yeah," Juan said. "In all the excitement I forgot to tell you. We know everything."

There was a long pause and then Hamlin cleared this throat and asked, "Um, what are you talking about Juan?"

A big grin spread across Juan's face. "You did it Hamlin. The moment they connected that laptop you had stuck that USB drive into to their network—I presume to access tools to scan for viruses—they opened the door for us. My hack got in."

"You are in their system?" Christopher asked. "I assume you mean their computer systems."

"Oh yeah," said Juan, his grin even wider. "And my little baby is spreading; every day I am getting deeper and deeper. Soon we will have complete access to everything on their network. We are going to be able to do a lot of fucking damage."

"One other thing," Hamlin said. He reached into the mysterious purse hanging around his chest. "There's this."

He pulled out a small crystal container with a shimmering, wispy form flashing inside. Instantly Christopher recognized it, and he should, it was a part of him. The shard of his soul taken from him. He couldn't contain his excitement. Despite all the pain, he leaned forward and took it form Hamlin. The glow brightened as he took the crystal into his hands.

The darkness inside of him, the part fused to his soul rose up in anger. But Christopher suppressed it, time enough to deal with that. For now, he had himself back, he needed to be whole as soon as possible.

"Thank you, Hamlin. Thank you."

Christopher smiled as he eased back against the wall of the van. They had intel on the Alliance, he had his soul back and would be whole soon. As soon as the Erises wake up all would be right once again.

He passed out with a huge smile on his face and his soul cradled in his arms.

32

The hospital room was dark. But not dark enough. Light from the hallway came through the open door, and the light from the machines surrounding Eris lit up the pale form on the bed. The only sounds this late at night were the gentle hum of the computer and the occasional quiet ping from the machines regulating the medicine seeping through the IV.

Slowly, silently the door to the room swung shut on its own, no one had touched it. The darkness behind the door began to coalesce and harden into a human form. At first it was an ill-defined dark mass shifting, changing. Then sharper lines, clarity. It was a man.

Jax stepped from the shadow. He pulled back the curtain, letting the moonlight in. The beams fell across the slight girl on the bed. That was better. He always preferred the light of the moon to artificial light. It held magic and he had always loved that kind of magic.

"I'm sorry this had to happen to you," Jax said. "It was unavoidable; I had seen it, but that does not make it any less unpleasant."

Jax leaned forward until he was only inches from Eris' face. "Such beauty." He said almost wistfully. "You are so beautiful, daughter."

His hands touched her shoulder, caressed her neck, then came to rest to either side of her face. He pressed his cheek against hers, feeling her tender flesh against his. His mouth touching lightly against her ear.

"Golyat has almost reached the end of his usefulness," Jax whispered. "The game is fun, but there has to be an ending. Or at least a pause. I have need of you daughter, you are my greatest creation and it turns out my greatest weapon. You will be my sword, my spear. Love has always been the strongest WMD."

He kissed her brow gently.

"Here is what I want you to do."

His tongue lolled out of his mouth, long and thin. It slipped into Eris's ear and into her brain. Licking its way into her sleeping thoughts and dreams.

Her eyes flew wide open, panic etched in every line in her face.

"Chris... no." She said. Then she started screaming, and she didn't stop for a very, very long time.

ALSO BY ERIK LYND

NOVELS

Asylum

The Collection

THE HAND OF PERDITION SERIES:

Book and Blade

Eater of Souls

The Demon Collector

SILAS ROBB SERIES:

Silas Robb: Of Saints and Sinners

Silas Robb: Hell Hath No Fury

SHORTER WORKS

The Hanging Tree

Dark on the Water

His Devil

Dreams

Siege of the Bone Children

In the Pit

ABOUT THE AUTHOR

Erik Lynd writes novels and short stories primarily in the horror, dark fantasy, and urban fantasy genres. Currently he is in the middle of two ongoing urban fantasy series; Silas Robb and The Hand of Perdition series. He also writes the occasional horror novel such as Asylum and The Collection. He lives in the Pacific Northwest where yes it does rain a lot and no he does not mind it.

For more information...

www.eriklynd.com

erik@eriklynd.com

Made in the USA
Lexington, KY
19 August 2018